WARTIMES

By the same author

Fiction

A Waste of Public Money
My Vision's Enemy
Big Breadwinner Hog
The Duchess's Diary
Christoferus or Tom Kyd's Revenge

Plays

High Street China
Gymnasium
Guests
One of Us

ROBIN CHAPMAN

Wartimes

Two Stories of World War II

SINCLAIR-STEVENSON

First published in Great Britain in 1995
by Sinclair-Stevenson
an imprint of Reed Consumer Books Ltd
Michelin House, 81 Fulham Road, London SW3 6RB
and Auckland, Melbourne, Singapore and Toronto

Copyright © 1995 by Robin Chapman

The right of Robin Chapman to be identified as author
of this work has been asserted by him in accordance
with the Copyright, Designs and Patents Act 1988

A CIP catalogue record for this book
is available at the British Library
ISBN 1 85619 505 8

Typeset by Deltatype Ltd, Ellesmere Port, Cheshire
Printed and bound in Great Britain by
Clays Ltd, St Ives plc

To Paulette and Michel Gentot,
in friendship and gratitude

Anne's Story

Sans Anne, peut-être n'aurais-je pas fait tout ce que j'ai fait.

Charles de Gaulle

ONE

Papa was her sun, her moon, her stars and she hated him. How dared he sail away without her? Without even telling her? Besides, the elephants would love him to death the moment he got to their land. They would make him their king. He would never come back. Not now.

As for her being— no, she wasn't, no, she refused, no, she wasn't a fairy from the east, no, it was not to be true, please God, say it wasn't! For one thing she was far too big, far too grown-up. Hadn't Papa said so? Hadn't he said she was a great lump of sausage when he'd heaved her up on his lap to pretend she could play his cards for him? Before he'd gone away?

But her nurse had shown her – oh, a long time ago – she had shown her a country full of people who were all like Anne. Who ate grass. Who rode wild horses white as milk. Who had slanting eyes. This fearsome place had stuck in her heart. It was on a coloured ball her father kept at home. Home, where she wished she was again, where she wanted to die. Nowadays Anne often pretended she was dying – all her other daydreams had gone – and in this manner she hoped to understand how it might happen when it did.

Anne was aware she wasn't going to live long. She knew

this in her insides. She had seen it in the eyes of all the doctors who had ever examined her. And other adults often said it out loud, over her head. They thought she couldn't understand. 'Her kind don't always last, or so we've heard,' they would say, and something speculative, interrogative, in their voices implied this might be no small mercy, perhaps even a blessing. When such things were said Maman neither agreed nor disagreed; indeed she appeared never to notice them, but that was because Maman was as proud as she was quiet, while Papa was as proud as he was proud. So they never said such things in front of *him*. They wouldn't have dared. *He* would have killed them.

After Anne had been shown her country of origin she had run outside to play, but sooner than she might have expected she found herself creeping back to look at it again. Not that she was ever supposed to be in Papa's library alone – she wasn't safe with books – but the information had been so shocking, so horrible, she simply had to stare at the place once more.

She turned Papa's globe round on its silver spindle with extreme care, telling herself to mind now, be gentle, Anne, you break things, you know you do. Where was it? She looked among yellow for seas, orange and blue for dry land and black and white for mountains which were so high you couldn't breathe on the tops of them. Where? She couldn't see this country in the east. She pushed again, faster this time, then again. Was she cross at not finding this place she didn't want to come from? She couldn't tell, except she felt hot, especially her face and beneath her arms. Soon she had made the world spin so fast it squeaked; she could hear a noise like a choir of mice. Anne forgot her quest and began to laugh, pushing and slapping at the globe. She felt better. The faster it spun, the happier the mice became.

All the coloured countries and seas whizzed by. They became a dazzling blur at her command. They were beautiful animals on a carousel: horses, zebras, camels, giraffes with spots. But she had to be careful because the faster she made them go round, the greyer, the duller, they began to look. And that seemed sad. Not that the mice inside minded. No. The faster she spun Papa's world, the more their squeaking became singing: marvellous, wonderful, triumphant singing, as if they had changed into surging crowds on wide streets under soaring trees, into great armies determined to burst out and march past Papa. And salute him. Her Papa.

Anne wanted to see them come out. Would they have a band? One last push and out they must come, surely? Her pudgy hand with the raw bitten nails pushed. The globe shuddered and fell. Her father's world fell over. It tumbled to the floor. It lay still. No mice came out. She was terrified. She backed away dumbfounded and toppled into Maman's leather chair by the fireplace.

Miraculously no one came running to ask her what had she done this time, so she was able to recover her breath, push herself upright and tiptoe shakily acoss to the fallen globe. It was heavier than she expected but she managed to lift it and put it back where it belonged. It seemed to be undamaged except for a scratch on an ocean, which she rubbed at with a licked finger – Anne's universal panacea for a myriad routine mishaps. Then she ran out into the garden again to resume her search for stag beetles.

From that moment Anne had continued to hope – it was hope against hope; she even put it in her prayers underneath the usual words – that she wasn't a fairy from Mongolia. Nobody else she knew came from that place. Why should she? Not from Mongolia. Please! Please, God, let me come sensibly from France like everybody else does. That was her prayer.

Today her English neighbour was carrying a tray with cups and a brown teapot on it. Anne had recently learned what teapots were and also that in England they had special hats to keep them warm. Maman had been given one and Anne had wanted to wear it. She kept trying to say 'tea-cosy' to herself and felt proud to know such a pretty-sounding English word.

When she had first attempted to peep through the hole in the fence her view of her neighbour's garden had been partially blocked by the knot itself, still lodged awkwardly like a shrivelled nut where it had once grown, but a poke with her finger had pushed it out on to the other side. The brisk effectiveness of her action had rather surprised her. The world didn't often obey Anne. Now when she knelt and pushed her eye hard against the hole she could spy at leisure on the little English boy who lived at the bottom of her new garden. The fence squashed her nose but it smelt reassuringly of old sunshine and cough mixture.

He was taking his tray towards his flower-covered house. Anne envied him his house – she wanted to visit it.

It seemed to stand in a trench. Bobby had to jump down to enter its ever open front door.

Anne drew breath. As so often, she had surprised herself. Simply with an unbidden thought. So this small boy she was admiring through the fence was called Bobby, was he? She hadn't realised this before. Until then. That instant. Until it had slipped sideways into her mind. What a pleasant occurrence. His name was Bobby. How convenient. How easy for her to say. Very well, from now on he would be what she had made him: Bobby. He was hers.

Bobby's house had no windows, so far as she could see, and the wavy wall around the door was painted in orange and black vertical stripes. The roof was a complete curve and thatched with nasturtiums. Anne didn't know their name but she recognised the flowers well enough from back home, where in summer there was always a bawling crowd of their orange and red faces outside the village post office.

Bobby carefully deposited his tray on the path and jumped down into the trench in front of his house. Then he leaned out to pick up the tray again and disappeared through the doorway into darkness.

Anne had no doubt he was taking tea with his toy bear, whom she had observed for the first time the day before, just as she sometimes gave her elephant, Babar, a large bowl of coffee. But now Maman kept saying she was too old for such baby games – now she was twelve and a half, or however much the date had got to.

Anne could not have said what the date was any more than she could tell the time, except when the hands of the clock reached places she recognised. But invariably – well, at least until the war came – someone had been present to explain that since her birthday fell on the first day of January it was easy to calculate how old she was. On this last day of August in 1940 she was exactly twelve years and eight months old. Such information, if given in company, usually provoked further practised smiles, gentle nods, head-cocked appraisals from the adults surrounding her, and if, by chance or mistake or distraction, Anne did not smile back, someone would be bound to pinch her cheek and coax her to. 'Smile, Anne, smile, there's a good girl.' At this command and fearing another tweak – grown-ups' fingers were crueller than they knew – Anne would smile, dutifully, lopsidedly. Until they said, 'That's enough smiling, Anne.'

Twelve years and eight months she might be, as she knelt with her eye glued to the fence, but her mental age was quite another matter, they said, not realising such yardsticks were too brutal a measure for the tangle inside her. The turmoil that was she. Her sense of self – what she called her 'me, me, me' – often overwhelmed her. This she had inherited from her father, upon whom such all-nourishing egotism looked necessary, even ideal, but for Anne it was a source of deep fear. It was like a dangerous, sleeping animal she didn't want to wake. But sometimes, despite herself, she did wake it – or did it wake up of its own accord? – and then she would struggle furiously to express, to tell them, these stupid, horrible outsiders, who she really, really was and to pronounce her name in full as if it were some sort of battle honour. She would stand, big, four-square, stamping her foot to force the words out that said: Me, I'm me. But they, so level-eyed, so neutral, never understood. No, never, because if adults looked at her too closely the words emerged in what Anne's family called her mumbly voice. And whoever was with her would deliberately translate her bumping, shunting syllables into polite things she would never dream of saying, such as: 'Anne is enchanted to meet you and your wife and she sincerely hopes that you are both well', or: 'Anne's troublesome cold will soon be better, thank you. That's what you really meant, didn't you darling?' She would try to shake her head, say 'No, no, no'; but as they never really paid her any true attention she would turn the shake into a nod, her angry denial into docile agreement, although she hated meeting other people who, unlike her, seemed not only sensible but also quite free from coughs and sneezes and tightness in the chest. When someone she knew complained of a cold Anne was delighted, but not once had she ever been introduced to anyone really and truly the same as she. There were big houses somewhere full of refugees like herself from that bad country in the east and she knew she would be sent to such a house if she became ungovernable; that was why she always had to be good in order to stay forever with those who loved her until she had to go, rather sooner than most, to Heaven. Which would be exactly like home had been, she knew.

But home had gone and here she was in a bright place called England, in the back garden of a house that had a number but no name. She couldn't remember what the number was, though she had asked several times and been told twice.

Anne drew back from her peephole and rubbed at her eyebrow and nose. They felt dented. Then she looked through again at Bobby's house. He must still be giving his friend, his bear in the red jersey, his tea . . . No, he wasn't, he was climbing out and running up the garden so as to disappear beyond rustic arches dripping with white and pink roses. He was shouting English words she couldn't understand. While he was gone, the roses told Anne they were sweets in a shop her mother had taken her to after buying dress material in a frightening place called Au Bon Marché, in a square called Babylon, which was somewhere Papa and Maman had lived before she had been born to be a nuisance.

Bobby returned carrying an elephant. At such a sight of such an animal Anne could hardly control her pleasure. She wanted to scale the fence, leap in delirium from the top of it and hug that elephant. And all the while she would be able to tell Bobby she knew everything there was to be known about such exceptional persons – hers was called Babar, what about his? The same, surely? Unless it was Celeste? No, not Celeste – she could see now that Bobby's toy elephant wore trousers. They appeared to be the wrong colour for Babar – he usually wore green – but no matter.

Anne hadn't been long enough in England to know that this toy was Edward Trunk, the special, indeed best friend of the bear, Rupert, a national figure whose never-failing exploits were reported each day in the press and then collected into official memoirs, known as bumper books, every Christmas.

Bobby vanished once more into his nasturtium-crowned air-raid shelter. Anne sat back on her heels to consider what to do. Could she, dared she, climb the fence and pay Bobby a visit? It was tall, but so was she. Or should she call to him through the hole? No, climb over, surprise him by her visit, that would be best. She got up and started jumping on the spot, trying to see more of his garden than she had so far. But this only afforded her snatched visions of the air-raid shelter, the rose arches and a woman in a deck chair on the lawn who was knitting with crinkly wool.

Anne recognised this kind of wartime wool – something was being made into something else. Occasionally she wondered if she also might be unwound and remade into something more useful, two purl, one plain, in the same way? Suddenly, as she jumped, she jarred her left heel so much it hurt her neck and head. For a moment she thought she was going to be sick but, no, she only belched. The sour taste made Anne decide she had better not try to climb over after all. She knelt down once again and peered regretfully, yearningly, through the hole.

It was clear to her that Bobby had invited the elephant to tea. One would. But his late arrival meant this distinguished guest must have been delayed. Perhaps the boat from Africa had got lost? Boats could get lost. The one that had brought them to England had got lost for hours, Maman said. And suppose Papa's boat taking him to see the real Babar got lost? But she pushed that thought aside. She didn't want to think it, so she wouldn't. It would make her feel sorry for Papa instead of cross with him for leaving her.

She felt she could see inside Bobby's house now. It was just like being in her own head: shadowed, but clear once you got used to it. Friendly, too. The tea Bobby was offering his guests would be tap water, like the coffee she always served on such occasions, and the cakes would be bigger and lumpier than hers but equally invisible, unless they were pebbles and seashells, of course. The conversation would be easy to understand and full of laughter. They might even tickle each other in the ribs.

Imagined thus, the prospect was irresistible. She simply *had* to join them, become the unexpected but utterly welcome visitor at Bobby's feast. Yes! She had to get there somehow even if she didn't dare climb over.

Could she fly in? She gave the thought wings but they wouldn't flap. Could she squeeze through? Let the entire bulk of herself follow her eye through the knothole? This seemed an admirable solution. Yes, why shouldn't she become elastic? And at once Anne found herself as pliable as forbidden chewing gum, as squeezable as sorbo rubber, as long drawn out as baker's dough. She flowed through the fence to emerge, *bloop*! the other side . . . where she was at once her white sausage self again. Or was she? Had the magic changed her? she wondered. She felt herself, chest, stomach, legs. Her hands said, yes, they were all the same, solid as ever. So was her familiar button nose, which wasn't going to grow, they said, if she persisted in catching flies in her open mouth. Anne had never caught a fly in this way (though she had tried in secret), nor in any other way for that matter, yet those who cared for her so vigilantly feared she might. Certainly her lips often fell apart, looking immodestly damp and pink.

Satisfied that her essential self had survived the magic passage through the fence, Anne shook herself into visiting shape, glanced back to see her own eye still watching her, and marched determinedly to the shelter, mouth shut, to knock smartly at the rectangular emptiness of the open doorway. To accomplish this she had forgotten to jump down, but that no longer mattered because Bobby appeared at once. How very English he looked, with his cornflower-blue eyes and his golden hair curling into a quiff. What was particularly gratifying was that he was definitely smaller than Anne. Perhaps about seven years old? Perfect. Adorable. Anne loved children younger than she was.

'Good day,' said Anne. 'How do you do? I am pleased to meet you. I hope you are well. You're my new friend Bobby, did you know?'

'Yes, please,' Bobby replied, sounding just like her.

'My name is Anne and my father is a giant.'

'I've seen him in the newspapers.'

'He is also a general.'

'He has a big nose.'

'Like Babar.'

'Does he breathe through it?'

'Of course. He is very famous.'

Anne knew you had always to bring a present when visiting someone's home for the first time. She pulled her handkerchief with the sweet in it from the pocket in her knickers. The milkman had given it to her that morning. This very foreign person kept a cigarette not thicker than a matchstick stuck to his lower lip. When he spoke, it bobbed up and down as if conducting his words. Sometimes smoke came out of it; at other times it looked dead and yellowy-brown, but always it was there.

An equally permanent pencil lodged behind the milkman's ear. He had to lick this pencil's point before writing in his fat account book, which had a broad rubber band to hold the pages still when the wind blew. What he wrote appeared in purple. 'It's an indelible pencil, Anne,' they explained; 'people use them back home, especially when writing out the menu for a restaurant.' But Anne had hardly ever been to a restaurant.

The palms of the milkman's hands (at home they got their milk from the cows next door) were as shiny and leathery as his satchel, which he shook in a horizontal, shovelly sort of way to make the heavy English coins slide out. He laughed and joked all the time, but none of them could easily understand what he was saying. 'He's a cockney,' they said. He called Anne 'duckie' or even 'ducks'. Anne preferred his horse. She felt she could understand this patient animal who never had to be told where to stop or when to start.

When it had first been explained that the sweets the milkman brought her were bull's-eyes, Anne had been so petrified she had refused, hot-faced, dumb with horror, even to touch the one she was offered, let alone eat it. To encourage her they said it would change colour as she sucked it – 'Suck it and see', the milkman said. But still she refused. He had patted her head and she'd shrunk away from him.

They had all laughed. 'Oh, Anne, you're so silly.' But Anne had once been held very close to a bull by the farmer next door at home. Its eye had been quite as wickedly bloodshot as this carmine ball she was now offering to Bobby. The farmer had assured her she was quite safe from the bull, which he had travelled all the way to Colmar to buy. There was a ring through its nose and from the ring ran a long chain. 'That keeps our Fritz quiet as a lamb,' he said, rattling the chain. But this reassurance hadn't stopped the bull's baleful eye following Anne through many dreams.

Although she had grown used to the strange milkman and his sweets, Anne still preferred to give them away if she could. She had tried offering one to a ginger tom cat, but he had only cuffed it contemptuously with his paw and stalked away, tail held high. After that, other politer recipients of her self-protective generosity had included pillar boxes, storm drains and flowerpots. But Bobby, having been appointed by her as her perfect neighbour, accepted the sweet at once and made his soft cheek bulge with it so satisfactorily she could laugh without fear. To make the moment even more memorable he thanked her with his mouth full. This was superb. For Anne, talking while eating was a cardinal sin, although she often noticed adults doing it. But they, of course, found it easy not to dribble and rarely spat out crumbs.

'They call them bull's-eyes,' she said. 'They change colour.'

'I know,' Bobby said, nodding.

Anne thought she would nod as well. The sensation was rather enjoyable. Soon the pair of them, she discovered, were imitating each other. They had, it appeared, achieved a perfect rapport. Bobby pulled at the corners of his eyes to make them slant like hers. At once she recognised herself in him, this clever baby. How kind, how supremely tactful, it was of Bobby to make himself so like her; never had she enjoyed such understanding, such flattery. She began to bounce up and down, but carefully because of her sore heel, and straight off, without any prompting, exactly as she had hoped and intended, Bobby jumped too. As they bounced, he with exuberant infant energy, she with maturer caution, they found that they saw literally eye to eye. Clearly they were perfectly matched – ideal companions.

But now, good heavens, Bobby was spluttering, coughing! Should she pat his back? Be the grown-up mother she could turn into if she chose? But no, there was no need. No. Because the bull's-eye, lemon yellow now, had shot out of his mouth and landed, by purest sympathetic magic, right in the middle of Anne's outstretched palm. And stuck there. Not rolled off down the slope of her fingers. She had caught it. This was unprecedented. She wasn't Anne Butterfingers after all. Had she ever experienced such co-ordinated pleasure before? She thought not.

Anne stopped jigging and stared at the glistening sweet. Merely by accepting it Bobby had rendered it safe; but now . . . now he had not only changed its colour but let her catch it too. She would eat it at once, without thinking any more. *Yes*! She gulped it from her open hand and smiled.

'You are going to be my best friend,' she announced grandly, as if she were the Queen of Sheba, whom she sometimes was but not today. Bobby agreed and led her into his house.

It smelt like a barn. Anne liked such smells – earthy, cool, haylike. As her eyes became used to the dimness of the house she decided she could see a deck chair, a broken wicker armchair and a stool with a cork seat exactly like the one in the bathroom of their house here in Petts Wood which Maman had found while Papa was busy telling Mr Churchill how to shoot Herr Hitler. Lolling at his ease in the sag of the deck chair was the bear in the jumper, together with the elephant whose check trousers were, she could now see, entirely inappropriate if he was to be who he really ought to be.

'Your elephant's trousers should be green,' she said severely.

'Really?' Bobby said. But she could tell he hadn't fully understood.

'And what about his spats?' she added. Her Babar always wore spats, unless equally correctly dressed for other activities such as tennis at Casablanca or motoring along the Corniche. Just as Papa always had the right clothes to do the right things in. Obviously this little English boy was unaware of such proprieties. She would have to bring him her Babar book so he could see what she meant. His elephant was far too lax. Elephants had to be impeccable at all times.

'Do please sit down,' Bobby said, hauling his Rupert Bear out of the deck chair by a very loose arm, and the elephant by his trunk.

Anne was shocked. 'You must never do that!' she said.

'Why not?' he said, waving the toys. Anne grabbed the elephant from him.

'You must never hold an elephant by his trunk and certainly not Babar,' she said. And suddenly she felt so protective she knew exactly how her father felt about her and everybody else at home. Papa often talked about France like that – with a furious sadness – on the wireless that Maman listened to every evening. His voice came through a little window of pale-gold brocade.

Anne sat down in the deck chair with the elephant on her knee while Bobby poured the tea. On receiving it, she crooked her little finger in imitation of a white-haired lady with three foxes on her chest whom she had seen sipping tea in London. The water tasted fresh and pleasant around the aniseed sweetness of the bull's-eye. Next she set her cup aside and took the sweet out of her mouth to inspect it. Apart from a patch of red coming through on one side it was now safely green. It was at this moment that Anne heard the air-raid siren.

All her pretences flew away. Bobby who understood her every word, his magic house, their perfect tea together, their shared bull's-eye, all were gone. Swallowed up, lost in the echoing moan, the fulsome whining of the siren. The terrible sound rose and fell, reaching out of the air at Anne, groping at her like some invisible monster with a hundred arms. An octopus of sound singing at her to make her cry before devouring her. Try as she might, she could not blot out this relentless cry which seemed to her more menacing than the danger it presaged.

Anne jerked her head up . . . and she was back where she had been all along, beside the fence – looking urgently at the sky. So far its virgin blue was quite un-smudged. As she stared upwards, searching for tell-tale vapour trails, she rubbed at her left eyebrow, which was again dented, rather more so than before, from being pressed too hard against the fence. Anne was praying, *Please don't let me see any aeroplanes, please.* And her stomach churned – it seemed to move in rhythm with the siren's insidious oscillations. She started to sweat and tremble; then staggering to her feet, she tried to run. She fell over, grazing her knee, got up, sobbing; her chest burned with breathing but somehow she managed to reach the back door, where her nurse, Marguerite, was standing saying there, there, it's only the silly siren, but Anne barged past her anyoldhow and ducked head first into the cupboard under the stairs. There she remained, hands over her ears, crouched, bottom stuck out, waiting for the all clear.

The air raids had begun again just a week before. After the dogfights. Though why several tiny aeroplanes buzzing at each other until one fell from the sky with smoke pouring out of it were called dogfights Anne couldn't understand. They didn't look at all like dogs. The English aeroplanes were good but made of old saucepans; the German ones were made from proper metal but were bad. There were far more of them too, but fortunately the English aeroplanes were full of blue boys who could make their old saucepans jump out of the sun and kill the bad Germans.

After the dogfights everything had gone quiet and summer had pretended it had sent the world away on holiday. Anne had started to feel almost happy again, but now the sirens had returned, crying throughout the day, and the night too, creating huge vacancies of dread.

When it was dark the sky got criss-crossed with sweeping swords of light and the blackout windows rattled as the tall guns at the tennis club fired at the streams of bombers swimming like silver fish across Anne's overturned world. The guns coughed and barked like angry metal frogs.

Anne was now perpetually terrified, but she had no need to be, they said. Herr Hitler's bombers weren't trying to hurt *her*, they said. 'They're going up to London. They're trying to hurt London, darling, not you.' But she didn't believe them. Of course the fish in the sky were trying to hurt her. Papa was Papa and she was Papa's daughter. Since he was important so was she and, besides, he'd told her she was his best girl. Herr Hitler thought Papa was still here, not gone to be king of the elephants, and so he sent his flying fish to find him and kill him here in England. But killing her would be just as good because that would upset Papa. And serve him right since he had deserted her.

Anne thought she could hear the all clear. She took her hands from her ears. Was that it dying away, like pain ebbing from a bump or bruise? She peeped out and her nurse was saying: 'It's all right, you can come out now, Anne. You'll be safe now. Besides, it's time we took Jockey for a walk.' And, hearing this, the bristly little terrier appeared from the kitchen. Anne had been given him by friends of Papa. He was there to help her like being in England. He was a clever dog but you had to be careful he didn't bite.

They put Jockey on his lead and went out round the corner past the church that had had its spire knocked off by a shot-down saucepan.

To buy things in England you had to have little books with dull-coloured stamps in them, which the man in the shop cut out with scissors.

Anne liked to watch him work the bacon slicer and the way he cut the hard English cheese with wire and tucked in the tops of the blue sugar bags with blunt, brown fingers. These were their week's rations, she was told.

The shelves in the grocer's shop were decorated with large square biscuit tins and huge round tea caddies. They looked brave and gay and Anne liked them, especially the biscuit tins with their flags and banners saluting the Kings and Queens of England, but she knew they were empty just from the look of them.

After buying their groceries they would go to the butcher's. Here there was often a queue but hardly any meat. Instead the shop was full of marble and shiny hooks with sawdust on the floor, to soak up the blood, Maman said. But Anne never saw much blood; there was a little when the butcher cut up liver, but mostly she saw only pale, pimpled chickens. What meat there was looked different from at home and so did the butcher. Back home he did everything very carefully and slowly, cutting and slicing with surgical reverence before tying the meat up into perfect parcels with string almost as thin as cotton. But here in England the man just went, bang, chop, skewer, and his string was thick and hairy. Anne could tell her mother didn't really like the butcher because she never tried to say anything extra to him, whereas in the grocer's she would talk quite a lot. Hearing her mother attempt to speak English made Anne glad because suddenly Maman seemed as eager and as misunderstood as she.

Their next stop that morning was the shoe-repair man. He had thumbs that curved right back – a bad sign in a person, Maman said. Here Anne had little metal moons called segs tapped into the heels and toes of her shoes and

Maman collected a pair of her own which had new heels now.

Anne walked back to the house with the segs in her shoes clacking sharply on the pavement. They sounded lovely – click, clack. She began to move faster, pushing the clicks and clacks closer together until they produced, she thought, an almost continuous roar like an aeroplane. Yes, she was spreading her arms for wings. She was a twin-engined bomber, yes. And her mouth could make engine noises too. Fancy her becoming what she feared most – but no, that wasn't it: she was a *good* aeroplane, going to Herr Hitler's house to blow him up.

Now she was flying, which meant running along the grass verge so her feet made no further sound because she was heavily – so many bombs inside her – beautifully, dangerously airborne as she growled and droned and hummed her way to her target, which would be the next gap, where the grass stopped by the belisha beacon . . . She could see it ahead, there, that would be Herr Hitler's house, and she would jump over it dropping all her bombs, bang, bang, bang, and he would be dead and she would have won the war for Papa and they would all go home again.

But Maman called and she had to stop, never reaching her target. Her entire strategy which had been so marvellously inspired by the new segs in her shoes, was spoiled. Anne flew slowly back to base with holes in her wings and only one engine working. Maman was cross. She was not – 'do you hear, Anne?' – *not* to go mooning along the road like that with her arms waving everywhere and making those ridiculous noises. What did she imagine she was doing, a big girl like her? Really! Anyone would think she was a seven-year-old, not twelve and more. Anne did not reply. She didn't speak at all for the rest of the way. Her recall from her bombing mission had blighted her trip to the shops. Now the war would never end and she would have to stay in England for ever.

'Let's make a garden,' he said. Anne agreed at once; and she was through the fence in an instant, without even bothering to be elastic. She merely pretended herself to the other side... and there they were together, kneeling to fill Bobby's old baking tin with earth from a pile beside a hole which he said he'd dug only that morning so they could enjoy another visit to Australia. Anne was surprised.

'We've visited Australia?' she said.
'Oh yes. You took me to a boxing match.'
'Did I?'
'You must remember.'
'I expect I shall in a minute.'
'It was between a man and a kangaroo. It was quite funny really. The man kept falling down when the kangaroo hit him. We laughed and laughed.'
'I've seen a picture like that in a book.'
'So've I.'
'The kangaroo wore big gloves like balloons.'
'The man did, too. They're boxing gloves.'
'Who won?'
'Nobody. We had to leave before the end so you could bomb Herr Hitler. We came back up through the earth just like that.' And to demonstrate the speed of their return

Bobby clicked his fingers in a snappy way that Anne's never would or could.

'That explains it,' she said.

Anne had no recollection of this momentous excursion but she decided that, if Bobby said it had been so, so it must have been.

Hidden from the world, between a row of going-to-seed lettuces and a tangle of sweet peas, they took turns with the rusty trowel scooping earth into the tin. Once it was full, they patted the earth flat and planted it with moss for a lawn and small stones for a path of crazy paving. In the flower beds they stuck daisies and tiny blue speedwell flowers. Bobby wanted to put in an enormous lupin but Anne said no. Instead she broke off six thin heads of the shot lettuces to make a row of poplars along one side.

Finally Bobby disappeared to return with two painted people and a pig from his toy farm. The people were him and her and the pig was really their dog, he said. Anne thought a pig couldn't be a dog and they very nearly began to quarrel, but then Anne was overwhelmed with homesickness because these people made of lead and indeed the pig, too, were identical with the toys she had left behind in France. She started to cry. Bobby patted her hand and she stopped. He placed the three of them in the garden and then they looked at the tableau from every conceivable angle. Neither had seen anything quite so beautiful before.

After a while Anne had a new idea. Why didn't they make it rain on the garden? Bobby, reading her mind, went at once to fetch the watering can to make a gentle shower with the sun shining through the raindrops. Anne lay full length on her side gazing at their sparkling home-made heaven.

Bobby wanted to show it to his bear and elephant, so they took it down to the Anderson shelter. The tin garden seemed very heavy and one of the poplar-tree lettuces fell over but somehow they managed to manoeuvre it safely inside. After a couple of quick repairs the animals were brought to view it. Both were speechless with admiration – as well they might be – especially the bear, whose head Bobby forcibly nodded in acclaim. Anne felt warm inside. Their model paradise was now a social success as well as a triumph of shared science and true friendship.

Bobby began to read his toys a story from a book he knew by heart. Anne loved to pretend to read too, and normally she might well have seized the book from him but just now she had eyes only for their miniature garden. It seemed to her quite as precious as the one at home which Papa had told her was hers and in which she would always be safe.

Even before the war Anne had been anxious and afraid – with and without reason. She didn't know why. It was like a spectral stomach ache that came and went yet its menace was always lurking somewhere within her. She hid this fear from herself and others, or so she imagined, by looking as pleasant as she could and smiling almost all the time. But Papa's telling her she would be safe in her garden at home meant he must have seen or smelt her fear. Or both. But then being so brave himself he would know a coward at once. Soldiers like Papa were never afraid.

One day in her garden, when she was looking for wild strawberries under the trees in the wood where the ivy and cyclamen grew, she had been startled by a rustling sound and there at her feet was a blackbird with a broken wing. It ran from her, trying to fly, but couldn't. Anne went to pick the bird up to nurse it better, but its erratic movements alarmed her. Instead she went in search of Marguerite, who was darning the family's socks under the walnut tree, but when they came to where she had seen the blackbird it had gone.

'You must have imagined it, Anne.'

'No.'

'You're sure?'

'Its wing was all dragged down, droopy.'

'Perhaps it was pretending? Birds do that sometimes.'

'Birds play "let's pretend" like me?'

'Yes. To trick you away from their nests.'

'Why?'

'So you won't steal their eggs or eat their nestlings.'

'But I wouldn't, would I?'

'How could the blackbird know that? I expect that's what it was, so you needn't worry about it.'

But her nurse was wrong. Several days later Anne found the blackbird lying dead with woodlice and ants all over it. They made a shimmering cover like a satin counterpane. She gathered up leaves to drop on it to make the insects go away, but they wouldn't. Having failed at this she tried to scrape a grave for it, but the ground was too hard and she didn't dare touch the blackbird, let alone carry it to somewhere softer, so she left it where it was.

This time she didn't tell her nurse or anyone else about it and the dead thing in the wood became her precious secret. She found herself thinking about it when she felt afraid. Very soon the dead bird had turned into the stomach ache inside her. And this secret vision of decaying flesh and loosening feathers with a livingness not its own thrilled her. She hugged it to her, loving it, feeling grown-up, not telling a soul. Day after day she returned to examine the blackbird's decomposition with rapt pleasure, until eventually she found only a ragged wing, some downy fluff from its breast and no insects at all except a daddy-longlegs.

Anne didn't know where the rest of the bird had vanished to. Nor, after a moment, did she care, because now the ache was nowhere to be felt inside her. It had gone too. And the cyclamen were all in flower.

Anne lay down flat on her now untroubled tummy to look at them. Viewed this way their marbled leaves became wide as dinner plates and their flowers' petals became angels' wings, like those of the doves that tumbled above the village when the church bell rang. The ground was damp. She would be scolded for muddying her smock – Anne was always dressed as if for a school she never went to – but never mind. What mattered were the flowers close to her and the golden meadow beyond, between the green trunks of the trees, where the grass was warm and hazy in the soft summer sun.

TWO

'What is England, Maman?'
  'It's a country, darling.'
  'Has Papa gone to England?'
  'We keep telling you, Anne, yes.'
  'Why?'
  'To help France, darling.'
  How it had rained as they'd hurried to the harbour. Once there, they had sat for hours in a wooden room while Maman went away. To distract Anne the others had kept pointing at the boat through the weeping doorway, but all Anne could see was sluiced greyness, a fat army lorry and, just once, a shivering sailor with a newspaper on his head.
  Anne felt something on her cheek and looked up to see if the roof was crying too. But it wasn't – it was still her own teardrops.
  'Do stop crying, Anne – Maman will be back soon.'
  'I want to go home.'
  'Don't be silly,' Marguerite said. 'By now it's full of Germans.'
  After that none of them had said anything, but Anne hoped the cats were happy and that they didn't mind being stroked by Herr Hitler. She thought they wouldn't because cats liked chair legs quite as much as people and

important people, she knew, often had highly polished legs. Papa's were sometimes as shiny as a piano's right up to his knees, where suddenly they went dull and baggy so he could ride a horse. Anne could remember seeing him once on a horse. He had looked like a brown statue.

When at last Maman came back they had to go to the boat straight away. It was always like that now. Either they made Anne sit for hours, asking herself what would happen next, or else she was chivvied along to catch a bus which was going to take her to a motor car which delivered her to a train which carried her to an aunt who gave Maman some money so they could all sail away from the seaside town full of raw-faced men in uniforms.

They splashed through the rain to the boat. Their luggage was much too heavy even though Maman said they had only brought what they stood up in, which was strange because most of it was inside all these suitcases whose handles hurt your hand. Stuck on the side of one was a picture of a girl in a spotted bathing dress looking very happy on yellow sand. When she grew up Anne wanted to be this beautiful girl. To her she looked like the Blessed Virgin Mary on holiday with a beach ball instead of Jesus.

As they left the harbour the sun suddenly blazed out from under the rain clouds so the granite walls and slate roofs of the town (which was almost at the end of the earth, they said) turned to dazzling gold and the oiled waters all round them grew rainbow plumes. They stood at the ship's rail, Maman, Anne, her big brother and her not quite so big sister, and her nurse, and waved at the shining town until the sun was blacked out again. This made it darker, sadder, but easier to be going. Her brother said they weren't really leaving France, it was France who was leaving them, but it didn't feel like that to Anne, oh no. She could tell, she *knew*, it was she who was going away. So, too, was the deck, suddenly, as they reached the open sea; wherever she put her feet it kept saying goodbye to them. She swayed, clung hard to things and people, and shutting her eyes tried in vain to believe she wasn't anywhere at all.

Later on, after being encouraged to eat some chewy meat that was difficult to swallow, she was supposed to go to sleep. But it was too early, too different, and everybody else kept coming in or going out of the cabin. She could hear them talking in shadowy voices about a strange place in England the boat wasn't going to after all because the captain thought it safer not to. The shorter the voyage the safer it would be, they said, but their voices didn't sound safe because they thought Anne was asleep and so they no longer pretended everything was all right when it wasn't.

When at last Anne was left alone in the cabin with her nurse, Marguerite took her prayer-book out of her handbag; but she didn't open it, no: she simply clutched it so tightly her knuckles looked like tiny cockleshells.

In her berth Anne lay on her back with her eyes shut and thought about her father because although she had been told many times that he had gone to England she kept wondering if he was dead. After all, he had changed from a soldier fighting Herr Hitler to a general with a star on his hat who'd turned into someone called a minister. Hearing the repeated refrain 'Papa is a minister in the government as well as a general now, darling', she had decided he must have died and gone to heaven. She hoped desperately

Anne's Story

these unintelligible words didn't mean this, but dwelling as she did within a closed circle of gentle untruths, adult mysteries and well-meant euphemisms Anne couldn't be sure. She knew people were always altering the world so she wouldn't be upset by it but these alterations only added to her confusion.

But then as Marguerite climbed up a little steel ladder to lie still dressed on the berth above her, Anne decided her father must be alive so she could go to sleep. She would tell herself over and over he was. And he was still her favourite giant and he had gone to the place they were going to, which was somewhere in the moonlit emptiness she could now glimpse through the porthole. Its solid, polished roundness and the bold brass bolts on it comforted her a little, made her feel almost safe, despite the creaking of Marguerite above her as she, too, composed herself for the night.

At one o'clock in the morning an angry donkey in a tin box ordered them to get up at once and go on deck to a muster station. They said this heehaw sound was the ship's klaxon and it meant they were being followed by Herr Hitler under the water. Hitler was going to shoot holes in their boat unless the English captain did something clever. And of course he would: 'You needn't worry, Anne, because England is full of wonderful sailors,' they said.

Sailors, Anne knew, were allowed to grow beards but soldiers were not; soldiers were only permitted moustaches like Papa's, which felt like friendly sandpaper when he kissed her.

'Has he got a beard?' she asked.

'Who, darling?'

'The sailorman.'

'No more questions now, dear. This isn't the time.'

The ship's wake glowed in widening zigzags under the moon as the officers quartered the surface of the sea with binoculars. Anne was familiar with these instruments, indeed she had looked through her father's – they made things with coloured edges come close to you. She asked if they would really be all right now the boat kept going this way and that, like an old man who had had too much wine and no dinner. They said the ship was fine. Ten zigzags later she repeated her question and they got angry with her: 'Oh Anne, how many more times must we tell you? It's all right! Now, shush.'

Anne was aware she ought to remember what she was told and this time she had, but sometimes she didn't, it was true. On those occasions it was as if her mind was busy somewhere else, knew really but couldn't at that moment locate what it was looking for. Often the effort of hunting through her head for thoughts she ought to have remembered made it hurt and she would get short of breath. Sensible people's minds were like Maman's tidy cupboards; hers was mostly a jumble with an order all its own. She went and climbed up on to her mother's lap.

'You're much too big for this, really, darling.'

'Papa doesn't mind.'

'Papa's stronger than I am.'

'But he isn't here, so you're next, Maman.'

'Next best? Second best, am I?'

'Yes.'

'Well, thank you for the compliment, young lady.'

'Where is Papa?'

'Darling, we told you. In London.'

'I forgot. Are we going to London?'

'Just as soon as we get off this boat, yes.'

'Is England London?'

'No, Anne, London is a city in England. It's a big, big city, like Paris. We'll go there in a train.'

'I like trains,' Anne said and bumped herself up and down, chuffing and chugging.

'If you're going to be a train you can get off my lap this minute,' her mother said. Anne stopped puffing immediately, without even letting off steam, which was one of the best parts of the game. She lay still, nuzzling into her mother's neck.

'What a silly old thing you are,' her mother said and sighed. Then she hummed a song she knew Anne liked. After that nothing happened for a long time, until a sailor came with life jackets and they tied them round each other. Anne felt fatter and clumsier than ever, but these rubber cushions would make her into a film star called Mae West, they said. And keep her afloat too.

'But I don't want to go in the water.'

'None of us do, Anne. It's just in case.'

'I can't swim, can I? You know I can't. Please don't let me go in the water!'

'You mustn't worry, darling.'

'I'll catch cold if I go in the water.'

'You'll be all right.'

'Don't let me go in the water!'

'Now, stop it, Anne! Be quiet! And don't stamp your foot. Just sit there – where you are.'

This time their voices sounded not just uncertain but openly angry, so Anne knew it was perfectly all right to be afraid. The sweet sickly smell of the rubber life jacket added a taste of nausea to her fear. Still the ship veered this way, that way, under the moon and the moon came with them as they went. Anne's nurse tried to put her arm round Anne but it woudn't reach because of the life jacket, so she held her hand instead. Anne felt like a disconsolate sofa.

Suddenly out of the moon came a grinding noise and an enormous aeroplane. The ship crackled orders and the klaxon brayed urgently. The sailors ran and stood everywhere, looking alert and ready – but for what Anne couldn't tell. She stared, transfixed, her mouth dribbling, at the enormous machine, which was almost like a boat itself except that it possessed huge wings and four propellers. It was coming straight at them.

'Will it fall on us?' Anne cried in a shriek that no one heard because the noise was so loud.

Then it was past them. A ship's officer shouted: 'It's one of ours!' It belonged to the Royal Air Force, he said, and it was a boat. A Sunderland Flying Boat. This was translated for Anne. 'The aeroplane is on our side, darling, and it's also a boat. So you needn't cry,' they said, 'it isn't going to hurt you.'

This monster with engines like giant bumblebees flew twice round the ship again before rumbling away. To Anne it still seemed too heavy to really fly. But somehow it had and now it was gone for good and she was glad, however friendly they had said it was.

An officer came and saluted Maman exactly as people

did Papa. She must come and speak to the captain, he said. Maman went and when she came back she was smiling all over, not just her face. It was wonderful. Anne hadn't seen her mother smile for a week. Not a proper smile. Maman said Mr Churchill had sent the flying boat to look for them because Papa had become Mr Churchill's special friend now and he, Papa, had begun to wonder where they were. Wasn't that nice? And the ship's captain had told the pilot they were all safe and well but they were still evading German submarines. They all agreed it was marvellous news, but Anne was puzzled: she couldn't understand how a boat flying through the air could talk to a boat in the water. She wanted to ask, but everyone was too busy being happy again, so she didn't.

Later the clouds came back on a rush of wind, which piled them up together until it rained and the waves grew taller and wider while the ship wallowed up and down, not going anywhere for hours. Everyone in turn told Anne the ship couldn't take shelter in the harbour – which was just over there, where they couldn't see it – until the gale blew itself out and, 'isn't this absurd because the one place we all want to be in a storm is safe inside a harbour.' Although she had been in one when they set out from Brittany, Anne didn't know what a harbour was.

When at last they did get in they were somewhere called Falmouth. A strange word. It went furry when she tried to pronounce it. She did try several times but was told firmly to stop. They hadn't expected to come ashore here, they said. The ship's original destination had been Southampton. But Anne had ceased to listen to anyone because she didn't want to be anywhere except home. She felt sick at heart again and couldn't stop yawning. She tried pretending the suitcase she was perched on was really the leather arm of her father's chair, but it wasn't smooth enough. Marguerite told her not to fidget, there's a good girl, but the way she said it made Anne think of shoes crunching on broken glass.

As the morning sky cleared, someone gave them a newspaper and everyone except Anne got shiny-eyed and excited. There was a photograph of Papa on it. His face looked grey and dotty. The paper said he had talked to France on the radio from London and told France she wasn't to feel lonely because she wasn't alone and everything would be all right so long as she listened to him. Anne agreed. She could have told France that. It was obvious. Papa always made everything all right for her. So she couldn't understand why everyone else was so chattery and red-cheeked.

Maman went away to telephone Papa. Anne looked between her legs at the Blessed Virgin Mary at the seaside but her upside-down smile seemed ridiculous now. Though she still rather liked her coloured ball. Anne decided she didn't want to be her after all. Nor did she want to be in England. She wanted to see Papa, yes, but not here: here was too different.

After a while Maman came back, but she didn't say very much. They went to a railway station with high platforms. Much higher than at home. Anne quite liked the look of the engine driver. He was eating sandwiches out of a tin box. His grimy face grinned down at her and he held out a sandwich towards her, but she shook her heavy head. He smiled again and cocked his thumb at her with an encouraging sort of shake, saying something she couldn't understand. The engine driver and the warm, insidious smell of soot and steam made Anne feel a little better.

To start with, the train was full of sailors; then, at the first stop, hundreds of soldiers got on, too. They all stood and sat and slept anywhere and everywhere, packing the corridors. The train went slowly and often came to a stop where there wasn't a station. It didn't seem to know which way to go.

England looked small. But as green as home. Anne looked at trees, at cows, washing on clotheslines, a real man climbing a telegraph pole and two pretend ones cut out of plywood carrying a plank with words on it across a field full of buttercups. The words said something about paint you put on houses, her sister Elizabeth said. But there wasn't a house anywhere near. Anne hoped the plywood men would reach one soon.

Next she stared at a row of thin gun barrels pointing at the sky. They gleamed in the sun as the train chugged past. Then came something to really encourage her – a true joy. Nothing less than a herd of elephants in the sky. Grey and bulging, with their ears at the back and wires hanging down from their stomachs instead of legs, but elephants nevertheless. You could tell that at a glance. 'Look!' she shouted. Of course she was told to shush but Anne didn't care, didn't even hear as she wriggled and pointed at the airborne elephants. 'Those aren't elephants, Anne,' they said, 'those are barrage balloons. The wires tangle round the propellers of enemy aeroplanes so they can't bomb the town underneath.' But Anne didn't listen to their explanations because she knew what the balloons really were.

They passed another town, but it didn't look like the sort she liked so she went to sleep and had just started to dream she had been taken to be examined by a new doctor, who roared with laughter when he saw her, only to wake up with a jolt in echoing darkness to find one of the English soldiers struggling to shut the window for them. Their compartment filled with smoke before it could be properly pulled up, but by then the train had burst out of the tunnel into blue-green sunshine and a brass stud popped through a hole in the thick leather strap to wink at Anne.

She had got a coal smut on her blouse, which Marguerite rubbed at with a damp handkerchief, but that only made it look worse – just as Maman had said it would. Marguerite sulked. The English soldier opened the window again, to let out the smell of smoke, and again the brass stud winked at Anne. She decided it was the eye of a small animal about the size of a guinea pig. Someone friendly certainly. Someone who would like to be winked back at. So she tried to return the wink, but this simple action did not come happily or easily to her. Her mother noticed. 'Don't make faces, darling,' she said.

When Maman had talked to Papa on the telephone he had been too busy to say anything except they were to come at once to London and he was glad to hear they were safe because the flying boat Mr Churchill had sent to look for them hadn't come back. Anne, remembering how heavy it had looked, asked if it had fallen on its back. They laughed, but it wasn't a silly question – not to her. It had reminded her of the upside-down stag beetles who came in from the lovely smelly farmyard next door at home; the ones she liked to help if she could by turning them over with a stick so they could fly again. First they would waddle as if they couldn't fly at all; then, with a sudden dry whirr, their backs would open and they'd take off into the air. But, no, they said, the flying boat wouldn't have fallen down: it had probably been shot down because Hitler was stepping up the war in the air against England.

When people talked like that, talked like the newspapers and the wireless, Anne didn't even try to understand them, although she recognised certain repeated sounds as if they were familiar flags bobbing and flapping above the marching words. 'Herr Hitler' was a black flag, which meant guns and tanks and Germans with boots living in her house and getting their milk and eggs from the farm next door. Would the farmer be kind to the Germans? she wondered. He was an obliging man, they always said. 'The war' was a bright red flag; and 'England', well, that was a new flag really. It seemed to her it might be pale beige-pink – the colour of underclothes you weren't supposed to see on washing lines or when ladies sat down without thinking or you were having a rest on a rug and they stepped over you. But she had no coloured flags for words like '*Luftwaffe*' or '*Messerschmitt*'. The first simply sounded like breathing, the second like sneezing.

London was tall shadows, white faces, sharp lights and a peculiar bed with oblong pillows and no bolster at all. But that didn't matter, everything was all right, because London was Papa. He was there! He had said prayers with her and told her the swan story. This ineffable creature had started out as a big, ugly gawk who the pretty little ducklings had despised. Once they had grown up, though, they were just ducks and she was the Queen of Light and Air. But it wasn't the prayers or the story that had released Anne from terror; no, it was his sitting there, him, so his great weight made the mattress slant down from under her as he held her hand and kissed her goodnight with his moustache still smelling wonderfully of tobacco like it always did, though the smell was different now, somehow sharper, brighter. And so were the funny flat packets of his cigarettes, which had the head of a king with a beard on them and were called Player's Navy Cut. Anne could neither read nor say these words, but she liked the look and sound of them because they were part of this new-old Papa.

She reached up to put her arms right round his neck and hold him tight. Papa was hers because she was so strong, she said. He laughed and pretended he couldn't escape her grip. By being with him she was special again. His special girl. The one whose eyes he looked into long enough for her to see herself reflected in his. He was doing it now and she remembered the very first time he had looked into her like that when she had been much smaller, after he had taken her to the top of the hill above the village at home and held her up on his shoulders so her heels could beat against his chest and her hands could hold on to his hair – 'Gently, Anne, gently' – to show her – 'Look carefully, Anne' – something he said was called France stretched out all around them as far as their eyes could see.

As they turned, Papa told her that the roof over there was their house, that spire was their church and everything else was the green hills, dark woods and meadows of home. Anne had laughed with delight, but her delight was more at being high up on his shoulders than at anything she saw, until he stopped turning and stood stock-still with his back to the evening sun.

She began to wriggle, kicking at his chest, but he gripped her shins yet more firmly and told her to hold her arms out wide. At first she didn't want to, she was afraid. 'No, I don't dare – I'll fall, Papa,' she said. But he promised her she wouldn't, that he would never allow her to fall, so she did as she was told, slowly extending her arms until they were as wide as Jesus's. And then . . . then Papa, just for an instant, let go his grip on her legs and he, too, held out his arms. And there, stretching out in front of them, was their shadow and it was like a long cross twice over – the one with four arms Anne had seen on postcards and sweet boxes.

She laughed and wobbled. Their shadow windmilled wildly as Papa caught her, laughing too, and swung her sweepingly to the ground as if she were no weight at all. Then he crouched down to her level and looked into her eyes for a long time before he said: 'Anne, you're France, too.' And there she was twice over in his eyes, though now her reflections were dissolving, blurring. He blinked and stood up, turning away from her to blow his nose trumpetingly.

On the way home he had bought her a Whirligig, a celluloid propeller on a stick. At first Anne supposed it was a kind of daffodil. But when she waved it in the air it spun softly.

THREE

The Queen of Sheba's limousine bulged as she sat with her knees squashed up under her chin. Her chauffeur, Bobby, was at the wheel in the driver's compartment, an old banana box, in front of the soap crate.

Anne was proud of her new English chauffeur and her big car. Already they had driven halfway to Timbuktu. Soon they would reach Babar's kingdom and find Papa. Already it was getting hotter and hotter as she bumped her carton along the garden path, pushing against the banana box, until suddenly it stuck.

'What's the matter?' she asked.

'We've boiled over, your majesty,' Bobby replied.

She got out and walked round to inspect the front of the car. The banana box looked perfectly all right to her. She couldn't see any steam coming out of it. True she had to shift the box from where it was jammed against a stone, but that was all. She climbed back into her carton.

'I've made it better,' she said.

But when Bobby tried to start again, nothing happened.

'Is it still too hot?'

'Yes, your majesty. Listen. You can hear the water bubbling.'

Anne listened and this time, yes, she was able to imagine

she could hear a hissing turbulence somewhere, because once upon a time she had seen a real chauffeur undo a metal cap and a sharp fountain of steam had shot up into the air making him jump back with a bright-red face.

Anne had grown even more fond of Bobby since her first sighting of him through the fence. Now when he wasn't being her invisible chauffeur she reserved seats for him as her best friend on sofas, beside her at table, in bed, on public benches, front-garden walls and buses. He came everywhere with her, often to the exasperation of Maman and Marguerite. But now, here they were, marooned in the desert. Very soon evil bandits on bad-tempered camels were bound to appear and capture them. Whereupon, even as she thought it, they were surrounded. Instantaneously. Exactly as she had feared.

The Chief of the Bandits came to gloat over them. He looked like her father, but not so tall – who was? – and much fatter. He was an evil sort of Papa made out of creased and polished leather, with eyes as black as jet and yellow as butter. On his terrible hands there were ten rings (he sported one on each thumb as well as on his fingers), which exploded in the sun like soundless fireworks, whereas Papa had only one plain gold ring, his wedding ring, which he wore on his right hand because the Germans had fired a bullet through his left one, oh long ago, long before Anne had been born. Nor did this desert chieftain wear a proper uniform like Papa. No, he wore a white sheet with a jewelled belt and a silver sword as curved as his victorious smile.

'How do you do,' he said. 'I am the Chief of the Bandits

and you are the Queen of Sheba. I need another wife, so I shall carry you off and marry you.'

'No! I want to marry Bobby,' Anne said. She hadn't realised this until she said it but it was true.

'No more silly talk,' the Chief replied.

Whereupon they were seized and the next thing Anne knew they were trussed like chickens and flung over the backs of camels fast as express trains. They sped across the desert, with the bandits galloping beside them screeching like owls, until they came to their stronghold, which was a huge sand castle exactly like the one Papa had built for her at the seaside when she was small and hadn't known his world could turn round, let alone fall over.

After she and Bobby had been put into a cupboard and given nothing to eat, Anne had time to think what to pretend next.

'We must escape at once,' she said.

'Immediately,' Bobby agreed.

'How?'

'Easily,' he answered with his cheerful English smile.

But then, alas, the cupboard door burst open and the Chief of the Bandits stood before them again, only this time he was eating smoked salmon, gulping red wine and grinning widely. And he was looking more than ever like Papa, who also loved smoked salmon because it was so easy to eat and didn't interfere with his thinking about how to rescue France from Herr Hitler and smoking cigarettes at the same time.

'Ha-ha,' the Chief said. 'You thought you could escape, didn't you?'

'Yes. We want to be free.'

'You can be,' he said. 'All you've got to do is marry me.'

'Yes, do! Never mind me, your majesty. Do marry him!' said Bobby. 'Look, he's getting cross.'

Anne was shocked. 'But I'm not the Queen of Sheba any more. I've stopped being her. I'm me again. I'm Anne from France. Ask Papa.'

'Exactly who is this papa of yours?'

'He's a giant. He's going to beat Herr Hitler.'

'How will he do that?'

'I don't know, but Mr Churchill likes him. He lets Papa talk on the wireless and the little yellow light comes on to tell us never to stop fighting. But most of us haven't even started yet – we just wait while the bombs fall down, houses burn, dead men fall out of the sky, I can't sleep and if my night light goes out the bangs in the darkness make me scream and scream.'

'You sound in need of comfort and help, young lady,' said the Chief.

'No, I just want to go home. I want to be as I used to be.'

'Me, too,' said Bobby.

'Nonsense. Impossible. No. Never. Don't you know there's a war on?' the Chief said.

And at a snap from his cruel fingers the bandits packed Anne and Bobby into kitbags stencilled with short names and long numbers and carried them off once more.

This time they arrived at a beautiful oasis, where a pond smooth as glass reflected palm trees weighed down with monkeys eating dates beneath an enormous moon bright as an orange. Here Bobby disappeared and Anne was dressed in shimmery clothes like net curtains threaded with gold and she wore coins on her forehead and silver bells on her toes, which were painted bright red. Then the Chief came out of a tent made of rugs and with great ceremony gave her a sheep's eye. But Anne, thanks to her experience with bull's-eyes, managed to pass it deftly to an alighting flamingo.

'My name is King Solomon,' the Chief said, but Anne knew he wasn't. He only said it because he still wanted her to be the Queen of Sheba.

'No, you aren't. I've seen him in the Bible and you look different,' she said, hoping desperately Bobby would come back and rescue her.

Bobby didn't return. Instead, a military band struck up and she was marched towards an altar to marry the Chief of the Bandits. Her knees were jelly and she wished she were dreaming but she knew she wasn't. She knew she had brought this upon herself by telling Bobby to drive to Timbuktu, so this was her fault entirely and, though she tried to unbelieve it, she found she couldn't. Twice she tried to say: 'I don't like this game any more. Goodbye everybody.' But the words didn't come out. Or, if they did, no one heard them because the music was so loud the ground trembled, the palm trees shook and the monkeys screamed. Worst of all, the Chief of the Bandits was shrinking into someone else, someone half Papa's size but almost as familiar and wearing a uniform like his and with exactly the same small moustache, which he kept cropped with nail scissors.

'Do you, Anne de Gaulle, take Herr Hitler to be your husband?' he said.

There was an awful silence. The monkeys even stopped scratching their bottoms. All the bandits were looking at

Anne's Story

her, enjoying this moment of dreadful truth. Her face burned, her chest tightened, she couldn't breathe, her eyes smarted, she didn't know what to say . . . and then, then, out of the darkness beyond the palms, came a magnificent trumpeting. It was savage, hoarse, quite wonderful. It was joined by other bellowings and now she could see great grey shapes trundling towards her.

The bandits drew their swords and fired their pistols, but the elephants were charging now, their ears wide, their trunks stuck out like gun barrels, their tusks glinting in the moonlight and their fierce little eyes glowing with the joy of battle. And their leader, oh their leader, he strode in the midst of them on his hind legs, which made him twice as tall as any normal elephant, and he was dressed in bright green, with a bowler hat and the whitest spats ever worn by any elephant in the world. He carried a malacca cane in one hand and his panama hat in the other. Impervious to danger, like Papa, King Babar strode into the battle as if presiding over a village fête.

At the sight of such stylish heroism and reckless courage Anne's captors fled, howling, into the night. Several of the younger elephants, accelerating like fleet-footed scout cars, gave chase. Only Herr Hitler remained. He was brave. He had a malacca cane like Babar's and, brandishing it, he advanced towards Anne's saviour. With great cunning he struck out at the tender tip of Babar's trunk, but Babar's cane met his, swept it aside as if it were a matchstick and then – oh delirious vision! – Babar swept him up with his trunk, whirled him round and round his head, so that Herr Hitler's arms and legs waved and waggled like an old rag doll, and threw him away in a soaring parabola into the pool. And even as Herr Hitler fell towards the moon-burnished waters, an enormous crocodile opened its elastic jaws and Anne's prospective consort was gone for ever.

Slowly the crocodile submerged to digest its prize in the dark depths. Had Anne been dreaming this at night such a happy conclusion might well have caused her to wet her bed with sheer relief, but now here to distract her was Bobby come back, pointing and waving cheerfully. How surprised she was. Especially when an old grey tennis ball hit her in the face.

Anne blinked, her eyes stinging, and at the same time she realised her young English neighbour was waving at her from the top of the garden fence. She stared at him. What had happened? He didn't look as much like her Bobby as she had thought.

And he was shouting something she couldn't understand. 'Can I have my ball back?' he called. Still Anne stared. What could he mean? 'My ball,' he yelled, pointing hard at the tennis ball. Anne, understanding his poking finger well enough, eased herself out of her soap carton and collected the ball.

She tried to throw it up to him but this, being reality, meant it bounced straight back at her. The little boy laughed. She managed – how her fingers trembled – to pick it up again and this time she carried it to the fence. Still he was laughing, giggling at her with his tongue protruding a little from the side of his mouth. Anne jumped and with two hands threw the ball high up at the same time. By a miracle it went over. 'Thanks,' he said. And that was that. He had gone as quickly as he had appeared.

Anne bent down to peer through the fence and just glimpsed him as he ran under the rose arches. But that was all. He had gone. Anne was alone again. There was no chauffeur, no beautiful motor car. All she had was a splintery banana box, a battered soap carton and herself.

In the greenhouse was the flowerpot concealing her father in the form of a large carrot with two legs. The rusty nail she had stuck into it after he had left her for ever was still there. She had banged it through his middle.

Her mother was indoors, sitting at the sewing machine with her mouth full of pins. Anne had wanted to turn the handle for her, but the manner in which Maman had flicked up the lever which pushed down the little metal foot that held the material in place so the needle could go up and down had warned her she wouldn't be indulged at all that morning, so instead she had decided to punish Papa again. She was going to be as fierce as Maman's mouth.

Anne pulled at the nail. To her surprise it came out quite easily. She was pleased. Now she could stick it in again and she did, hardly noticing that she had begun to cry. The pressure of her hands – they didn't look like hers, they were dark-veined and strong – was making the carrot wriggle and also crack across its waist, but nevertheless she managed to push the nail right through as far as before, and then she propped her skewered effigy against the flowerpot.

Contemplating it, she continued to sob but without tears now and wishing she didn't hate Papa, wishing she could stop, thinking she might as well be dead. Because if he had really gone to visit Babar, why hadn't he come with Bobby and the elephants to rescue her from the bandits?

The carrot slid to one side and fell over. The top of Papa had split off from the bottom. Inside was clean, bright orange. She picked up the top half, the nail fell away with a ping on to the floor and suddenly Anne had an irresistible urge to nibble the carrot. She rubbed at the dusty outside with her sleeve. Then she bit it and crunched. And chewed, She was eating Papa! Serve him right! This was better than when she had first pushed the nail into him!

She bit again. Her mouth was filling up with chewed carrot. Now she would be able to see in the dark like he could ... only, no, she gulped, no ... She tried again, No, she couldn't swallow it, her throat was too tight, shreds of carrot were tickling it too far back. She was going to cough and, as she started to, her stomach moved as if she might be sick as well ... but no, all she had to do was to open her mouth wide, as wide as she had seen Jockey do ... and out came the mass of carrot in a sort of slimy ball.

Her eyes stung with fresh tears. Her nose dripped. She snuffled, staring at the ball. Had she really meant to eat Papa? She would never have dared. It was just another pretence of hers, wasn't it? Yes. No.

Hot with fear, she found a trowel and scraped up the mess she had made and carried it to a dark corner, where she let it slip into obscurity behind some old, earth-encrusted seedling boxes. Then she sat as best she could on the garden roller.

How could she make herself dead? she wondered. Really, properly dead? Could she do it to herself without hurting? If she stuck the nail into her middle, would that kill her as she had killed Papa? She was bigger than the carrot so perhaps she would need something bigger than a nail? A big knife from the kitchen or the shiny one in the dining room in the polished wooden box on the sideboard? Could she do it? Anne told herself, still weeping, that she must. She had been worse than naughty and although the others, Maman, Marguerite and Elizabeth, knew nothing about it – they never did know what really happened inside her, though they thought they did – their ignorance made no difference because she knew she had killed Papa and eaten him.

Anne tried to wipe her nose on her sleeve and her tears on her skirt and then got up from the roller. Yes, she would creep into the house and steal into the dining room. She would take the big knife and do to herself what she had done to Papa. That was only fair.

But when she reached the back door, there was Marguerite saying it was time for her dose of malt. For a moment Anne forget herself and Papa, because she loved her extract of malt that would make her like all the other children in England who also had it every day. Eagerly she settled herself down at the kitchen table while Marguerite got out the big brown glass jar with the turn-around lid. As the spoon went into the dark stickiness Anne felt herself dribbling in anticipation, but then, when the glistening, sweet-smelling blob of malt was presented to her mouth – 'Quickly, Anne, before it drips. Mouth wide open' – and pressed in upon her, she found she couldn't swallow it. Try as she might, she found herself choking and coughing.

'What is the matter with you today, Anne?'

Anne pushed the spoon away and spat out the malt and

her nurse was cross, asking over and over again the very question Anne had posed so wretchedly, so inchoately, to herself: 'What are we going to do with you?'

After two further attempts that were as messy and as unsuccessful as the first, Marguerite hauled Anne up to her room and told her she was to stay there until she was more sensible.

The bars at her bedroom window reminded Anne of the ones at home. As she stood there looking out at the quiet suburban road the terrible thoughts she had had earlier slipped from her mind, to be replaced by nothing at all except the whirring of Maman's sewing machine in the spare bedroom.

FOUR

Soon after their arrival in England they had gone to stay at a brown hotel smelling of cabbage next door to the King and Queen. Anne had seen their high garden wall with iron spikes on top and with big gates, bigger than those at home and painted black not green, which were opened by funny English policemen when the King's horses needed to go in and out.

The King was small and called George, which was a name Anne could understand. He couldn't talk properly, they said. He stammered and stumbled over his words like she sometimes did, only he did it all the time. Anne felt sorry for him, which was a nice feeling she was rarely able to enjoy. The Queen was round and friendly and she always smiled whatever happened. There were also two princesses, but when Anne was shown a photograph of them she thought they looked too ordinary to be real ones.

One day, while Maman went looking for a house for them to live in, Anne was taken across the road to look at the palace. It was very big and grey and bleak. And the soldiers on guard seemed to her to be as dull as sparrows. She had expected bright red ones with black bears on their heads instead of hats. Marguerite said it was because the war was here, too, in England. 'It's wartime, Anne,' she said.

Anne knew it was wartime well enough. And that before there had been something called peacetime, but she wouldn't remember that, they said. She did, though.

When she turned her back on the palace the view across the park was happier. She could see pinnacles sharp as kitchen skewers and a tall tower with a clock that went *bong-g-g* and, above it, a herd of beautiful barrage balloons. They were put in the sky just there to look after Mr and Mrs Churchill, who lived in Big Ben, going in or out all the time, rain or shine. Marguerite took her hand and they crossed over the wide road to go into the park. They had brought some bread to feed the ducks, who were the last bright things, apart from the giant red buses, left in London.

That night in the hotel Anne woke up as Big Ben struck two o'clock and couldn't get back to sleep, although everything was quiet except for Marguerite's steady breathing. There were no sirens, no bangs going upwards or downwards, but still she couldn't sleep. Yet the odd thing was she felt quite calm. It was strange. Then she remembered why. Papa was sleeping next door.

Anne got out of bed. She tiptoed to the door and lifted up the little brass latch that stopped Germans bursting into your bedroom in the middle of the night to take you away and peeped out into the hotel corridor. It had just one green sign at the end, which gave a light so dim it made the row of fire buckets beneath look black not red.

Outside her parents' door were Papa's shoes, with her mother's beside them. How tiny Maman's were. Anne couldn't have tried them on even if she had wanted to; already her feet were too big. But inside her father's shoes her feet were lost. Nevertheless, wearing them, she at once became a giant with seven-league boots as big and shiny as the rowing boats on the lake near the hill with the big stone arch, which was where they had buried a soldier whom nobody knew because he had lost the little metal saucer on a string with his name and number on it. That was back home, not here. England didn't lose her soldiers like France did.

Anne clumped up the corridor, waving her arms to help her feel bigger still and making giant noises – dangerous growls, essentially – very quietly so as not to wake up anyone and get into trouble. Anne loved to be big and bad whenever she could. Most of the time she had to pretend to be small and good, otherwise adults quickly became angry despite their continuous cooings at her.

Her giant growlings made her laugh – they were very good, entirely convincing, undeniably funny – so she fell over on purpose, engulfed by self-congratulation and laughter. Rarely had she felt so happy, sprawling in her nightie on the carpet that smelt of dust, her feet half in, half out of, her father's shoes. The feel of the carpet's texture through her nightdress was wonderful. She wriggled, making herself flatter so she could feel it more, but then her chest twinged and she stopped laughing and began to cough. Dust caught in her nose, her throat. She coughed and coughed but still no one came – how lucky she was – and she was able to put Papa's shoes back beside Maman's, hold her breath and return safely to her room.

As she crept back into bed Marguerite asked her where

she had been and Anne lied proudly, saying she had gone to the WC all by herself instead of using the chamber pot under the bed, and wasn't she clever and brave too, this being a strange hotel in a foreign country full of smells so English they were disgusting? Her nurse replied: 'Be quiet, dear, and go to sleep. That's enough now.'

Soon afterwards – the days seemed to knock each other over like dominoes – Anne rode in a car called Packard which belonged to a friend of Papa who had lots of diamonds hidden under his shop in London, to their new house Maman had found. It seemed a long way from Buckingham Palace and the brown hotel. They told Anne she now lived in a place called Petts Wood, but since Anne found it difficult to pronounce Petts Wood, though she tried many times, she decided it was easier not to be anywhere at all.

All the others insisted they liked this place that wasn't there. So convenient for London yet quiet, rather like the country really, with lovely gardens, big trees and hardly any motorcars, they said. The buses here were mostly green, or green and cream, and the skies were always blue. It was ideal. Just the place for a family and Papa could travel up to London each day with all the other fathers, although most of these had been called up. Lots were now in hospitals all round Anne because Herr Hitler had dive-bombed them at the seaside near where she had played in the sand with Papa.

Anne wondered why they hadn't hidden in her sand castle. They would have been safe there. She decided they must be foolish soldiers although some had been sensible enough to escape in little boats. All this had happened while her mother was taking her to Brittany and her father had vanished, only to reappear in London. To Anne it seemed that everyone had run away from France to England: she had, Papa had, Maman had, and even these English soldiers had.

The house in Petts Wood had a long front garden and an even bigger back one. It would be as safe for her as the garden at home, they said. Anne inspected it carefully. It was nothing like home and therefore not at all safe, but her inspection (cracks in paths, caterpillars swinging from rose leaves, a steel spike with string wound round it) did reveal the knothole in the fence.

To begin with, Bobby had been nowhere to be seen and Anne had been content to contemplate his house: to admire its unique proportions, the satisfying curve of the nasturtium-thatched roof, its lack of windows and unusual setting, snuggled as it was into a hole. Then suddenly one day there he had been, standing in the doorway – well, the upper half of him.

In this very first sighting of him he was wearing an English policeman's helmet. These peculiar domes always made Anne laugh. Then he climbed out and Anne could see that he was not only a policeman but a cowboy too. His trousers had fringes and he was waving a silver gun. To Anne's delight he proceeded to stalk an invisible enemy, darting forward, crouching abruptly, slinking sideways and then leaping to his feet to fire his magnificent revolver: *chow, pow, wow*!

The repeated noise he made was difficult to imitate; it sounded most frequently like *chow*, but it came from further back in the throat and with a crackle of phlegm around it. When Anne tried to make the sound it turned into her usual cough, but Bobby could repeat it easily and whenever he chose, which was often, especially whilst crouching beside an apple tree. From this vantage point he decimated his invisible quarry, riddling him with these explosive glottals and never pausing to breathe let alone reload.

The apple tree had a trunk white as icing sugar and was topped with a band of black tarry stickiness to trap insects. Anne, who was an earnest student of natural misfortune, had often seen ants wriggle in such places for hours. Flies, too, and great moths with bodies like woolly slugs.

In the middle of what was clearly a total victory for her new neighbour, somebody called him and he danced away waving his gun – it flashed in the sun – and kicking out his fringed cowboy legs. Here was the finest English person Anne had yet seen.

She kept her knowledge of her neighbour to herself. Even though she hadn't yet found him a name or made him her best friend he was already her secret. Having secrets made Anne feel excited and, better still, though this was part of the excitement, important. She knew others had secrets, especially adults – they were full of them – so she imagined that if she had one of her own she would be more like everybody else. Others would recognise her as something unignorable, something serious, like Maman's handbag or Papa's kepi.

Such recognition had become more desirable than ever because a few days before, under a flood tide of English breaking over her head, she had picked out that word – it had bumped up against her like a dead jellyfish wreathed in seaweed – the word 'mongol'. So they could say it about her in England too, could they? They knew what she was, what she didn't want to be, even here, did they? Certainly these English eyes, fixed on her now, were just the same as those in France: full of concern for Maman.

Anne wanted to go away and hide, but she couldn't. She had to sit there and nod and smile. Her hair was ruffled twice, but luckily, because this was England, she wasn't required to say anything as she might well have been in France.

When Anne had first seen inside the house in Petts Wood they had said it was quite like home, wasn't it? And their voices had warned her to agree. She had nodded, but it wasn't. Well, perhaps the banisters were a little. And the wooden floor in the hall. But that was all. Because in this house the rooms opened out from the middle, whereas at home they came sensibly one after another as you went along the corridor.

As for the sitting room here, why, it was frighteningly angry. Fiercely angry. It was orange and black and gold, especially the fireplace, which was like a temple in China, her sister said. The shiny furniture glowered at Anne as if it knew all about her. But worst of all was a mysterious cabinet that stood by itself. It had a small pearl-grey window, with a row of knobs below it, very like those she wasn't allowed to touch on the wireless.

Two days later Anne plucked up enough courage to touch the largest knob on the cabinet – she loved the feel of softly ridged bakelite – but, when she did, nothing happened. Emboldened, she tried the other, smaller knobs, turning them until they stopped. Then back the other way. But whatever she did the cabinet remained the same, although what she had expected it to do she could not have said. Finally she tried looking through the fat little window, but all she could see inside was the blurred face of someone who might have been her.

Had she been imprisoned in this box? she wondered. Was she even then looking out from inside it? She was tempted to try to look at the back of it, but no, there was no need: she could tell she was really outside it, firmly, corporeally herself. It was, however, entirely possible that this strange, opaque window, so like an eye, belonged on an ogre – an English ogre who kept his spare eyes in polished cabinets such as this. After all, she had once known a man who could take out his left eye because it was made of glass. He had had a spare one he kept in a box in case he ever lost the one he kept popping in and out of its socket to make her laugh. Once he even put it in his mouth and sucked it as if it were a sweet. Anne begged him not to, to put it back where it belonged, and, when she'd cried enough and stamped her feet enough, he had. But then, when it was back in its place, it had stared at Anne as if it would never forgive her.

The dining room was friendlier. It glowed and glinted with brass and there was a big table with tall chairs standing to attention round it. The best thing about the table, apart from the grooves in the top you could roll a penny along, were its legs. They were like bulbous old ladies in the park. The dining table at home had similar legs but these English ones were fatter. Anne liked patting and hugging them and when she heard the air-raid siren for the first time in Petts Wood she went at once to hide under the table. But they told her she would be safer in the big cupboard under the stairs. There everyone could just squeeze in, which was comforting, except Papa wouldn't join them. He stood looking out through the front door, saying it was all right. Anne supposed it was – for him. Whenever there was a particularly loud bang or a rattle of window panes he would smile to himself – and breathe deeply, as if inhaling the violence in the air all round them like cigarette smoke.

Papa had shown them how the blackout worked. The black material was stretched on frames that fitted against the windows at night so the German bombers couldn't see you. When you took them out in the morning the light blazed in and you stacked the floppy rectangles of blackness against the wall. To Anne it seemed that the next noisy night was waiting inside them, waiting for the old men in navy-blue to come down the road and shout at houses where any light showed – even the tiniest chink or faintest glow. These men wore tin colanders without holes on their heads and carried a satchel with a special mask in it to turn themselves into rubber pigs in case Herr Hitler dropped bombs full of mustard on them.

But at that time, when the Battle of Britain had only just begun, the most menacing things for Anne were not the air raids but the telephones. There were two. Uniformed men from the post office had come and unrolled wires and left this pair of gleaming toads black as tar squatting in their house. When they rang – and very often they did so when it wasn't at all convenient – their clangour hurt Anne's ears.

These big toads were more frightening than the tin

donkey on the boat. Even Maman was afraid to answer them, but this was mainly because she might have to speak in English. Her sister Elizabeth didn't mind. She spoke very good English. As for Papa, he never hesitated. He would seize the phone at once and, whatever was said to him, reply only in French. He understood English but never spoke it, they told her.

Mrs Churchill spoke French and used to tell Mr Churchill what Papa was saying. Mr Churchill thought he could speak French but no one could ever understand him; that was the trouble with him, apparently. But one day Mr Churchill told Papa, by way of Mrs Churchill, that France was really Papa's now – or, at least, she would be once they had won the war. Papa was furious. He didn't need Mr Churchill to give him France, he said. Anne decided she wouldn't speak English either, which was a great relief because she couldn't anyway.

When Anne got earache and they poured warm olive oil down – 'It'll loosen the wax, darling' – she knew it was the black toads' fault. It was they who had made her ears hurt. The pain was terrible, worse than toothache, but the oil did soften the wax, which came out on the end of a hairpin. It looked like the little disc you had to take off the end of a winkle before you could eat it. And the pain went away. She could go to sleep again without crying. But she could hear better now and that was a pity. The telephones' bells were louder than ever.

Naturally Papa was famous. He talked regularly on the wireless, but they had to have a long wire on a stick poking out of the window to hear him. He had to be on a different wavelength, they said, to talk to France. Always he told France to be good, to be brave and to listen to him. Anne listened as hard as she could and tried not only to be good and brave but also to look as worried and concerned as everybody else did when Papa told them what to do. In this way she came to believe she understood what her father was saying.

Mostly he told France to come to London. Everybody was to come, like they had. Well, no, not quite everybody, because there were wicked men in France who had made friends with the Germans. One of them had once liked Papa and when Papa had written a book all about fighting he had wanted to put his name on it instead of Papa's, but Papa had told him he couldn't and this man had got angry. Now he was old and foolish, but still he was much more important than Papa and kept giving Herr Hitler all France's guns and warships. And in return Herr Hitler had allowed him to live in a place where adults went when their sore stomachs needed fizzy water instead of wine.

Meanwhile, Herr Hitler marched all over poor France stamping on people with his shining boots. But Papa said the good people back home were not to take any notice of Herr Hitler because France would get better soon. Papa's globe showed him there were lots of places in the world whose inhabitants didn't like Herr Hitler and these people would all come to France and help France push Herr Hitler back into Germany, where he belonged.

In another broadcast – Anne had now become rather more accustomed to the house in Petts Wood and no longer minded the diamond-leaded window panes – Papa said France had gone into hospital and the stupid and bad old men had made her breathe something which had put her to sleep so Herr Hitler could cut her up into pieces without her knowing it, but one day she would be stitched together again and already some of her young men had started to fight for her while helping England and Mr Churchill. And inside France (here her father's voice changed) there was a secret, a precious secret, and this was that underneath, deep down, France was beautiful and brave – just as Anne was – even if at the moment she seemed ugly and frightened – just as Anne did. One day France would turn into a swan like Anne, his ugly duckling, was going to do. That was what Papa meant.

Throughout July and August he went up and down on the train to London. In the evenings he would tell her stories, tickle her and her new puppy, let her play whist, pretend to teach her patience – he loved to play patience because you had to try to beat yourself, he said – and, on Sunday, take them all to church. Occasionally he was too busy to come back and he would stay in London at his headquarters. This word intrigued Anne. She supposed it meant a big house. She had been taken just once to somewhere in London with pillars and seen her father's desk. On it were pieces of paper, more black telephones and one red one. There were little flags of France as well, and some had the cross Papa had made with his and her shadows on them. Anne liked seeing that cross with Papa's long arms below her short ones. She thought of it as hers. It made her feel proud.

After visiting Papa's office they took her on a bus to look at a tree made of metal in a park. On top of it stood a little English boy just like Bobby, but this one was called Peter and wore a smock and there were animals and fairies nestling in the tree's shiny bark. Then they had tea in a shop.

Flowers and parcels kept coming to their house. At first Anne thought the parcels were presents for her. 'No, darling, they're for Papa,' said Maman. But why did Papa need gold earrings and bangles with diamonds? It was explained that they were for Papa's soldiers. Again Anne couldn't understand. Hadn't his soldiers run away from him? Certainly he'd been very cross with them. They were supposed to have fought the Germans but, like the English, they had been afraid to. 'No, darling, they're rallying to Papa. They're coming to England like we did.' But why did soldiers need bangles? 'They don't, dear: they'll be sold for money. The money will help to feed and kit them out.'

Anne didn't try to understand any more – these explanations had become the sort she didn't like. All she knew was that Mr Churchill had talked in Big Ben and now Papa was allowed to have proper French soldiers and sailors underneath him. Anne was obliged to take this latter piece of information literally, but though the words seemed to offer her a picture in her head, she still couldn't quite make sense of them. How could the soldiers and sailors be *under* Papa? Would he stand on top of them or lie down on them? Either way he would be sure to squash them.

After lengthy but intermittent consideration Anne decided this information belonged to that part of the adult world she would never comprehend, so she screwed up her eyes to blink the puzzling picture away. 'Why are you doing that?' they asked. In response she ducked her head sideways, which was her latest way of not answering things. 'Don't do that,' they said.

One hot day her father showed her a photograph. She saw that he was standing in a field with a white flagpole behind him flying the Union Jack, which was, he said, Mr Churchill's flag. He was taking the salute, he told her. And there were his men – not *underneath* Papa: he was standing on a box, so they were lower than he was, that was all – marching past him with their heads turned hard to one side to stare pop-eyed at Papa, with their right hands held up like spoons in front of their ears. Anne giggled, but Papa frowned. Sensing danger she asked him where was her flag with the four arms, but this only made things worse.

Suddenly Papa was angry. Not with her, although it felt like it. Papa was as angry as only he could be angry – she could see the blackness in his eyes; did hers look like that when she was angry? – and he told her the stupid English hadn't been able to find one, not even a simple tricolour, let alone one with the Cross of Lorraine on it. He would never forgive them. 'They give with one hand only to take away with the other,' he said. And to make his meaning clear he gave Anne an apple, then snatched it back from her. This became a game. They laughed and he let her do it to him several times, until she snatched too hard and the apple fell to the floor. It rolled away under the sideboard and Jockey, who was still a puppy, chased after it furiously.

On another evening Papa had come home, marched straight through the house without a word to anyone, not even to her, and gone out into the garden. Anne had watched from a window. Jockey kept pestering him, pretending to snap at his ankles and trying to bite his shoelaces. Finally Papa scooped up the puppy in his great hands and gazed at him intently. Was he going to hurt Jockey? He looked – Anne had never seen him like this before – so ferocious, like a wolf or an angry bear. It was terrible. She thought he might strangle Jockey or bite him back. Perhaps even bite his head off.

She wanted to open the window and shout, but she couldn't manage the hasp. Then as she watched, her father's face began to alter . . . it seemed to be breaking . . . She didn't recognise him any more. This was worse still. What was happening to him? What? *What*? Oh, no! Could it be? He was crying. Her father was *crying*. This was impossible. She must be dreaming. Papa couldn't cry. He mustn't cry! No! But he was, yes. The tears rolled down his cheeks, leaving snail trails. And he let them fall. Then he put Jockey down and pulled out his handkerchief and blew his wonderful nose with a roar as loud as a land mine exploding. After that he mopped his cheek and his eyes. Now he looked like himself again. His face had come back. Anne wanted to run out and hug him. But she didn't. She knew she mustn't.

Later everyone agreed Mr Churchill should not have done it. He had sunk a lot of their warships without telling Papa and killed a lot of their sailors – over a thousand of them. And the good ships and innocent sailors hadn't been doing anything except floating on the sea. Was that what had made Papa cry? she wondered. She would have asked, but she wasn't sure if her father had cried for the ships and sailors or for himself. He had looked so angry before he cried. So perhaps he was cross with Mr Churchill and sorry for himself? Papa often talked about Mr Churchill as if the two of them weren't friends at all. For once Anne was glad to go to bed.

It was when the aeroplanes first appeared over Petts Wood that people said Herr Hitler was trying to bomb Papa – well, the milkman did. This news made everyone, including Papa, shake their heads and laugh. But Anne didn't. To her it wasn't funny at all. To her it was true.

And how carefree these English people were. There they would stand, in the middle of the high street or out in the soft suburban avenues, gazing up at the gathering war above their heads as if everything was safe. They laughed when a German fighter fell down; they sighed and said 'oh dear' when it was an English one. And on the wireless voices kept count, telling everyone how many aeroplanes had been hurt that day. The pilots were boys, 'our boys', they said, little more than children but so brave you could cry for them. Only they didn't, they clapped, they cheered, as if it were all a game. But when one day Anne saw pictures of the pilots in the papers they looked quite old, and this gladdened her because it proved what she had just decided: wars were going to be nothing to do with her, they were purely adult concerns.

Every night, as the raids multiplied, Anne prayed that a bomb wouldn't fall on them. But her prayers did not prevent her from walking in her sleep, to wake in horror, crouched and cold, in the cupboard under the stairs. When, in the blackout, she had felt where she was she grew more frightened than ever. But at that moment the kitchen door creaked and suddenly Jockey, warm, rough-haired, was squirming against her, licking her face. She hugged him to her. Now she could manage, now she would be brave. She felt her way to the kitchen and put on a light so bright it made her jump and Jockey bark. This brought Maman in her dressing gown and soon Anne was back in bed, scolded but kissed.

The next day Marguerite was red-eyed and irritable until lunch. Anne knew they were both to blame – she for sleepwalking, her nurse for not stopping her. To please Marguerite she tried to be no trouble at all and for the most part she succeeded, though she should not have blown her nose on the face flannel.

Ever more frequently she found herself drawn to the fence to look through the peep hole at the little English boy. Sometimes it was the sound of the lawnmower that called her and she would see not him but his mother mowing the lawn, and once this lady came very close to Anne to dump a heap of grass cuttings beside the fence. They smelt wonderful. Then he himself came out and this time, really it couldn't have been better if she'd imagined it, he had a box from which he took strips of something that fitted together and shone in the sun. Railway lines, she realised. Her neighbour had a clockwork train set!

Slowly, painstakingly, he fitted the rails together. This seemed to be difficult to do, his hands being slightly too small to span the wide rails. However, after much frowning perseverance he had laid a track that came from the lawn and passed under the rose arches to reach the air-raid shelter, where it curved to a halt. Here he placed a signal and a tin station before jumping down to bring out for the first time the bear in the red jumper. He placed the bear beside the station.

Anne's heart warmed to both the boy and the bear. Clearly, like her, he recognised the necessity of having someone to play with, while the bear, equally clearly, appreciated the invitation. For his part, the bear looked good-natured and reliable, but he did not possess – how could he? – the suave magnetism of her toy elephant. Nevertheless he looked after the station competently enough while the boy disappeared again. Anne decided the bear must be meant to be the stationmaster and this was confirmed when he was brought a brass whistle on a string, which Anne's new acquaintance first blew for him and then hung round his neck.

This done, the boy went again and was away for a long time, although she did glimpse him occasionally going to and fro beyond the rose arches. The bear waited patiently but Anne couldn't. What was the boy doing? She wished she could go to the bear and help him blow his whistle to hurry things up. Where was the boy now? She peered through the hole until her eyes watered. What had happened? What?

Then it came: an engine, black, silver and green, with cotton wool stuck in its funnel for smoke, pulling a mobile crane, a coal truck and a passenger carriage. The truck was full of lead soldiers, not coal, accompanied by a zebra and a giraffe, while the passenger carriage carried no one.

Anne couldn't breathe for admiration. It was a triumphant progress – quite magnificent, even if the plume of cotton wool was detaching itself slowly and inexorably from the funnel. But what did that matter? The train, with the little boy jigging beside it, willing it along, shepherding it round the curve, was coming towards the station. And it almost reached it, but by this time the clockwork engine was running down – she could tell from the noise it made or, rather, was ceasing to make. The circular spring inside was easing itself out and out between the wheels and soon – now, no, not yet – there would be no strength left in it and the train would stop. It did. Not far from the station but still too far.

The boy spoke to the bear, who appeared to offer him advice. Certainly whatever he said proved decisive, because the boy seized the train, uncoupled the engine and wound it up again, holding it tightly against his babyish pot belly. The click-clack of the ratchet as he rewound was delicious. Then, holding the wheels firmly, he set the engine down and, pressing it to the rails, twisted round to blow a strident blast on the bear's whistle. Then he let go.

The engine, unencumbered by freight or passengers, shot away down the line to hurl itself off the rails and into a tuft of parsley at the curve. Here upended, it squealed its pent-up energy away like Jockey rolling on his back and pedalling the air. The boy picked it up and disappeared with the engine beyond the rose arches. A few minutes later the engine returned and, coming from the opposite direction this time, it didn't fall off at the curve and it did reach the station. Anne was so pleased she said 'bravo' aloud.

He had heard! He was looking round, but he couldn't see her. His querying look so vaguely directed made her giggle. But now he was coming towards the fence. He mustn't find her. She backed away from her spyhole and crouched, listening. She heard him brush against weeds and lettuces before returning to his railway. Anne waited, then peeped through again. He was talking to his bear and taking the soldiers out of the coal truck. Keeping as quiet as possible, Anne pretended she was helping him and when he succeeded in making the train go again with the empty coal truck and the mobile crane but not the carriage she felt she was with him, walking beside it, helping him admire its progress. It was the very next day that Anne discovered for herself he was called Bobby and she gave him the bull's-eye, whereupon he became her perfect friend.

But it was also that night that she dreamt she was holding Papa's head in her lap. And she was sticky with blood. The old man of Vichy had chopped it off. Papa's eyes were open but they were no longer shiny and they didn't move. She couldn't see herself in them, though she kept trying. Then they told her no one would guillotine her father, she had misunderstood, her Papa was a soldier: therefore, if anyone wished to kill him – they did, the wireless had said it and so had Papa – he could be put in front of a firing squad and shot.

'Yes, cowardly, nasty people in France have condemned him to death, darling,' they said. 'Yes, at home, according to the law, he is dead, yes, dear, but he isn't really.' Then they laughed because there he was – 'Look, Anne' – letting himself in through the front door. And he picked her up and kissed her. But then he noticed his blood all over her and said, 'Oh, dear.'

FIVE

As balloonists, their first descent was to be beside the treasure tree in Bobby's garden. Here they would take on board the provisions necessary for their next, much longer expedition. The balloon itself – pink and pear-shaped – was tied to a stick and by rights should have been floating serenely above their heads, but instead it hung down rather shamefacedly, reminding Anne of herself when embarrassed. The basket was the old soap carton she had made into her limousine the week before. At that time it had been too small for her, but now one side of it was broken so there was enough room for them all – herself, Bobby, Babar and Rupert Bear.

They soared over the fence, gaining height above the shelter and the arches, and landed without incident on the lawn in front of the treasure tree. This was a rotting, pulpy tree stump devoid of bark, which Anne had liked and frequently inspected in the woods at home. You could pull at it and huge lumps weighing nothing would come away in your hands. It smelt like an enormous mushroom and sometimes there were spiders to make you jump. This pungent phenomenon now magically transplanted to Bobby's garden stood in a position conveniently imaginable from Anne's usual observation post.

The day before, she and Bobby had decorated the tree in a manner derived from Anne's visit to Peter Pan in Kensington Gardens. They had made models in plasticine of various creatures, persons and fairies and perched them on and around the tree. After that they had begun to hollow out the base of the trunk and already they had excavated a capacious cave in which to conceal their treasures: a thin penny which was said to have been run over by a train, four custard-cream biscuits and a bottle of lemon barley water called Robinson. All these items were now required for their mission, but as they loaded them into the balloon Bobby said: 'We'd better take a gun, don't you think?'

'Yes, we must,' agreed Anne. 'Have you got one?' she added, knowing perfectly well he had his cowboy revolver.

'*Chow, pow, wow*!' answered Bobby and raced indoors to fetch his gun. While he was gone, Anne practised these noises until she thought she sounded as professionally explosive as her friend.

When he returned he was not only flourishing his revolver but, to Anne's delight, he was wearing his gas mask. Anne loved gas masks provided other people wore them. They made her laugh.

They climbed into his ballon and, provisioned, protected and armed, took to the skies again.

'Where are we going today?' asked Bobby as they floated over the white cliffs of Dover.

'It's a secret,' Anne said.

They passed a pigeon carrying important messages for

Papa. They waved at it but the pigeon, intent upon its mission, took no notice.

'Is it far?' asked Bobby as a warship passed below them.

'Wait and see,' Anne replied, happy to use a phrase so often used by grown-ups to ward off her own questions.

'I'm hungry,' her friend said. So was Anne, so she ate two biscuits – one for him, the other for her.

Suddenly a cloud covered the sun and all the bright nursery colours and contrasts of Petts Wood vanished. Its painted gables, scumbled beams, sparkling pebbledash, golden privet and seed-hung laburnums were gone. Everything below had become dingy, melancholy, unkempt. But fortunately by this time the balloon was somewhere else, driven on the wind high above . . . where? Where were they?

Home. Of course. Home. Her village. Her house. There it was below them. There were the woods and fields. There was the church with its spire as neat as a blue-grey goat's cheese and the churchyard where the tombs were stone mattresses they put on top of you not under you so you couldn't get out until Jesus said so. And there was the path leading to the top of the hill where Papa had hoisted her up on to his shoulders.

'We're going to land here,' Anne said.

'We can't,' Bobby said. 'It's full of Germans.'

'But it's home. Look, there's our house with the long roof.'

'The Germans will shoot us.'

'Not if we're brave.'

And Anne took command of the descent, letting the air out of the balloon by vibrating her lips in a manner so rude as to be delicious. As a result they hurtled towards the ground and the rush of their descent made the hair on their heads stand on end. They landed with a crunch on the gravel outside Anne's front door.

The house looked exactly as it had when she left it three months before except that now the Virginia creeper was beginning to turn red. Its lovely thick blanket of leaves still covered everything apart from the windows, which stood in a row like soldiers on parade with the front entrance as their commandant in the middle. The eight panels of the double doors not only looked like the pockets of Papa's uniform, they were the same colour; but he never had more than four.

Once they had recovered from returning to earth so thrillingly they all climbed out of the balloon to stand, tense, alert, looking and listening. Nothing seemed untoward. In fact it was so much the same as ever that Anne quite expected cook to emerge from the kitchen at any moment.

'Where's Herr Hitler?' whispered Bobby.

'I don't know,' she said. 'Perhaps he's gone out for a walk?'

'Let's hide the balloon.'

All four dragged the carton and balloon on its stick behind a holly bush. Then, carrying their animals, they started to cross the gravel forecourt, hand in hand, trying not to sound too crunchingly loud, but halfway across Babar and Rupert insisted on being put down and then there were four pairs of feet announcing their progress to the front porch.

The doors were shut. Holding her breath, Anne pushed

at the right-hand one. At once it eased itself heavily open. No squeak, no groan. They peeped in. The hall and stairs hadn't changed. But did they dare go in? Anne's followers looked to her. Yes, yes, they would. Suddenly fearless, she led them in and down the corridor to the right. There she showed them the dining room's heavy stone fireplace; next, the salon, which she had never liked because the furniture was so well-behaved you had to sit quite still on it; after that the library, which she loved. And there was Papa's globe waiting to be shown to Bobby and the others. She turned it round for them, taking care not to mention the country Marguerite had said she came from in case one of them found it for her. Bobby, however, noticed the scratch.

'Who did that?' he said.

Anne wished he hadn't asked, but a moment later, to her surprise, she knew what to answer. And said it. 'Oh, the Germans, of course,' she lied. They all nodded, innocently accepting her false explanation. 'I expect they were looking at it and knocked it over,' she added for good measure.

Pleased with her new-found capacity for masterful deception she allowed herself and her troops to sit for a moment in Papa's and Maman's armchairs. Here she tried to pretend it was peacetime again, but all the while the others were looking round and listening hard for Herr Hitler's footsteps in the corridor. But nothing was heard, except for the tick-tock of a clock while pigeons crooned sleepily outside.

Now it was time to show them upstairs, especially her room, but when they reached the stairs Anne was too afraid to go up. Instead, looking as determined as she could, she told Bobby she had a superior plan: they would go outside and inspect the grounds. Out they went, past the walnut tree (under which Anne had once tried to pod peas) and round the end of the house, into the garden proper with the meadow and woods beyond.

Here there was more to do. Bobby and Rupert Bear performed somersaults and encouraged Anne to try, but, crouch and bend as she might, she couldn't push her bottom over her head. Fortunately Babar was superbly athletic – he could do three somersaults without stopping – so French family honour was preserved.

Then she led them on patrol through the woods, to the huge green gates that opened on to the lane. And someone had left them open, too. Papa would never have allowed that. But before they ventured out into the lane, Anne showed them the dark walk beside the ivy-covered wall of the farm next door and explained this was the best place to look for stag beetles. Straight away she found one happily and suitably upside down, ready to be rescued.

Bobby got a stick and, instructed by Anne, poked the beetle up and over on to its legs. Away it flew, just as she had said it would. Bobby and the others exchanged glances brimful of admiration for their leader who was not only resourceful but also a mine of information concerning the natural world. Cheerfully following her they marched up to the village, where they soon located the church. Anne recognised two old ladies – one, as always, had a basket full of leeks – chatting on a corner. She waved to them but they didn't return her greeting.

They entered the church and Anne, while knowing

perfectly well where she was headed for, made a show of counting six pews in from the door before saying: 'This is where we all sit on Sundays.'

So they sat in the family pew and admired the plump pillars, round vaultings and the man-sized Jesus on the cross above the altar. Jesus had a forked but friendly beard and, all things considered, He didn't seem to be too uncomfortable.

At this moment, to their astonishment, Anne's father appeared in the pulpit. He looked around, then down – his eyes pierced them to their souls – and, having cleared his throat, he spoke.

'Once upon a time not so long ago there lived a princess, who, sad to say, did not look like one. She should have been beautiful but, alas, she wasn't. She possessed an outsize head, not much brain, squinting eyes, crooked teeth and a sausage body. And her hands and feet were webbed. Her parents loved her dearly.'

'Papa means me,' Anne said proudly, sticking out her chest, which action somehow always included her stomach. 'I'm his princess.'

'Her name was France.'

'He still means me.'

'But while her body was ugly, her soul was beautiful.'

'There, what did I say?' said Anne.

All the time her father was speaking the church was filling with people. First came every one of the villagers Anne had ever seen and if some of them looked pleased to see Papa, others frowned. After them, files of German soldiers appeared. They wore uniforms and no expressions at all. Soon the church was packed and still Papa was telling everybody that one day Princess France would be free and happy and all would see she was as beautiful as she was always meant to be.

'Your Papa could be in grave danger,' whispered Babar wisely, eyeing the soldiers standing six deep and shoulder to shoulder in the aisle. Bobby agreed. But Anne knew she didn't have to worry about her father. Papa, being Papa, could, if he chose, vanish from the pulpit as smartly as he had appeared in it.

'No,' she said. 'We're the ones in danger. Come on – quick!'

Hand in hand they threaded their way out through the crowd, trying to look as inconspicuous as possible – which was easy for the toy animals and even for Bobby, who was relatively small, but Anne felt larger and lumpier than ever as she pushed and squeezed past German buckles, silver buttons and black leather revolver holsters. Then, as they reached the door, an old woman screeched 'Who goes there?' and all the soldiers turned and shouted things in German.

'Run!' said Anne. And they did.

They tore across the churchyard, leaping over the graves as the Germans poured out of the church. Bullets buzzed and whined around them and Anne dropped Babar, but Bobby, proving himself the coolest of captains under fire, dashed back waving his revolver and, crouching, cowboy-fashion, behind a family-sized stone mattress (the family Dupont – sincere regrets) fired off six bullets, each of which found its mark, thus enabling him to grab Babar by an ear and haul him away unharmed.

On they ran, out of the churchyard and down and round

the village, with everyone giving chase, villagers and Germans alike, and all of them shouting: 'Stop! Traitors! Stop!' As they ran, Bobby reloaded and turned to hold back their pursuers, while she, Babar and Rupert Bear retreated in good order, as Anne's father would have said.

During this strategic withdrawal (though, heavens, how they panted, how their chests heaved and hurt) Bobby was wounded in the shoulder, but he carried on firing and running, as if it were nothing, just as real cowboys did. He didn't even bleed; he merely held his left hand to his right shoulder while he and his revolver went *chow, pow, wow*!

Thanks to Bobby's gallantry and limitless ammunition they reached the balloon ahead of their enemies and took off at once, on a sustained burst of hot air, shooting straight up through the trees, with branches and leaves catching at them as if Mother Nature herself had joined Herr Hitler and wanted forcibly to detain them. But no, they erupted through the tree-tops and rose serenely into the blue. Below them their enemies shook their fists in impotent rage while Anne and her valiant men toasted each other in lemon barley water.

Safe now high above the clouds Anne tended Bobby's shoulder, which it turned out had suffered merely a graze and only needed kissing better, when Maman called: 'Anne, it's time to get ready. Come along.'

Marguerite washed her and dressed her and as soon as the white socks and patent strap shoes appeared Anne knew the worst. They were going for a drive.

'I don't want to go in the car,' she said.

'Hold still while I do your hair.'

Her nurse brushed her hair hard, so it would hang down

straighter than ever from the crown of her head, and then lodged a pink bow on a clip in it. At once Anne shook it off.

'Don't do that, Anne.'

'Don't want a bow.'

'Of course you do.' Marguerite picked it up and tried to clip it back in place but again Anne shook her head.

'No! Don't want it.'

'Anne! Now, be a good girl. You liked it yesterday. You said your friend liked it.'

'He didn't. Bobby hated it. So do I. Nasty bow – baby bow!'

'Hush. You mustn't talk like that. No tantrums, young lady.'

But Anne's insides were writhing with fury. Her stomach was alive with eels, coiling, uncoiling. Her face was red, her mouth was dribbling. Why shouldn't she be cross? Papa got cross, so why shouldn't she? She was his daughter, his, as proud and furious as he. Anne stamped her feet in a wild tattoo and screamed: 'No, no, no!' Marguerite waited. Anne fell silent.

'Very well, Anne,' Marguerite said. 'You needn't wear the bow if it upsets you. But you're a very silly girl. You look nice with a bow. And we all want you to look nice. Your Papa wants you to look nice. You ought to want to look nice.'

For an instant Anne felt triumphant. She thought she had won. She burst into tears. Marguerite comforted her, mopped her cheeks and mouth and then clipped the bow into place after all. Anne, devoid of further protest, was led downstairs.

In the car the bow fell off of its own accord without

anyone noticing. So Anne allowed it to slide from her shoulder to her seat and then nudged it into a leathery space under an armrest.

They drove for hours in an England without signposts. Anne liked the hedges and the cornfields but wished she had her friend Bobby with her. She had been too upset to keep a place for him. As they went along, looking for somebody called Our Lady of Zion, Anne tried to imagine she was back in her balloon, but her mind wouldn't even transport her to the garden of Petts Wood let alone send her on a proper adventure with Bobby.

For hour after hour she was where she was. And now the adults were talking about a German aeroplane that had suddenly appeared out of the sky and tried to shoot two children going to the corner shop to buy ice lollipops. Luckily the wicked aeroplane hadn't hurt the poor, frightened children and afterwards they had collected the spent bullets, which had danced in the road like hailstones, to keep as souvenirs. And this in broad daylight not far from their house in Petts Wood, they said. What was the war coming to if Herr Hitler tried to machine-gun children? At this point Maman glanced at Anne and changed the subject so she wouldn't be upset. But Anne wasn't. Anne quite liked such stories. She was glad the children had been as frightened as she would have been.

When they found Our Lady of Zion she turned out not to be an important person but a school for Elizabeth to go to. Maman talked to the headmistress like she had talked to the captain of the boat that got lost. And then, to Anne's anguished surprise, it was announced they would stay the night because it was now too late to drive back to London. When it got dark, cars were only allowed little slits for eyes, which made them slow and dangerous, they said. Like me, thought Anne.

The mattress smelt familiar. It almost smelt of home, of something green and fresh. But it was also lumpy and crackly at the same time, so she couldn't go to sleep. 'It's stuffed with bracken,' they said. 'There's a shortage of proper mattresses, so we all sleep on bracken,' they explained chirpily, with that don't-you-know-there's-a-war-on smile which the milkman always wore.

The English, Anne had discovered, smiled whatever happened; they hardly ever shrugged their shoulders or waved their arms, never held their hands out for you to shake and if you offered them your cheeks to be kissed they didn't know what to do. It was said they were all kind at heart, but as Anne only knew Bobby she couldn't be certain of this. Besides, Papa often said you shouldn't trust them. In any case, she couldn't understand what they said when they talked to her – and, curiously, many did. They seemed to think she would be glad to be spoken to no matter what the language.

Eventually Anne went to sleep in that vaulted dormitory full of other girls more sensible than she was. Unlike her, they didn't need night-lights and they giggled a lot before saying their prayers.

On her return to Petts Wood the next day Anne saw something hanging on the wardrobe door in the front bedroom. It looked like Papa without a head or legs and it was the colour of pale sand. It hung on a big wooden hanger which had a little tin label on it.

'What is it?' she said, her heart pounding.

'Papa's new uniform, darling. He got it at Simpson's. Look, it says so.' Anne stared at the little label but of course she couldn't read it. 'Simpson's is a big shop in London. The uniform is for when Papa goes to Africa.'

This was the first time Anne had heard that her father was going to visit the land of the elephants. She was immediately drunk with happiness. She went about hugging herself. She couldn't wait for him to come home and promise her that he would take her, Bobby, Babar and Rupert Bear with him. When he did return that evening and Anne said she was coming too, wasn't she, he laughed and said, 'Shush, we will see,' and this kept her happy.

SIX

A man was climbing out of Bobby's flower-camouflaged house. He wore a khaki shirt and baggy old flannels. His bare feet were white, his face and arms bright brown. He was followed by Bobby, who had a large black beret all over his head. He had to keep pushing it up to see where he was going. The beret had a silver badge. The man was full of rattle-bang laughter and jabbing movements. He said things to Bobby in a gabble, then seized him by the wrists and whirled him round and round. Bobby's feet flew away, the overlarge beret fell off and he shrieked, but whether in delight or fear Anne couldn't tell.

Beyond them she could see Bobby's mother bouncing a green and pink beach ball on the lawn. From time to time she called. And finally the man went to her, with Bobby tucked horizontally under his arm. Bobby's sandalled feet paddled the air. Anne wished she could go and play with them, although despite his friendliness this newcomer seemed unnervingly brusque. Nevertheless she would like to have worn his beret, which still lay where it had fallen among the lettuces.

Now they were playing ball. Bobby was in the middle, trying to catch it, while his mother and the man (Anne hadn't asked herself if he might be Bobby's father home on leave) threw and caught it. Bobby jumped and lunged and screamed with laughter, but always the adults kept the ball out of his reach. Soon his joy turned to misery, but still they wouldn't let him have the ball however much he pleaded. In the end he simply stopped jumping and plonked himself down in a sulk with his fists screwed into his eyes. Only then did they offer him the ball, but he pushed it away.

The man slid his arm round the woman's waist and she leant her head against his shoulder as they gazed down at the sobbing child huddled before them. As they watched him the man's hand caressed the woman's behind, rucking up her flowered skirt between her legs. She turned to kiss him and they embraced closely. When they separated their hands remained together as the man said something to Bobby. Still he wouldn't respond. Together the adults went indoors, leaving the child alone with the ball in front of him.

Anne longed to go and comfort her friend, but he looked so real in his sadness she couldn't pretend to be with him. Bobby, she had found, was easier to imagine when he was doing nothing in particular or else simply wasn't there.

After a while he stood up, rammed his hands into his pockets and kicked at the lawn. At this moment Anne almost called out to him, but she stopped herself just in time. Bobby, having vented some of his jealousy at his parents on a patch of clover, picked up the ball and threw it anywhere as hard as he could. It hit one of the rose arches and a gentle shower of petals fell. Next he stomped along the path and jumped down into his house.

He emerged with a new gun. It was longer than his

revolver and made of raw-looking wood. Anne hadn't seen it before but she had seen pictures of guns shaped like this. Soldiers carried them sloping up against their shoulders or else they lay down with them stuck out in front and looked down the barrel with one eye shut. Anne couldn't shut one eye independently of the other. She had often tried in order to wink as others did but always both eyes shut together.

Bobby didn't lie down with his gun, however. No, the first thing he did was to wave it as if it was his revolver and shout *chow, pow, wow*! as usual. From generalised slaughter he progressed to particular targets, killing various bushes and fruit trees in turn before putting the gun over his shoulder and marching up and down. This time he made military-band noises, blowing out his cheeks, and sticking out his stomach. He became so fat and hot, Anne laughed.

Bobby heard. He stopped in mid-stride and peered round carefully. Then he came towards the fence and Anne lost sight of him as first he looked in one corner of his garden and then began moving along the fence examining every crack and cranny. As he got nearer Anne listened harder. He was shuffling and snuffling. She giggled. She heard him stop, breathe in. Now they could both hear each other listening. He was very close. He was trying to hold his breath, but it kept seeping out.

Anne giggled again. Then some earth showered down to her right. Was he throwing it over the fence? At her? This was decidedly odd, certainly uncalled for. Bobby wasn't meant to do that. He was her friend. Her best friend. More loose earth came over, pattering like dry rain.

She heard Bobby laugh. Oh? So it was all right, was it? It was another game. She understood. Yes. Bobby was only pretending to bomb her. Anne felt privileged and happy to be her friend's target. Bits were landing in her hair and tickling the back of her neck as she stared through the hole, trying to catch sight of her teasing neighbour.

Still she couldn't see him. Where was he? And what was this? Blue, bright . . . An eye? His eye. Bobby's eye staring straight into hers. For an instant they were transfixed – blue eye, brown eye – then Bobby said something and Anne drew back. But *he* didn't. His eye remained watching her. She tried to say something polite to it but her words were glued together, stuck with surprise. She put her eye to the peephole again, thinking this action might serve instead of words, but this time Bobby withdrew.

Anne wanted to say: 'No, no, don't go! Stay where you are, close up. Look into my eye. It's fun, isn't it? I'm Anne and you're Bobby and we're best friends, did you know? And we go on expeditions and adventures together and we shall be married one day.' But suddenly the wooden barrel of his gun stabbed through the hole and if she hadn't somehow sensed it coming it would have really hurt her instead of simply grazing the side of her eye socket.

'Ow,' she said, more in surprise than pain.

'Buzz off,' Bobby said. And the gun's barrel wiggled in the hole while explosive noises beyond indicated that she was under heavy fire. Anne hadn't understood Bobby's dismissive words but she was in no doubt now they were unfriendly and beyond pretence of any kind. She held her hand to the side of her face, felt tears sting her eyes, and very nearly cried; yet somehow didn't. She mumbled something placatory but he didn't answer except to give a final burst of *chow, pow, wow*s before withdrawing his gun.

The next thing she knew, leaves and grass were being pressed through the hole. They dribbled and drifted down and a few wisps of grass caught on the grainy surface of the wood. Anne sat where she was, unable to move or protest, hugging to herself her disappointment at this encounter, until some small stones began to patter around her. One touched her arm. Then half an old, yellow brick came over and landed beside her with a thwack. Bobby laughed loudly, unpleasantly.

Anne stood up, saying, 'No, please, don't,' to her former friend. Miraculously, the shower of stones stopped raining. She listened. He didn't seem to be moving about. Nor was she. But she would . . . She was going to look through again, but carefully this time, not too closely, so he couldn't hurt her.

The thing was, how could they be friends after this? Then she had a flash of inspiration. Give him a real bull's-eye instead of a pretend one. She had hidden one in a faded seed packet only that morning. She would pop it through to Bobby. He'd be bound to like it. He had before, hadn't he? That was how she had made them friends in the first place. Of course. How simple. Anne went happily to the greenhouse and found the sweet. Hurrying back, she kept a look out for further aerial bombardment, but there wasn't any and she reached the fence safely.

The hole was blocked! Bobby had jammed a stone into it. Part of it protruded on her side. At once she pushed hard with her thumb and it fell out on his side. Anne laughed. That was better. She wondered whether to peep through again but decided it was safer to post the bull's-eye through first. It came straight back. This was strange. She listened, straining her ears, but could hear only her own breathing. She pushed the sweet back through again.

'Please, it's for you,' Anne said. No reply. She waited. No sounds of any kind. But the bull's-eye didn't return. Was he eating it? She wanted to look but still she didn't dare. Then she heard a squelching sound. But it was far too loud to be Bobby sucking the sweet. What was it? As it continued she plucked up courage and with great circumspection crouched close to the fence and, tight in the chest with fear, peeped through once more.

Bobby was making mud pies. He was pouring water from his old watering can into a chipped pudding basin full of earth and stirring it with a stick. It looked like a thick, dark chocolate. Anne felt offended. She wanted to play, too. Help him stir. But now – oh, perhaps he was going to invite her, after all? – he was bringing the bowl of delicious mud to the fence. Yes, they would play together. *Yes*. He was after all her best friend and he'd accepted her peace offering. *Yes*. He hadn't posted it back, not the second time, had he? And the first was probably a joke, wasn't it?

He knelt and it was clear he was surveying the fence. Close to, he looked younger than ever. Such a baby face . . . except the eyes seemed to be filling with calculation and he was starting to frown. Then, in an instant, his face changed; he smiled to himself not her and, dipping both hands into the bowl, scooped out the mud and held it, dripping, in his cupped palms. Next, he leant back on his heels, cocked his head to one side – still she could see him; could he see her? – and slapped the mud at the hole. *Slurp. Thump.*

This was worse than the gun. The mud splashed right through. Some of it hit Anne's open eye. It stung. The rest splattered her face and even got into her mouth, making her splutter. And the grit set her teeth on edge. She cried out, but Bobby was laughing and slapping more mud into and around the hole so that the fence shook.

'Nosy parker, nosy parker,' he chanted.

Anne was too preoccupied by the mud all over her to be shocked by the tone of his voice. She didn't need to understand his words to realise that her friend now hated her. She stood up and began to cry. The thudding against the fence stopped and she heard Bobby laughing as he skipped away shouting words that sounded raucously triumphal.

Anne retreated indoors and when challenged about the state she was in she said she had fallen over. But no one believed her, because she hadn't grazed her knee as well as her face. She could hardly have done one without the other, they said. But it was the mud that really caused concern. Anne was taken upstairs, where she was promptly and firmly washed, after which she was given a clean blouse to put on. Usually she could do up the buttons herself, but not today. Then some golden liquid from a round-shouldered bottle was poured into a saucer of water; this turned milky-white and the tingling mixture – the bottle's label had a magic sword on it like King Arthur's – was dabbed on to the graze beside her eye. Again her knees were examined for damage but none was found.

'You can't have fallen over, Anne.'

'I did, Maman.' But her heart wasn't in her denial.

'No, you must have done something else. Besides, what about all that mud? Where did that come from?'

For a while Anne didn't reply. She wanted to remain loyal to Bobby. After all, they had been such friends, done so many wonderful things together. Why, he'd driven her to Timbuktu and rescued her from brigands. He had even been to church with her at home among the Germans.

'Come along, Anne. The truth now.'

'I didn't do anything,' she said.

'Someone did.'

'It wasn't me.'

'Who, then?'

'My friend.' There, she'd done it. Given her friend away. 'Bobby threw mud at me.'

'Oh, no! Not your friend again!'

'Yes! Yes!'

'You're making it up, darling.'

'I'm not! I'm not.'

Her truth wasn't believed.

'You're too old for such pretending. Only little children have pretend friends.'

'But he did. He tried to poke me in the eye.'

'What with?'

'With his gun.'

'But he's your friend. Why should he try to hurt you?'

'Don't know. I hate him. I hate him!' she stamped her foot.

'Shush, don't be silly. Besides, you can't hate somebody who isn't there.'

'I can,' said Anne and thought of her father. He wasn't there either and she hated him now, too. Quite as much as Bobby. In fact she hated everybody. She pushed abruptly at her mother and would have done the same to her nurse, but Marguerite caught Anne's hand and immobilised it firmly.

'Oh, no. No, no, no, young lady. Early bed for you.'

'Please. No. Won't.'

Anne went to her bedroom, wailing, shouting, stamping.

'Who's a crosspatch today?' they said.

Anne flung herself on to the bed and cried as heartily as she could, but to her surprise her tears were less plentiful than she would have wished. Her mother and Marguerite had been right – she was more angry than sad.

She rolled off the bed and stomped leaden-footed to the window, wishing she could make the whole house vibrate like Papa did in his boots. Through the diamond panes she could see Bobby. He was sitting on top of his house with his toy bear and toy elephant. Flying in the breeze beside him was a flag which she recognised as being the one Papa said was Mr Churchill's. It had the same blue, white and red as Papa's but its complex pattern frowned at you. It was a flag that seemed to warn you to behave yourself or else.

Bobby took occasional, lazy aim with his long gun at things in the sky, firing at loop-the-loop swallows or stalling sparrows. Watching him, Anne found herself, despite herself, making the firing sounds for him. But then, recalling her grievances against him, she abandoned this friendly, vocal complicity, pursed her lips and began to plot her revenge.

First – the plan was now taking shape in her mind – she would creep, no, she was already creeping, downstairs. In the kitchen she stole a knife from a drawer; a small sharp knife with a black handle they had brought from home. A French knife. Then she let herself out through the back door and tiptoed down the garden. Sirens sounded and searchlights played, but she had no fear, not now. The fence was no barrier at all. She simply scaled it as if she were a soldier. Once in Bobby's garden, she crawled her way forward commando-style to his house and peered down through the open doorway to where he lay asleep, safe from Herr Hitler but not from her.

For a moment she gazed down at him, savouring her power but wishing she had put burnt cork on her face. She said not a word; she was made of silent brass, mute steel. Now she felt herself to be finally her father's daughter. He too was renowned for saying little or nothing, she had heard. He had taught himself to be strong and silent when he was young so people would listen to him when he was old. And when he did do something, especially in battle, he never talked at all.

Anne was in action now, she was a soldier, so she wouldn't say anything either. She'd be like Papa. No, she *was* Papa. Look, her giant shadow towered over Bobby, the knife in her hand flashed in the moonlight and as she struck— Oh, no, her victim was moving! Suddenly he was standing up on top of his Anderson shelter while her daydream Bobby simply turned over with sigh and Anne's knife disappeared as she blinked at the real one scrambling down to answer the man who had burst through the rose arches shouting at him.

The man was all in khaki now. He sounded both anxious and angry. He shouted and pointed and shouted again. He and Bobby, followed by his mother, who also wore different clothes – slacks and a blouse instead of her flowery dress – were looking all over the garden, hunting for something. But it wasn't a game. They were too urgent, too hectic – there was a desperate impatience in it. Anne was glad she wasn't with them, even wished she wasn't watching when they found what they needed so badly: the black beret among the lettuces.

The man grabbed it savagely and moulded it on to his head with quicksilver hands, but already his anger was turning to relief, to smiles, to kisses. He scooped up Bobby with one arm and with the other he hugged the woman to him so compulsively her feet danced to keep her balance. At this Anne revised her opinion. Now she longed to rush in, to bury herself against them, among them, these violent English people, and say: 'Me too. Hold me too. Love me too.'

But she was far off, shut away behind diamond-leaded glass, and besides all three of them were going now. As she lost sight of them Bobby's garden seemed to grow darker. Much of it was already in shadow anyway, although the nasturtiums still blazed in glory on top of the shelter.

Anne reminded herself of her revenge raid, even tried to re-envisage her friend asleep and at her mercy, but no return to that bitter pretence was possible or desirable now. The rage in her had died. She loved Bobby again. Had done so all along really. Wanted to hold him, but now he'd gone. Intead she put her arms around herself as far as she could, but her fat hands would scarcely reach further than her fat sides. Anne rocked to and fro, crooning to herself in a way that made her salivate as her lips loosened their grip on everyday propriety. Feeling the familiar spittle dampening her chin she tried to lick it, suck it back. She retrieved some and swallowed it. This made a gurgling sound in her throat, which on the instant transported her to the top of Bobby's shelter.

And he was sitting beside her, smiling, quite his old self again, with the pudding basin between his knees. This time, though, instead of mud there was warm, soapy water in it. Bobby had a white clay pipe such as she had seen held on a card by elastic bands in the village shop at home. Bobby drew it upside down across the frothy surface so that after a moment he could turn it the right way up and blow a careful bubble that would teeter deliciously on the bowl of the pipe. Anne was open-mouthed at his prowess. Gently he shook the pipe and the bubble wobbled itself free. It drifted towards the arches and Anne thought it was going to burst among the roses, but, no, it managed to glide over them and rise up and up between the birch trees before vanishing in a golden haze of last-minute evening sunlight.

'It's like our balloon,' she said.
'Better,' he answered.
'Shinier. And with more colours.'
'Like little rainbows inside it.'
'Just what I was going to say. May I blow one, please?'
'Of course,' said Bobby, the perfect English gentleman once more. Perhaps he was a milord and hadn't told her?

She decided not to ask: it might be impolite. He handed her the pipe.

Her first bubble started off well, just as good as his, but then it burst before detaching itself. She tried again and this time, with his hand steadying hers, her bubble slid smoothly away and floated towards the top of the fence. There it stopped and balanced for a moment, sinuously changing shape before bursting into a nothingness that was like a hole in the air.

Bobby laughed and congratulated her; then, having stirred the soapsuds with a wooden spoon, he invited her to blow another. This one was a masterpiece. It was enormous, majestic, richly glistening, and its viscous walls seemed to be washed within by sliding veils of liquid light. The bubble floated up and up and she and Bobby scrambled to their feet to watch its progress – higher, higher – when, out of the blue, a swallow swooped down on razor wings, jinked by it, turned, and one curved wing tip caught the bubble so that it burst in a spray of water sparks as the bird stalled, fluttered in a chaotic thrash of wings and then banked away on a glide as smooth as silk.

'He did it. The bird did it!' Bobby shouted, clapping his hands together.

This gave Anne an idea. 'Let's burst some, too,' she said.

So they did. They blew bubbles purely for destruction, smacking at the shimmering spheres as they broke free from the pipe. Eventually Bobby blew a sustained burst of them and Anne galumphed around the garden systematically annihilating every one in an orgy of hand-flapping excitement. Meanwhile, Bobby trod in the basin and it tipped over. At once all the water was lost, spilt among the nasturtiums, so that ants shepherding blackfly scurried for their lives. Bobby cried at wetting his sandal and sock, but Anne climbed back up and kissed him better. Once he was comforted, she took out a brass curtain ring she had meant to hide one day in their treasure tree and gave it to him to wear as a wedding ring on his right hand like her father did.

'You can't wear it on your left hand,' she said. 'Because it was wounded when you fought the Germans before.' She helped him slip it on to his finger. 'There, now we're married. Just as I've always wanted. I told the Chief of the Bandits as much, didn't I?'

'But you haven't got a ring,' he objected.

'We'll share yours,' she said.

Bobby agreed and Anne took the ring. Bobby admired it on her finger. The correct one. Then she helped him remove his sandal and sock so they could dry in the sun. And there they would have sat for ever and a day if the air-raid siren hadn't sounded. And if Marguerite hadn't come into the bedroom.

'Anne, wipe your mouth,' she said.

Papa was wearing his new tropical uniform. Maman examined him with a dressmaker's unforgiving eye while he observed himself stoically in the wardrobe mirror. Anne and Babar stood in the doorway not quite certain if they should be there or not. Anne thought her father looked like God carved out of sandstone, but her mother was clearly less impressed. She kept tugging hard at the hem of the jacket so that it fell, as she put it, more smoothly over his 'situpon' – which seemed even to Anne to be rather a childish word for such an enormous and adult rump. After this her mother required him to step up on to a stool in order to check the length of the trousers. Meekly Papa obeyed and Anne hoped he would suddenly pretend to be an elephant at the circus, but he didn't. One of the legs was longer than the other. With swift decisiveness Maman inserted pins to mark the difference. She would shorten it after dinner. Mind you, it was the kind of material that would require continual pressing once he reached the tropics, she said.

At the mention of the word 'tropics' Papa shushed Anne's mother, saying that this was meant to be a secret and walls had ears. Anne hadn't heard this slogan before, so she looked around the room hoping to see sponge-like ears sprout at once from behind the bedhead, above the picture rail or beneath the dressing table. But none appeared. Her parents, realising why she was looking, laughed and Papa explained disappointingly that in fact walls couldn't grow ears, no: it was just a phrase warning people in England not to say things out loud that might help Herr Hitler, who was trying to listen to people wherever they were – in shops, on a bus, anywhere.

Immediately Anne wanted to look under her parents' bed to see if by mischance Herr Hitler was there with them in the room. She knew they didn't mind her being childish but she also liked them to think she was becoming more mature, so instead she picked up her father's cap and tried it on. It fitted. 'Now I'm a general too,' she said, and tried to salute herself like Papa did when he was in uniform. But somehow – was it because she could see herself from three different angles in the dressing table's bevelled mirrors? –

somehow her action overreached itself, her hand hit the peak of the kepi, it swivelled on her head and fell off. Papa retrieved it quickly and Maman went downstairs to put on the beans for supper.

Her father brushed his oak-leaved cap unnecessarily and offered it to her to wear again. Anne shook her head, at which he picked her up, saying, 'Well, well, you're heavier than ever. Soon you won't be my little Anne any more, will you?' She couldn't answer this and, besides, there wasn't time even to think of a reply because Papa was pitching her and Babar on to the bed and tickling her, making her arms and legs thrash the air in a delight close to pain. Maman called upstairs, telling Papa not to make her overexcited. He shouted back that he wasn't (though he was) and suddenly he stopped tickling her toes, drew himself up to his full height and then plunged on to one knee most dramatically in front of her.

Anne, bewildered, sat up. He fixed her with his eye and began, still resplendent in his godlike uniform the colour of sand and camels, to recite the strange words she had heard before, words which came to her like light from distant stars. Papa's voice had changed. It was richer, rounder, darker, and his arms and hands danced in time with the things he was saying, which were as enticing as deliciously flower-scented chocolates. Anne was astonished. She couldn't believe her good fortune. Papa only ever play-acted like this on very special occasions. This – this was the pretence he had played at last New Year, when he became a funny man with a big nose who begged her for a kiss. And she hadn't been Anne any more but someone beautiful called Roxane.

His mysterious words wound round her heart. They moved all about her, stroking her, caressing her, telling her to slide without fear from smiles to sighs to tears to kisses. And wonder of wonders, yes, she remembered, yes: this was the charade in which she was allowed to hush Papa, to shut his mouth! Because she was pretending not to want to be kissed, when she did, she did. Sometimes she tried to shush him too much, just as people would her, at which his voice would grow marvellously, overwhelmingly loud and she would fall silent, awaiting the moment when, his voice descending to a heartfelt whisper, he told her she was really the Queen of France and he was one of her lords who loved her from a distance, deeply, sadly, faithfully.

At this he lifted up his eyes so that the whites showed underneath (like those of a doll she had once had except her china head had broken) only he looked not like a doll but more like a tall, lugubrious hunting dog. Anne laughed, saying, 'Oh, Papa, Papa!' But he said sternly, 'No, no, don't laugh. I'm not Papa, I am' – how his eyes glittered! – 'I am Cyrano de Bergerac at your service, ma'am! But you can't see me in the dark, you can only hear my voice, because I am hidden from view beneath your balcony. And you are my cousin, the beautiful Lady Roxane, whom I love without hope.' Then she had to tell him to climb up (Anne, ignorant of balconies, was never quite sure where she actually was in this game, but Papa always put her on a chair or bed so he could kneel below her) and claim his kiss.

This was the best bit. When he pretended to climb. His knees and feet went up and down while his hands kept changing places with each other. 'I'm climbing a drainpipe,' he told her. And whoops, suddenly, there he was with her, and he put his arms round her and then – it was always a surprise, though she knew what was coming – he grabbed Babar and thrust the elephant at her to receive his kiss instead of him because he'd jumped off the bed and was being funny, pretending to be left out while his friend, on whose behalf he had spoken, received the kiss. He got sadder and sadder, until she thought he was crying. He was a ghost, he said, he was Lazarus at the Feast of Love, boo-hoo.

'Don't cry, Papa,' she said, horrified even by his pretence. At once he stopped, stood up with a flourish and a twirl of his moustache and seized a coat hanger. He struck a wonderful pose – his left leg straight back, his right crooked at the knee, one arm in the air behind his head and the other held straight out with the coat hanger, which was now his sword, pointing forwards. 'On guard,' he shouted. And, lunging at nothing, he fought an invisible opponent. He stabbed, he parried, he cut, he thrust, he feinted and laughed, turning on the spot, saluting her with his sword held up to his nose while his enemy, bemused, stumbled past him. The whole room shuddered, thudded and shook. Then he lunged again, piercing his foe to the heart; Anne saw him fall, before Papa stood over him and pulled out his sword from the wretch's non-existent heart.

'Have you won?' Anne asked.

Papa had. The man had been impertinent, he said. Again his mood changed. He began to speak. More magic spells. But these were worse and better than before. He was wearing marble boots and lead gloves, he said. But, even so, he was going to fight all his ancient enemies. There were thousands of them and they had strange names such as Treachery, Compromise, Prejudice and Cowardice. And again his coat hanger slashed and lunged. Did they imagine he wanted to make a pact with them? Never! An armistice? A shameful peace? Never! And again he struck, this time at the someone he always called Field Marshal Old Fool, shouting that he would fight and fight and fight! They could strip him of everything – his honour, his love, his laurels and his rose – but despite them all he would take with him to heaven something that was pure, without stain.

'What? What is it?' Anne cried.

'Oh, my dear little Anne –'

'What?'

'My way of being me, Anne, my way that says: "when you have nothing, demand everything".'

'Will God like that?'

'I hope so,' he said. 'After all, it's His way too.' And saluting her superbly for the last time, he spun round on his heels and fell down dead, wooden coat hanger in hand. She ran to him. Was he all right really? Of course he was. It was all a pretence. He came to life, pulled her to him and kissed her and then heaved himself and her to their feet and started to dance with her, singing an absurd song full of words even Anne could tell were nonsense. Round and round they went, singing and laughing, until with a last gigantic effort he lifted her off her feet and they flopped on to the bed. There they lay, recovering their breath side by side, and Anne was as happy as she had ever been.

Two days later Anne learned that her father had gone to the land of the elephants. He was sailing over the sea with hundreds of English soldiers and sailors and some French ones too. But not with her. He hadn't taken her, his Queen of Light and Air.

When she informed Babar of this betrayal, even he couldn't comfort her. She threw her toy into a corner.

SEVEN

Anne lay on her bed in broad daylight and still they were talking about her in the living room below. Would they never stop? She had heard them before; she could half hear them now.

She was supposed to have been behaving nicely, helping wind wool while Maman talked to a visitor who spoke French. They thought she couldn't understand, but she could, oh, she could. With Anne, many words went in though few came out.

'My mother has always maintained,' Maman said, 'that *that* was why Anne was born as she was.'

'Because of a fight between soldiers?'

'It was very alarming at the time, I must say. We were stationed at Treves. My husband's first command. The 19th Rifles. He's still an infantry man at heart, you know. Anyway, while expecting Anne I was rather surprised one evening to find myself in the middle of a brawl. They were drunk, of course. Some of our men had started a fight with a group of Germans – veterans from the first war. The town was near the border.'

'And the shock affected your unborn baby?'

'So my mother insists. Mind you, all the doctors we've ever consulted – and we've tried so many – they all dismiss the idea. They say a mongolian child is really a question of biology.'

'I'm sure you're right. She must be a burden to you?'

'No.'

'No?'

'Well, only sometimes.'

'Has it affected your husband's career?'

'Not at all.'

'I'm so glad. Of course, his coming over here has been something of a risk, I dare say?'

'Of course.'

'Where is he at the moment? I haven't seen him in the newspapers recently.'

'I'm afraid I'm not allowed to say.'

This was when Anne stopped holding the wool. She had just understood what had been said the moment before concerning her and that country in the east that she didn't come from. No! No, she wasn't from Mongolia. She came from France. She turned and protested in an impassioned mumble of denial, but the wool fell from her outstretched hands and she caught her foot in it as she stood up. She kicked to free herself, but it wouldn't let go, and this increased her panic and screaming, which was why Marguerite had been called to take her upstairs to bed.

Another of her tantrums, they called it. The latest of many since Papa had gone. She had become bad and obstinate. She wasn't Papa's poor little, dear little Anne at all any more, they said. Very well, she wouldn't be. She would be a fierce dragon instead.

But as Anne turned over to crouch on all fours and become a dragon breathing fire, she heard the siren and then the aeroplanes. At once her fire-breathing evaporated. She rushed to the window, though she knew she shouldn't. You were meant to stay away from looking at what could hurt you. There they were. The golden sky was darkened by them. Hundreds of bombers, all in rows. They growled and groaned overhead while the ack-ack guns at the tennis club croaked at them.

Marguerite came in. 'Anne, come away from the window this instant,' she said.

They took shelter under the stairs. Maman and the lady talked of invasion. Herr Hitler was going to come with his men in big barges and his aeroplanes would rain bombs down on the poor English, as they were doing now on London. She could hear a distant, continuous rumble like thunder. Anne began to cry, but as quietly as possible, and this time her mother put her arm round her and told their visitor her little Anne was frightened of the air raids, which was true. Especially at night. She snuggled against Maman, hoping she would sing her a song, but she didn't.

When the all clear sounded they scrambled out and stretched, but no sooner had it stopped than the warning started again because all the German aeroplanes were coming back on their way home, and this was dangerous because sometimes they unloaded any bombs they had left over on to Petts Wood. Several nearby explosions were even now making the windows rattle.

At last they were gone and the siren said it was all right again, and this time it was. Maman said something about them moving somewhere else soon, but Anne wasn't listening – she was too busy asking if she could go out into the garden again to see if her friend was all right.

She had quite forgotten he had blocked up the hole. The mud had dried – from dark chocolate to milk chocolate. It looked hard and permanent. She examined the fence, hoping to find another cranny to peep through, and after a while she found one. If she stood on tiptoe she could put her eye to the gap, but it only afforded a view of the upended, rusting wheelbarrow. She decided to try listening. Perhaps she would be able to hear Bobby? Once or twice she thought she did, but then she wasn't sure. She went back and regarded the dried mud again.

This time it did not occur to her to clear the hole. Part of Anne felt she deserved exclusion from her friend's world. And this obscure feeling seemed to connect mysteriously with her father's desertion of her. If Papa could deceive her, then why shouldn't a little English boy turn against her? She had felt so pleased to be in command of Bobby, making him do whatever she wanted just like Papa made everyone do what he wanted. She had been so proud of herself, but now once again she was that silly nobody they called poor little Anne, the one who made them sigh and smile too brightly, the Anne she didn't like or believe in either.

When eventually she returned to the house the kitchen was unoccupied. But she found there a basket full of carrots, onions and potatoes. And this was the moment she discovered the carrot she had turned into Papa. At first it had been simply a funny thing, an absurd vegetable with protrusions like legs she had smuggled out into the garden. In the greenhouse she had found it a hiding place under a flowerpot. But once there, stored away for later unspecified use, it had grown in her mind until the fearsome intention had become hard and clear.

It was a wicked plan, she knew, but it comforted her as the sirens howled and nobody slept while the sky danced with light and sound. She would do it. Yes. Papa had deserted her. Papa deserved it. Could she make a general's cap for it first? she wondered. Perhaps. Then she would get the nail. And afterwards ... what would she do with it afterwards? Would she bury him? No. She'd keep him where he was under the flowerpot so he was neither alive nor dead but in prison. In her power. Yes. And with this thought – between one air raid and another – Anne slept.

Then one morning it was raining and she had to stay indoors. In case her chest caught cold. But the ideal children depicted in her new colour-in book depressed her. They looked far cleverer than she would ever be. She scrawled at them until the red pencil went right through the page and stabbed the next. Then she ripped the pages out. For this she was smacked and she spent what was left of that dismal morning self-exiled in a corner, pretending not to be there, which meant keeping her hands over her eyes but peeping between her fingers every now and then to see if the sun had come out.

When the rain stopped, they had to go to the shops. Anne fidgeted all the way there and all the way back. Her mother declared she did not know what had got into her that morning. She wouldn't even hold Maman's hand to cross the road.

At last, after a scarcely eaten lunch and an unwanted rest, she escaped to the greenhouse and her secret. She discovered she was sharing it with several ants and a small red spider. She shook them off the carrot and went to get the nail. It was intended as a hook for a coil of garden wire, but when she had pulled at the wire the day before the nail had nearly come out. One more try and it would. It did, falling from her hand to the concrete floor. Anne picked it up. It was dulled by rust and not quite straight but it was sufficient for her purpose.

First she had to conjure up her father. Anne stared hard at the carrot, telling herself she was a witch and willing herself to think of a wicked spell that would transform it into Papa. But she wasn't and she couldn't; well, not yet. She propped it up against the flowerpot. That in itself was better. 'Stand on your own two legs,' she told the carrot and it did – leaning back a little awkwardly, admittedly, but upright enough. She considered it. Of course. It needed its general's cap. That would do it. That would turn it into Papa.

Out in the garden it was difficult to find any flower to resemble a peaked cap. In her mind it had been an easy, even an obvious, solution but in reality daisies were too small, roses became fragrant confetti in her hands and snapdragons, which had at first looked ideal, refused to stay put on top of a carrot. In the end she was obliged to make do with a white campanula.

Placed in position the bell-like flower looked nothing like Papa's kepi with its shining peak and gold oak leaves. But it did fit beautifully. So Anne quickly revised her requirements of it, told herself the flower was not his cap but his face. Yes, it did look quite like Papa now. Yes. White face, orange uniform. Oh dear, ought she to wash it? No, he was dusty from journeying to the land of the elephants, wasn't he? Of course.

Now for the spell again. She mumbled the few bad words she knew, but the few bad words she knew weren't powerful enough to make the transformation she needed. Finally she tried chanting the nonsense song he had sometimes sung to her. Her rendition, unlike his, was as fierce as she could make it. *Ou Pachou Pachou Paya* she went, repeating the words until they sounded like a fit of sneezing. Her eyes smarted with the effort. She felt dizzy. And how her hand was shaking as she picked up the nail! She would have to hold it still with her other one as she pointed her – what was it? It couldn't be just a nail any more – her sword, yes, her sword called Dettol . . . no, her bayonet, yes, her bayonet with no name like the Germans had stuck in Papa before, yes, her bayonet!

There! Stick him in the middle! Again and again! There! The carrot fell over. She stood up and lunged again. Again Papa fell over. He was lying on his back and his face had fallen off. 'Stand up!' she said. 'Stand up!' But he didn't. He defied her. Very well then, she would kill him lying down. And she stabbed at him with the nail gripped tight in her sweating fist. This time it worked. The nail went in and the skewered carrot came back up with it. She banged it down again and the nail pierced it still further. 'Kill! Kill! Kill!' she shouted, feeling frightened. 'Bad Papa. Bad, bad, bad. Serve you right for leaving me behind. Look, you're dead, you're dead. Dead. Look. Dead.'

Now she was truly lonely. In a limbo of her own creation. Her head was throbbing, her hair was damp with perspiration, her stomach was a knot that would never untie and her throat was made of sandpaper. When she tried to swallow, it hurt.

She put the flowerpot over Papa and felt no better. Jockey appeared. This made her think someone was coming, but she was wrong, no one was. The dog barked at her but, receiving no response, departed, leaving her with herself again. She tried to force tears into her eyes but it was no use. Tears were not allowed any more.

For the rest of that day, and for several days after, Anne told herself at frequent intervals that killing Papa had been just one of her pretences. How could she have done such a thing? Well, of course, she hadn't. Not really. But part of her felt she had. No. No. She wasn't old enough or clever enough to do what she had done – you had to be grown-up for that. Look at Herr Hitler. And besides, Papa wasn't a carrot, was he? A carrot was the last thing he would be. What a foolish game it had been – not a nice pretence at all. 'I've just been silly,' she told herself. Soon, having reproved herself repeatedly, and ever more gently, she found she could live with her crime. It seemed she could allow it to slip from her mind like something she'd grown out of.

EIGHT

The black limousine called Packard came ever more frequently to Petts Wood. Sometimes Maman went in it without Anne; at others Anne had to go too, across an England that was starting to turn brown. They were looking now for another house to live in a long way from the bombs, Maman said. Anne no longer replied that she wanted to go home to France. She just sat where she was put, feeling heavier, duller, fatter. She had become a real lump and was rather enjoying it. Soon, perhaps, they wouldn't be able to move her at all.

They went to inspect an old grey house with a pond. It had goldfish, green lily pads and a rowing boat. The stone house was huge after Petts Wood and the garden bigger still. You couldn't see any other houses from it. Anne wouldn't have immediate neighbours or imaginary friends if they lived there. Suddenly she wanted to return to Petts Wood and find Bobby.

When they got back she could see him from her bedroom window and he looked too distant to belong to her any more. But what was he doing? Was he really throwing everything out of his house? First the beach ball appeared, bouncing wildly, then his toy elephant was flung out and, following that, a deck chair, which he pushed, red-faced with the effort, up and out on to the path. After this came the old tin tray and Rupert Bear. Was that all? No, a moth-eaten blanket appeared and then, wonder of wonders, a big straw hat with an ostrich feather stuck in it. Anne had never seen this spectacular object before. Seeing it made her angry. She felt cheated. Why hadn't her friend shown it to her so it could have figured in her dreams? She could have worn it to Timbuktu, or to church – now she remembered she had gone in hatless: what would God, let alone the villagers, have thought of that?

Bobby meanwhile climbed out, picked up his toy animals, jammed the astonishing hat on his head and marched away with the ostrich feather bobbing like a purple banner. Anne nearly cried out with vexation. What a waste! Why, it was just the kind of hat Papa needed when he was the funny sad man with the coat-hanger sword. She could have imagined him wearing it. Then she remembered that such thoughts were now forbidden her. Because, thanks to her, Papa was dead. He would never come back. The horror of her crime returned.

When Bobby appeared again he no longer wore the hat. Instead he was holding hands with a little girl. And both of them had labels on. The labels were the kind you tied on suitcases, but these ones were round their necks. The two of them were laughing and skipping as they came through the rose arches, Bobby pointing at his house. The girl was as fair-haired as he but she had plaits with two green velvet bows. And she looked as pretty as a first Communion picture. She came and looked at all the things Bobby had cleared out of the shelter and peeped in, but turned away, not wanting to enter. How dare she despise their wonderful house? But now Bobby was holding out his hand again and helping her climb up and sit on top.

The girl picked a nasturtium; sniffed it and threw it away. Then she laughed and pointed at something in the sky before turning to kiss – to *kiss* – Bobby on the cheek. Anne was beside herself with rage. She could feel herself choking with jealousy, unable to breathe for hatred of her rival. When she forced herself to look again, they were inspecting each other's labels. What did they say? Although a refugee herself, Anne had no comprehension of evacuation or evacuees. She could not know that the labels identified their wearers.

Bobby's mother appeared, calling to them, again and again. The two children scrambled down and ran to her. She took both by the hand and they all wheeled round to greet another, older woman, wearing grey and green, coming out of the house. Bobby's mother spoke to the children, then to this new, official-looking person, who crouched briefly to meet them at their level. Then they all went, all hand in hand, and Anne knew she would never see her friend again.

Once more they were on the move. 'Look at it all,' her mother said, at the boxes and suitcases. She had said the same yesterday, she was saying it again today. She did not know how they could possibly have acquired so many possessions in so short a time in England.

Anne was helping them pack, fetching things that 'we don't need quite yet, thank you, darling.' She had put Babar out of the way on the bed only now it was being stripped. Flapping sheets and tumbling blankets surrounded her as she tried to rescue Babar. '*Do* mind out from under our feet, Anne,' they said.

She did as she was told, taking Babar by the ear in a way she thought she never would, and sat with him under the stairs as the house echoed with unease. Every day now she nagged them about Papa. Where was he? Was he safe? If they would tell her something definite, she could stop worrying about what she had done to him in the greenhouse. But they always said he was bound to be all right. Anne knew this couldn't be true but the asking was a kind of comfort.

A man in a melon hat came to make sure they hadn't broken anything during their stay in Petts Wood. Anne remained where she was, remembering the glass she had bitten, two plates she had broken – one by sitting on it – and a flower vase her elbow had swept to the parquet floor. It was when the man was going into the kitchen with Maman that Anne realised the front door had been left open. A most surprising oversight. Why, if she chose, she could venture out into the front garden by herself. Something she had never done in all the time they'd been there.

She crept out of the cupboard and along the hall. In the porch she hesitated but, telling herself not to be afraid, she went down the path to the front gate. She peered up and down the road. It looked as quiet and leafy as it did when Maman or Marguerite took her shopping.

Should she open the gate? She knew how the latch worked. And here she was, lifting it. And now she was going down the road. She hadn't really decided to go to the shops by herself but that was what she was doing. She knew she had no money, let alone her ration book, but even so she continued down the road.

She passed familiar hedges, the wall with the coloured-glass butterflies embedded in it, the fat red postbox on the corner. This object she had always liked, so she gave it a pat and decided she must not only be visiting the shops but also running away. But was she? She hadn't brought Babar and where was her suitcase? These thoughts disturbed her. Should she go back? Was she really sensible enough to run away, with or without her most precious possessions? Anne knew other children could, and sometimes did, run away, but they were different. Silly but clever. Whereas she was, well, she.

Anne stopped and looked back as doubt welled up within her. Oh, how she wished she could think sensibly, decide clearly. She shut her eyes, hoping this would help, and when she opened them again she was staring up at the sky, which was suddenly full of rushing sound as well as sunshine.

There had been no siren to announce this aeroplane's approach. And its noise told Anne it wasn't one of the small twisting-and-turning sort, nor one of the heavy kind, but a betwixt-and-between one. A medium noise heralding pure terror. And here it was! She could see it. It was diving down towards her. Aiming at her!

Now she knew what she was doing. Yes. She was running out into the road with her arms wide – she was running towards it as if to embrace it. Her fear was welcoming it, saying *hello, good morning, how nice to see you, how do you do?* And the Heinkel was upon her, stooping at her like a bird of prey. She could see everything about it and it was spitting bullets at her alone; they sparked on the kerbstones, ricocheting everywhere.

She stood transfixed, certain she could feel the bullets going through her. The noise was deafening but she didn't cover her ears, no, she turned full circle, performing a surprising pirouette to watch the studded underbelly of the Heinkel as it roared away over the roof tops. Anne stayed stuck where she was in the middle of the road. Then she fell down.

The rough breath of the milkman's horse on her cheek roused her. She opened her eyes to stare into its leathery nostrils and hairy upper lip. The milkman's hand helped her to her feet. He was saying things she couldn't understand or answer. But it was clear he intended to take her home. His voice was kind and he let her ride on his milk cart.

When they reached the house he helped her down, gave her another bull's-eye and accompanied her to the front door. Here he explained to the alarmed eyes and open mouths of the others that he had found Anne lying unconscious in the middle of the road. She had fainted, he said. Marguerite led her into the living room while Maman continued trying to understand the milkman's story and pay their last milk bill at the same time.

'What did you think you were doing?' they said.

'I didn't mean to go out.'

'You must have. And what were you doing in the middle of the road? Suppose a car had come? You could've been run over.'

They were very angry with her but, strangely, no one mentioned the dive bomber or the bullets dancing everywhere.

'Did you see the aeroplane?' she managed to ask in between their barrage of questions.

'What aeroplane?'

'It came down low. It shot bullets.'

'Don't be silly, Anne. There wasn't even a siren.'

'But I saw it!'

'Nonsense. There hasn't been a raid.'

'It was shooting at me.'

'That's enough.'

'I was going to run away, then it came instead and I told it to shoot me because of Papa. That's when I fell down.'

'Now we really are getting very, very upset, aren't we?'

And this was true. Anne was close to hysteria. 'I'm not, I'm not,' she screamed.

A hand slapped the back of her leg and she stopped. She went quiet. Her wet face was wiped.

'You must have imagined it, darling.'

'I didn't,' she said, but so quietly no one heard.

'It certainly sounds as if you've made it all up.'

'No.'

'You must have been thinking about what that lady said in the car. It's preyed on your mind. It didn't really happen to *you*, Anne. It was just one of your daydreams.'

NINE

Now that they were far away from the bombs, everyone agreed Anne would be much happier. In this house there wasn't even a wireless to unsettle anybody. All you could hear at night in Shropshire was the bark of an autumn fox or an early cockcrow. But when the cocks crowed, Anne thought of her father and trembled. He had been called the Cockerel at school, she remembered. When he had told her this he'd promptly uttered a magnificent crowing sound, jigging her on his knee. She had been much smaller then, of course, but she remembered how he had stretched his neck so his Adam's apple quivered as he crowed. She'd laughed and tried to clap her hands.

There weren't so many of them now. Her brother and sister were gone and her father was still stuck in the land of the elephants. But of course Papa was dead really, as Anne knew perfectly well, even if no one else would admit it in case she was upset. After all, she had killed him and eaten him, hadn't she? And her evil wish would have reached him wherever he was and he would have fallen down dead at once.

Without Papa and with her sister away at school and her brother in his boat, this strange old house contained just her, Maman and Marguerite. And the gardener, who kept the grounds so beautifully everybody smiled at him. She could pronounce his name – Tom. She often said it. When he spoke he was as incomprehensible as the milkman in Petts Wood but in a different way. It seemed to Anne that very few people in England spoke real English. Tom often gave her sweet little apples and, just once, some blackberries.

The house smelt of paraffin because there wasn't any electric light and Anne had to be very careful never to touch the lamps, especially when they were lit in the evenings – which arrived sooner than before, they said, though Anne hadn't noticed. The lamps were hot and dangerous and if you didn't snip off the burnt edges the wicks made the ceilings dirty and you got black specks on your face. The lamps were a different shape from Aladdin's but even so they could perform one magic trick. If a grown-up held a cigarette over the top of the glass funnel it would light of its own accord.

When Anne went up to bed Marguerite would bring a candle. It cast tall shadows up the stairs and made the pictures on the wall even more frightening than they were in daytime. They were crowded with people shouting and hurting each other a long time ago at home in France. Maman had explained that the poor people had attacked the rich people, especially the King, and cut off their heads, which then fell into baskets. It was because of these baskets full of heads that France didn't have a king and queen any more, although England still did – Anne had seen their palace in London, remember? Yes, Anne did. The pictures on the stairs looked hard, unfriendly and silvery-grey but very polite compared with the frantic people depicted in them. When you looked at them, Maman said, you were looking at history, which was why Anne tried not to. She didn't like the look of history.

Once safely in bed Anne wanted to know if people were always fighting. Marguerite said, 'Yes, most of the time they are, the more's the pity. Your papa wouldn't be a soldier if they weren't, would he?' And she kissed her good night to prevent further questions. but Anne held on to her, saying, 'Please stay. Don't go yet.' Because she, too, had an ulterior motive: a sudden compulsion to confess. She wanted to say: 'Please tell everyone I killed Papa. Please chop off my head, please.' But when she started to say it, Marguerite told her it was time to go to sleep and, extricating herself from Anne's frantic grip, went across to the window and closed the curtains.

'Go to sleep now,' her nurse repeated.

'But Papa's dead! I know he is!'

'What nonsense. Now good night. And no more talking.'

The minute the door shut Anne got out of bed, pulled open the curtains and let the moon back in again. She loved the light it gave and it seemed to appear more often here than in Petts Wood. At least she saw it more. Just as she had at home. Tonight it was exactly full – not a lopsided lemon any more but a beautiful round grapefruit. Remembering those fruits almost surprised Anne. She hadn't seen a lemon or a grapefruit for months and, as for oranges, they came as juice in brown bottles. But she wasn't entirely surprised to remember such things. Increasingly, she found, memories just slipped unbidden into her mind. Before coming to England she hadn't seemed to need them; the present had been enough, so they hadn't bothered to enter her head.

The moon made the gardens look tidier than ever and the waters of the lily pond shone like black glass. One late lily flower floated there pretending it was a star fallen from the sky. The pond fascinated Anne. It was beautiful and treacherous. She was not to go near it by herself, they said. This prohibition enhanced its beauty in her eyes. Anne imagined she was floating on it in the little boat she had seen moored at one side, or else she was swimming with the goldfish – not that she could swim except in dreams. She couldn't fly either but, even so, she was opening the window and wishing she could. She leant out eagerly, but then timid common sense pulled her back – she had tried to fly once before, down the stairs at home. The resulting bruises had turned into wonderful colours once the pain had faded.

But as Anne gazed out at the moonlit garden the recent horror of what she had done returned. A shifting image of her pretend revenge in the greenhouse mixed in her mind with one of Papa clutching his stomach and falling to bits in a place full of palm trees. A doctor was examining the orange mess that was his body. He said it was strange but Papa had all the symptoms, rarely if ever seen before in his experience, of having been nailed through the middle, broken in half and eaten by an unknown person who had proved unable to digest him. This was, of course, a case of murder and whoever had done it deserved to die.

Anne caught her breath. Once again she had accused herself. Once again she longed to confess. But no one would listen to her. No one would believe her. How could she make them hear her? Make them realise that this time, this once, she knew more than they did? No reply came. Her mind wouldn't stretch that far. Had it refused to think of a way? Yes. But her eyes hadn't. No. They observed the pond, armoured with lily pads. Of course, yes, things really could be as simple as she was. Of course. Tomorrow. Yes. Tomorrow she would force everyone to believe her. Well, afterwards they would. Anne returned to her bed and went to sleep.

In the morning her head wouldn't tell her what she had resolved to do the night before. She was conscious of having made a momentous decision but, try as she might, she couldn't recall what it was. Then, when her mother went away in a taxi, leaving Anne with Marguerite, she remembered. Yes. She was going to Heaven, by way of the lily pond, to see Papa. She couldn't wait to gallop across God's golden floors, to be swept up and hugged by her father, who would introduce her to all the angels – and even to Jesus, whose forked beard was so friendly. It was this happy ending that made her desperate plan such a comfort.

One familiar difficulty remained, however – how to be left unsupervised in this new place.

Anne tried everything she could think of to elude Marguerite. She asked very nicely if the two of them might play hide-and-seek or catch-me-if-you-can, but this was refused. She volunteered to help the gardener sweep the paths; again the answer was no. She offered to pick some flowers, but Marguerite said the vases were all full.

Much of the morning passed and Anne was beginning to fear that her mother would soon come home, when the doorbell rang. A visitor! This meant Marguerite had to go through the house to open the front door.

Without waiting even an instant to see who it might be – Jockey was barking his head off inside – Anne ran to the pond. She meant to stop at the edge and consider, to tell herself important things, to say goodbye to Babar, but the heaviness of her headlong rush propelled her straight in. She flopped face downwards with an elongated splash that seemed to dig a trench in the water. The lily pads danced; the goldfish fled. The watery impact stung her face. Her floundering hands slithered along roots and sank into fibrous mud. Her feet were caught, held, dragged down, and although she twisted her head wildly, choking, swallowing, coughing, she could feel herself going under, under. She thrashed and struggled.

This was not how she had meant it to be. She had intended a pleasant calmness, a floating into nowhere, into peace. She had hoped to collaborate gracefully with destiny, but instead here she was, fighting, kicking, spluttering – and refusing to sink with all the strength she had. How it hurt. But sinking she was, ah, yes, she was. Despite every effort. Yes. She could sense herself slipping now into a luminous darkness in which dim shapes seemed to pulsate to be born and these patterns, these nameless visions – what are you, who are you? – were the very things she had hoped for without knowing it.

Yes, this was how she had proposed to herself it might be. Soft and dark and swirling, but not cold any more – no – more like just before going to sleep. Perhaps these glowing green and purple shapes would become a mermaid soon? Or a friend? Or a drowned palace? Was that a goldfish staring at her? No. Oh, no! It was a doctor. A black and white doctor with glinting old spectacles. And she was little again. Small. Very small. And they had taken all her clothes away and made her stand naked for inspection on a dusty carpet in a cavernous room made of terrible books and dark cabinets holding glass jars full of brains and snakes. The doctor stared down at her as he measured her head with a tape measure.

'Anne, do you call her? Anne?' he said.

Her parents agreed they did. After noting the circumference of her head, he lifted her up on to a cold leather bed to observe her again at his level. He prodded at her chest, listened to it through a rubber tube, kneaded her tummy, turned her round, felt her back, patted her buttocks, examined her hands and feet, parting the fingers and toes.

'They can be webbed,' he said.

Next he shone a torch in her eyes. She blinked and started to cry. The doctor laughed and told her to open her mouth. He peered into it, using the torch as a spatula.

'We shall need to remove her tonsils in due course,' he said. 'You may dress her now.'

'Is there no hope?' Papa said.

'None,' the doctor said as Maman began to pull her clothes back on to her. 'Your daughter will never be like other children. She might as well go back where she came from.'

Papa's world was spinning and wobbling again, but this time it didn't fall to the floor. Instead Anne caught it and held it, clutching it to her as if it were in her power to make it better. And when she replaced it without a scratch she could see Mongolia quite clearly and great green waves rolled up to greet her, to sweep her off her feet, and she was drowning happily now, not in water but in grass, and someone just like herself came to take her hand and help her mount a beautiful horse, and as they rode away towards a great city of her own kind and a fairytale welcome, huge hands pulled Anne out of the pond and anxious voices asked her how on earth she had fallen in. 'Oh, really, Anne, how could you!'

Anne fought against rescue as she had against drowning, but it was no use. She was revived relentlessly, unforgivingly. She was bathed, dried, put to bed, fed warm milk with honey and even some brandy in it, scolded, kissed, scolded again, cuddled . . . condemned to life.

Anne, dumbfounded by failure, felt guiltier than ever and dreadfully frightened to be under such repeated orders to remain alive. Now she would never see Papa again. Well, not until she died properly.

The next morning Maman received a letter. It said Papa would soon be back in England.

A fence appeared around the lily pond. They unrolled chicken wire and tied it to posts. Anne was fond of chicken wire: the patterns it made were friendly; you could post things through it; it offered a ladder to convolvulus or sweet peas. But she wasn't to go anywhere near it, they said, not even to look through.

This veto could not prevent her noticing that the star flower which had fallen from heaven was disintegrating and two mallard had arrived. The drake kept chasing the duck, even though it was nowhere near springtime. In fact everyone kept telling Anne she was to cheer up because it would soon be Christmas. This news had little effect upon her, although she did wonder if there would be a chocolate Christmas log to eat. When she voiced this small hope, they laughed encouragingly and said: 'Wait and see.'

Once or twice Bobby came back into her mind and Anne was tempted to imagine him as her friend again. But she knew he wasn't, so she didn't.

One day Marguerite asked after him.

'We don't hear much of your Bobby these days do we?' she said.

'No.'

'Isn't he your best friend any more?'

'No.'

'I dare say it's a sign you're growing up.'

'Why?'

'Because big girls don't pretend things.'

Anne knew this already. She had noticed that now she was remembering more she didn't seem to need to pretend quite so much. It was as if the remembering was really pretending backwards. The more she kept imagining how things used to be, the less she projected herself into adventurous futures. But this inventing of her own past gave her no comfort. It simply said: you were like that once; now you're like this. Nothing was explained. And the leaves still fell from the trees. If you could catch one it meant you would be happy for a month next year. Marguerite caught them for her. Five in all.

Every day they said her father would arrive soon. He had been to Africa and back. They could say it aloud now, it was no longer a secret; all the walls with ears in the world could hear it if they wished, they said. Papa was in London and soon he would come on a train to visit them. He was still very busy with the war, of course.

Anne didn't dare believe their words. She told herself they were making it up, until one misty morning she was suddenly, inexplicably, left alone in the garden for the first time since she had fallen in the pond. Abruptly Marguerite had made an excuse and left her by herself. Obediently Anne began to follow her but she was told no, stay there, I won't be a minute. Anne was upset. She no longer wanted to be left alone. She didn't trust herself any more. She ran after Marguerite again, calling, crying, telling her to come back, please. But her nurse was gone laughing, behind the black yew hedge.

Anne heard her name. Her name was calling to her – her name was coming to her from his mouth. She turned, pierced with joy, only to stand petrified. What was this? A ghost tall as a tower, black as death, was striding out of the sun at her. All about him shimmered dancing terrors, terrors she knew were worse than stabbing searchlights, wailing sirens or dive bombers out of the blue. This advancing apparition was worse than anything Anne had ever pretended to herself, worse than her dreams. And still he was coming for her. Would he devour her? Bite off her head? Eat her alive?

She shrank back, her slanted eyes grown round as marbles, her knickers damp, her liberty bodice sticky with sweat, but still he advanced, still he was addressing her, 'Anne! Anne!' his voice booming in the air like the klaxon on the boat that had brought her over the sea to this terrible land full of bombs and guns and gardens not like hers.

Now he was crackling like a wireless – spitting and spatting like water spilt on a hot stove. Was he shooting at her? Was this pain in her chest a bullet? Should she fall down? As the sunlight around this dark giant exploded she could see he was made out of tanks and guns, out of bayonets stuck on the ends of chattering rifles, out of charging, falling, screaming soldiers, out of trumpets, drums, barbed wire, even out of holes in the ground full of blood-red water where tin hats floated, like soap dishes in the bath did.

All these things, pushed together, crumpled up in her mind, made this monster, this huge war man, into her war, Anne's war. The war was here. Now. Anne opened her mouth to scream but no sound came. She wanted to vanish. She tried desperately to shrink into herself, until suddenly she saw that this giant ghost was himself shrinking, was becoming simply her father, two metres tall as usual, in a suit grey as any elephant.

'My poor little Anne, what is it? What's the matter?'

Anne couldn't reply. She shook her head, dumb with remorse.

'You've grown,' Papa said, lifting her up in his arms and kissing her. 'Don't cry.'

But Anne hadn't even begun. She could feel the tears behind her eyes but she hoped that they could wait.

'Haven't you got a kiss for me?' he said.

Anne kissed him. His moustache still smelt of tobacco. But his face looked darker.

'It's all right now. I'm back. You're safe now.'

'Am I?' Anne said. And with that her tears arrived.

Tonya's Story

The matter was then in the hands of individual soldiers who were under military discipline which obliged them to obey orders without question.

> Nicholas Bethell

ONE

The battalion was out in force watching Adolf burn on top of the bonfire they had ordered the villagers to build in the square. The fire burnished the men's weatherworn faces, glowed on the colonel's Jeep and the three-tonners lined up beyond it. Everyone agreed Sergeant Major Rankin had made a bloody good job of Herr Hitler. The bugger was virtually life-size, with a kitbag stuffed full of God-knew-what for a torso buttoned into a stormtrooper's jacket. Adolf's head was an enormous mangelwurzel carved and painted to a perfect caricature. His cowlick hair and toothbrush moustache were spot-on. The arms, sporting a swastika armband each, were a stick, jammed, scarecrow-fashion, through the top of the kitbag. Military police gloves did duty as huge white hands. The legs were empty fatigue trousers with a suggestive stain spreading down from the flies. Rankin was pleased to inform anyone who would listen that this was his finest touch: 'Trust Adolf not to contain himself come the crunch,' he kept repeating.

Behind them, the villagers of Selsen had crowded in beside the army vehicles or were even now appearing at cautiously unshuttered windows. They were mostly old men together with women of all ages, a scattering of young children and a few older boys who had escaped conscription. As the flames spurted higher they all drew closer, their eyes fixed on the martyred effigy of the Führer. Unlike the English soldiers, they gazed at Hitler with a certain solemnity. Not one of them laughed, although one or two smiled self-consciously. Later, Jack was to realise why these Austrians had been unwilling to jeer. No doubt many had wanted to, but being among others who had supported the Third Reich to the very best of their ability they had remained circumspect. All of them were, however, prepared to celebrate the Allied victory in Europe in a general, how-pleasant-it-will-be-to-live-in-peace-once-again sort of way. But burning the Führer was too uncompromising a gesture for general comfort. It was best to let the straightforward English do the cheering. They seemed to be very good at it.

Colonel Billy stood on a Jeep leading the cheers while Jack Kempe, Tom Surtees and the other officers doled out local rotgut from fifteen-litre flasks which had been freely donated by the Mayor of Selsen, who knew perfectly well that, had he refused, these English would have commandeered the stuff anyway. The wine was inky-red, raw with tannin and had drops of olive oil floating in it – for want of corks a three-fingers' depth of oil had been used instead and these occupying soldiers were not yet adept at voiding it before the start of serious pouring. Not that they cared. It was enough that the long war was over. The wine, oil and all, would do.

For the third time the colonel shouted, 'Hip, hip . . .' and the men responded hugely: 'Hooray!' At the same time, ill-matched music struck up from a tin whistle, a violin and a concertina.

'Right you are, chaps. Victory vino top-up – all ranks at the double,' Colonel Billy yelled. Everyone cheered again and Billy jumped down from the Jeep and hugged Jack. 'We've done it, Grandad! We've done it! We've won the bloody war! Still hasn't sunk in. When the news came up from Brigade, I said: "Of course – and pigs have got bloody wings, correct?" I really did. Oh, Jack!'

Jack was laughing as if he were already hooched to heaven. 'I did keep telling you we'd win, Billy.'

'Want you to give the victory toast, Grandad.'

'Oh, no. You must give it, sir. As our colonel. The blokes expect it.'

'No, Jack. It's got to be you. And that's an order!' And without waiting for any further objections Billy jumped back on to the bonnet of his Jeep. 'Your attention, please,' he shouted. All turned to him. 'Has every man got a drink? A proper drink?' Inevitably this provoked comment. Suddenly everyone in the 5th Battalion of the Duke of Buckingham's Rifles was a wine connoisseur – informed tastings confirmed it as 'rabbit's piss', 'bleeding petrol' or 'liquid carbolic'. Colonel Billy, by now a practised commanding officer, took this as positive confirmation that all glasses were suitably charged. He said, 'Right, then. I've asked Major Kempe to give us the victory toast because he's been with the battalion through it all. From Egypt to Tunis to the Alps. And also because at his advanced age –' cosy, predictable laughter interrupted Billy for a moment – 'because, I say again, at his age he's Grandad to us all.' More cheers. 'Officers and men of the 5th, Major Kempe.'

The colonel jumped down and Jack jumped up, determined to show that even at thirty-five he was still as spry as Billy at twenty-nine. Billy had come out to the battalion after the desert war, joining them in Sicily to displace Jack as acting CO. Their previous colonel had bought it holding the Mareth line before Monty's relief column came steaming through the night, headlights blazing, to save what was left of the 5th and do for Rommel once and for all in North Africa. They had lost a lot of people in that engagement.

Jack held up his hand, grinned, waited, and the blokes quietened down.

'As usual,' he said, 'the Colonel's laying it on a bit bloody thick. Blow it, I'm in my prime, it's just he's still the new boy – right?' Further indulgent laughter rippled fleetingly round the square, to resolve into a silence that the occasion itself appeared to have commanded. The crackling of the bonfire steadily consuming itself and its grotesque effigy seemed only to serve to emphasise the need for something formal to be said, however banal. Jack raised his glass. 'I invite all ranks to lift their glasses to victory on this day – the seventh of May in the year of our Lord 1945 – and to our Colonel-in-Chief, His Majesty King George the Sixth. Riflemen all, I give you Victory in Europe and the King!'

All, except for a rowdy few at the back, drank respectfully. Several of Jack's fellow officers offered private murmurs reiterating or elaborating loyally upon the toast.

Jack said, 'And now let us drink to those of the 5th who didn't make it to the end but whose sacrifice has brought us here. To those who fell not by the way but *on* the way to give us victory.'

All drank in almost unanimous silence.

Jack added a third toast. 'Finally, we drink to peace at long last. Real peace with real honour, this time round. Not the lousy Munich variety. To peace.'

Everyone drained the dregs in his glass.

'And now, comrades-in-arms, I've got one last order: get bloody blotto!'

The battalion exploded into more cheers and laughter, the heavy wine flasks – 'more like sodding carboys', someone said – circulated again and the impromptu musicians were reinforced by the aged remnants of the village band. Old men came shyly forward dusting off their instruments fetched down from hooks or up from cellars. Some of the riflemen invited the village girls to dance and, once two or three had accepted, genuine fraternisation began. Not much later the language problem had dissolved in wine.

Jack was halfway through his sixth glass – he was determined to obey his own order to the letter – and deep in conversation with a toothless granny half his height, when Colonel Billy announced he had got another job lined up for him.

'Not tonight, I hope,' said Jack.

'Oh, no. No.'

'Imperative to get stupendously sozzled tonight, Billy. You too.'

'Quite agree. Why I'm speaking now. It's for tomorrow.'

'Ah, well. Fine. Tomorrow's another day, isn't it? Always has been, I believe. Tradition with tomorrow.'

'Strikes me you're already well primed, Grandad.'

'Could easily be, sir. You don't think they've spiked this stuff with brake fluid or some such? Interesting kick to it.'

'Liaison, Jack.'

'Really? Refill your glass?'

'Please. Yes. Liaison is what it is. Tomorrow.'

'Right you are, sir. Liaison it shall be.'

'But the best of it is she's a peach, Jack.'

'What exactly are you on about, Billy?'

'Your interpreter.'

'For what?'

'I told you. Liaison. Spot of liaison. Maintenance of public order, organisation thereof in these parts. Pleasant task. And I don't think I can trust any of the younger chaps on this one. Besides, as second-in-command you're free to swan around, aren't you? Got bugger all else to do now, really.'

'Could you kindly make yourself clear, sir?'

'Of course. The fact is, the Brigade Major has informed me that we, in our battalion area, are responsible for the welfare –'

But Colonel Billy's pronouncement was cut short by the immolation of the Führer as he toppled headlong from his incandescent perch. Everyone, soldiers and villagers alike, now yelled in eldritch triumph, dancing, embracing, singing and miming heartily rude farewells. A usually po-faced corporal from HQ company rushed forward and pulled what was left of the blazing torso clear of the flames and then proceeded to piss lavishly upon it. Others joined him. Soon the great dictator was doused by arcs of fire-lit urine bright as tracers. Jack and Billy strolled away, leaving the men to their hard-won excesses.

Next morning Jack found himself at the wheel of his Jeep with a thundering headache and Tonya Parvic, his official interpreter, beside him. If this was the first day of peace, then for Jack it had arrived far too soon and most disconcertingly in the person of this oddly serious girl sitting on his left. Jack had not experienced, let alone enjoyed, any consistent female company for almost four years. He'd had no letter from his wife for six months, nor had he seen, save in a snapshot, his baby daughter, by now aged three and a bit. As for the idea of working in harness with a woman, which was what this new task implied, well, there had been the occasional in-course-of-duty contact with nurses and a couple of rather stern female drivers in the Western Desert, but apart from that it had been chaps, chaps all the way, so he wasn't entirely sure how this particular exercise would work out. Jack decided, approaching the next bend, that he would have to play it by ear.

Meanwhile the girl seemed to him to be formidably good-looking. Not an English rose, of course; more the Greek-goddess type. And though he was yet to see her smile there was, he felt sure, a warmth within her. What she might be thinking of him it had not yet occurred to him to wonder.

Tonya spoke good English in a fluent, questioning manner, which flattered Jack into refining her use of the language. Already he was beginning to feel like a world-weary teacher about to be revitalised by an eager prize pupil.

She wore what looked like a farmhand's old cord trousers, tucked into boots, with a sapper's battledress blouse over an old grey jumper. On being introduced, Jack had made an ill-judged joke about her assorted dress, asking if it was standard uniform as issued to multilingual interpreters attached to the British army. Tonya had replied: 'Oh, no. We are given nothing. I wear anything I can get. What you call "scrounge", I think, yes? Is that correct, major?' The quick shadow of practised sadness in her voice and eyes had embarrassed Jack. He had hastened to assure her that, in the context, the word 'scrounge' was indeed correct. And had offered a smile in apology without receiving one in return.

But now the sun was shining, the sky was becoming bluer than a hedge sparrow's egg and the Alps lay ahead, patched and streaked with snow. Hazed by distance, the mountains seemed as insubstantial as clouds. The air was sharp in his nostrils and it was good to be in shirtsleeve order on such a brand-new morning pushing the Jeep up the road through rocky gullies and steep meadows.

Jack's driver-cum-batman sat in the back, his rifle across his knees, a reluctant chaperon for military form's sake. Corporal Gibson felt far worse than Jack. He was earnestly praying both that he hadn't got a dose from that village bint last night and that the major wouldn't overdo the slinging of the Jeep through the bends. It was all right for Grandad, he'd got the wheel to hang on to and the crumpet to soften up. Another hairpin like the last and Gibson reckoned he could well throw up over the bloody pair of them.

'I know you're called Tonya,' Jack said. 'But I didn't quite catch your surname when Colonel Billy introduced us.'

'It is Parvic. I am Tonya Parvic.'

'Of course. Indeed. Parvic. Forgive me. Should've got it off pat straightaway. Awfully bad at names. Mind you, it was something of a night last night. One for the book.'

'Which book is that?'

'Turn of phrase. Meaning "memorable". Quite a beano.'

'You have head like a Bolshevik bear, I expect?'

'That's one way of putting it. Did you celebrate down at Mittelthal? I imagine Brigade laid on the odd drink?'

'Oh, yes, there was a big celebration. I danced until midnight, but then I left because of getting up early to report to you, Major Kempe.'

'Like Cinderella?'

'What?'

'Duty called you?'

'Yes. Also many of the men were so in need of women it was not so pleasant.'

'But the chaps behaved themselves, I trust?'

'Oh, yes, they were very British.'

'From which I'm to deduce what?'

'They look at you like dogs.'

'With their tongues hanging out, do you mean?'

'Almost. And they also paw at you.'

'Indeed? Got the picture. Not pretty. Mind you, once one gets up to Brigade level, standards can and do decline alarmingly, I've found.'

'Please? I don't understand now.'

'Nothing. A pleasantry.'

But Jack was wondering why he couldn't talk straight. What was the matter with him? Was it the hangover or Miss Parvic's presence or what? Words, sentences, kept coagulating inside him. He seemed to speak on stilts. Then, as he changed down for another bend, he realised why. Of course. The reason was plain as a pikestaff. He had spoken only military English for the best part of four years. He had hardly had to bother with anyone outside the battalion except the enemy – whom one attacked wordlessly. Of course. That was the reason why. 'I'm sorry,' he said. 'I haven't been home for some time. You get sort of – well, you lose touch. Especially with matters civilian.' Still he sounded stuffy.

Tonya said: 'But worst of all they never *said* anything.'

'Ah well, yes, that *is* very English, I agree. We don't go in for idle chitchat. We've always left that sort of thing to foreigners – oh, sorry, I didn't mean you as such. You mustn't think –'

'But I am foreign to you, Major, aren't I?'

'Possibly. But even so – please: kindly forget I spoke, would you?'

Tonya nodded, said she would. Jack concentrated on his driving. At least that was fluent, co-ordinated. Meanwhile Corporal Gibson wished profoundly he was somewhere else, preferably back home in Aylesbury. If this interpreter piece hadn't been with them he could've asked the major about demob. Just how soon could he really expect to be back? Christ, he couldn't wait. Sod this new job, whatever it was.

As they roared out of another hairpin Tonya pointed suddenly across the still-shadowed valley to the opposite sunlit skyline. 'Look! Over there!' she shouted above the noise of the engine.

Jack brought the Jeep to a halt but kept his feet on the clutch and brake pedals. The handbrake had given up even pretending to function seven hundred-odd miles back in the Abruzzi.

'What? What?'

Tonya pointed again, slightly to the left of where they were facing. Jack followed her arm and eventually picked out three distant figures on horseback as they appeared in silhouette against the blue.

'Ah, yes. Got you. Militarily speaking, you should've said: "Unidentified personnel at ten o'clock." '

'What has the time of day to do with this? Besides, it is fifteen minutes after eleven just now.'

'No. You haven't understood. What I mean is, in the field we use the positions of the clock to pinpoint natural features, enemy positions, men on the ground or what-have-you. It's a way of orienting yourself. And others, of course. Straight ahead is twelve o'clock, with anything either side being one, two or three o'clock and so on – or else eleven, ten or nine o'clock etcetera, as appropriate. Easy, really, and effective.'

Jack had now got his field glasses out. A quick twiddle and he had brought the three figures into sharp focus. 'These chaps part of your lot, would you say? Peculiar-looking characters. Pretty damn wild-and-woolly. Take a look.' He offered Tonya the glasses. She took them and looked. 'Or could they be partisans from just across the border? It's no distance really, is it?'

'No. They aren't Italians. No. They are Cossacks, definitely. Many are hiding in the hills.'

'They aren't from this camp we're going to?'

'No.'

'How do you know?'

For the first time Tonya smiled. 'Because they have snow on their boots, of course, Major.'

Jack laughed. 'Fancy you knowing that old chestnut,' he said and stalled the engine. 'Damnation! Now look what you've made me do. Your fault, young lady. I tell you this calls for some pretty nifty footwork, given where we are. I'm right, aren't I, Corporal?'

'Yes, sir.'

'Please explain,' Tonya said.

'It requires a certain finesse – if we aren't to go careering off into nowhere, right? No handbrake, you observe? Useless. Kaput. And all Jeeps have foot starters. That tit there.' He pointed to a shiny, boot-burnished stud to the right of the accelerator. 'Therefore it follows, given a line-up of starter, accelerator, brake and clutch all in a row, you, as driver, would ideally have at least three feet if not four in order to start said vehicle on a sharpish incline with damn-all behind you; but, as the Lord in His Wisdom has only granted us two feet, we shall, as it were, have to tiptoe through the tulips with some dispatch. OK? Right. Here we go. Hold tight!'

And Jack's right boot jabbed at the starter before both feet performed a staccato ballet across the other controls as the engine roared into life and the Jeep rolled sickeningly back to within a foot of the abyss. But mercifully the clutch gripped as first gear engaged and they jerked forward and round the bend in a clacking spurt of stones and a sideways plume of dust. Gibson belched dourly and even Tonya had paled.

'You all right, Corporal Gibson?'

'Yes, sir. Just feel a bit rough, sir.'

'Don't we all!'

Ten minutes later they had reached a wide upland valley of undulating meadows where trees and coppices softened the bulk of huge rocky outcrops. Ahead of them in new-found clarity the snow-clad Alps stood shoulder to shoulder, shining in the sun. Jack breathed in deeply, exhaled and, miraculously, much of his headache was gone.

'Please,' Tonya said. 'When you said "nifty" just now, what is that?'

Jack decided to risk another joke. 'You are, Tonya,' he said, and grinned at her.

She smiled back carefully. She found this Englishman truly strange. Absurd, dangerously unserious, as if he were a boy and not a man at all. 'Is that a compliment, Major?'

'If you like. Yes. I think so. Now – now you tell me about these Cossacks we're about to liaise with.'

'Soon you will yourself see them.'

'Indeed. But you know them, I believe?'

'Oh yes. I've visited the camp many times. And once I even stayed with them. They gave me shelter.' She could have said more but decided then was not the moment.

'They fought with the Germans, I understand?'

'Yes, but not against you. Not against the British or the Americans. No. They fought against Stalin. It is Stalin they hate. And Lenin. They have resisted since the revolution, do you see?'

'A chequered history?'

'No. Very consistent. They are too proud to be told what to do by anyone. And they have kept their faith in God.'

'I see.'

'But it is Stalin they hate most since before the war. They hate him for his crimes against them, against the Kazak people. But, of course, everybody hates Stalin. That is obvious, isn't it?'

'Is it? I wouldn't say so. We don't, for a start. Nor do the Yanks. He's our ally. As far as we're concerned, Uncle Joe's a sterling fellow.'

'But that was for convenience in the war, yes? Now it is over you will fight him, I know. Everybody says so.'

'Who does?'

'All the poor people with nowhere to go.'

'Well, they've got it wrong. Fight the Russians? Heaven forbid. No. We're all for getting back home – bloody pronto, if you'll pardon my French.'

'I know what "pronto" means but it is not French, is it?'

They both laughed this time and Jack explained to Tonya's mystification that the expression he had used was a typically English apology for swearing. Behind them Corporal Gibson, more vulnerable to the gentle undulations of this straight stretch of road than to the previous hairpin bends, vomited copiously over the rear of the Jeep.

'Feeling OK, Corporal?'

'My breakfast, sir. Gone with the wind.'

'Best place for it. Those local sausages in axle grease were hell, weren't they?'

'It was the dipped bread did for me, sir.'

'You'll soon feel better.'

Their destination proved magically beautiful. It ought not to have been. Already officially designated by the Allied occupying forces as a prisoner-of-war camp, it should have appeared bleakly functional. The occupants, however, unaware of this recent reclassification, hadn't viewed it in this way at all. For almost a year now they had decided it had to be home. Their home from home. Certainly several pledges made by the previous authorities had fostered this belief. Pledges that would be upheld, because they now found themselves in the British zone and everyone knew that the British were the only people in the world who were entirely honourable, who always respected previous promises (no matter who had made them) and who never broke their word. Consequently they had continued to keep their encampment beautiful.

Inevitably the local farmer detested these foreign gypsies, as he called them. He had complained savagely to the mayor of Mittelthal, only to be told that he must accept them for the moment. He had explained that these were his summer pastures for the sheep, for his cows. The mayor had shrugged and pointed out that the Cossacks had fought gallantly for the Führer against the Russians, so he must be patient. But what the farmer really objected to was not the men – he could tell they were soldiers, however bizarre – but the entire caravan of women, children, priests, carts and livestock that had come with them as if they were some sort of army out of the history books.

Jack, though, was bowled over. Nothing he had heard had prepared him for a sight such as this. Here was the golden age spread out before him. Or was this Elysium out for a picnic? Suddenly for no reason, except that his mind often worked as much by assonance as association, Jack remembered an English lesson with the pale eyes of a long-forgotten schoolmaster surveying him through sunbeams alive with chalk motes. 'What country, friend, is this?' Jack, had read aloud. The chap detailed to reply had been slow at Shakespeare. 'Buck up, boy,' the master snapped and the answer had come, haltingly, prosaically – unforgettably: 'This is Illyria, lady.' Aged eleven Jack's blood had run cold. He had thrilled right down his spine. But why? It was strange. The statement, after all, was merely one of fact. The notes at the back said *Illyria* was the Latin name for modern Yugoslavia. And yet that name had remained with him ever since as a kind of sensuous code word for an ideal place. An improbable somewhere such as this. And, after all, Yugoslavia was not so far away – fifty miles or so. A train from Mittelthal – not that any were running just yet – could undoubtedly get there in an hour or so.

'The camp is called Grubenfeld,' Tonya said.

'Oh? Right. Grubenfeld? It deserves a nicer name.'

The first specific things to catch Jack's eye amidst a general impression of dun-coloured tents, flags on poles, washing and smoke from cooking fires against the dark of nearby sweet chestnut woods were three dromedaries grazing among cows and several quite passable horses. Where had they come from? The Caucasus, perhaps? Asia

Minor certainly. Next he registered wooden stockades coralling yet more horses. Then two small stone barns, shepherds' refuges, he supposed – but no, the nearer one had a cross attached to the rooftree and the other was distinguished by a substantial flagpole planted directly in front of it from which flew quite the largest of the many flags flying there, the double-headed eagle of Imperial Russia.

All around he could see women and children working and playing. Some of the children appeared to be in charge of the numerous goats, rangy sheep and white geese, while the ubiquitous chickens simply scratched and pecked where they liked. There was music, too, teased out by the breeze; an unseen mandolin offered frugal accompaniment to three male voices all exactly tuned.

'You like this?' Tonya said, hoping he would. After all, he had no knowledge of her parentage so he was certain to speak freely, truthfully. What would this stiff Englishman say?

'I had no idea,' Jack said.

'But I told you, Major Kempe. I said we have the Cossack nation here. Well, you know, a small part of it. Do you like them, though? That is what I ask.' She knew she sounded too impatient. But then she was.

'It's all very pretty. But how many have we got to cope with, do you know? Has there been a head count?'

'I don't think so.'

'Well, that's number-one priority. Unless they can tell us – within some degree of accuracy, that is. Either way, we'll have to find out.'

'There are many more camps like this.' Tonya's arm

indicated almost anywhere beyond.

'I'm sure. But this one looks – well – yes – charming. Jolly. Idyllic.'

So he did like it? Tonya smiled relief. 'Oh, it is, for *them*,' she said, just stopping herself from saying *us*. 'They think they are in paradise,' she added. 'They had a bad war, you know.'

Now a group of riders, thirty or so, looking to Jack like magnificent brigands out of an adventure book, were charging towards them. Ahead ran a pack of frenzied dogs. As they drew near, the Cossacks broke their gallop to a canter and then to a trot. The dogs fell silent. Jack pulled up and the horsemen rode round the Jeep three times before forming a neat phalanx in front of it. Jack could scarcely credit such archaic cavalry, such chivalry.

'Can you ride, Major Kempe?' Tonya said.

'I have done, a little, in my time. These blokes aren't bad at it, are they? Quite a circus. Ah. Looks like you'll have to do your stuff any minute now, Tonya. Interpreter-wise.'

A patriarchal figure with a full set of grizzled beard and moustaches was riding forward to salute Jack. Beyond him and the horsemen, children were now approaching, running, waving, laughing.

'*Wilkommen, Herr Major.*'

'German?' Jack turned to Tonya.

'He thinks perhaps you speak it rather than Russian.'

'Well, tell him I don't. And if I could, I wouldn't. Tell him I prefer him to speak his mother tongue for you to translate, OK? Much the best.'

Tonya explained this and the man grinned, evidently pleased by Jack's request. He jumped down from his horse. Jack and Tonya got out of the Jeep.

In English Tonya said: 'This is Brigadier Bakturov of the Cossack Third Division.' And in Russian: 'This is Major Kempe of the Duke of Buckingham's Regiment.'

'How do you do, sir,' Jack said.

Bakturov, while shaking Jack's hand in both of his, pronounced himself pleased to greet a British officer because the British were the finest people in the world after the Cossacks.'

'His Russian is very old-fashioned,' Tonya said, having translated this. 'He is, you must know, Major, not only the military commander here but also the camp's *ataman*, which means leader or headman. These soldiers who accompany him are his officers.'

'Right you are. Understood. Kindly inform him that, as of yesterday, my battalion is responsible for this area and this encampment in particular. For the maintenance of public order and public health. Until further notice we are the competent authority to whom he should apply if any problems arise.'

While Tonya related this, a small girl crept up behind Jack and silently, before he realised she was there, took his hand. Surprised by her touch, he turned. She looked up at him wonderingly, then smiled.

'Hello,' Jack said. 'Who are you?' He bent down and ruffled her hair, which shone like gold in the sun. The little girl held out her arms, plainly asking to be held. He lifted her up to perch in the crook of his arm. She felt soft, warm. Everyone laughed and some of the men leapt on to their saddles, to stand there, balanced, applauding.

'Ask her what her name is, would you?'

'She's called Varya.'

'Hello, Varya,' Jack said and the child kissed his cheek. Just like that. Her trust quite took his breath away. He had forgotten how quick to love a child could be. He said: 'Tell them I hope to bring up a chocolate ration shortly for the children, all right?'

This news brought more delight, more clapping. The word 'chocolate' snapped and crackled like burning brushwood as the information went round. Brigadier Bakturov spoke warmly to Tonya.

She said, 'The ataman says he is pleased to accept the British administration. They think it will be better here than before and also better than over there, beyond the mountains, in the American zone.' Tonya pointed northwards.

Jack agreed. 'Or the Russian zone over there.' He gestured with his free arm towards the east, grinning.

'I shall not translate that,' Tonya said. 'That is not a joke for them, Major.'

'Oh? Right. Take your point. Didn't mean to offend. Tell them I shall now conduct a general inspection of the camp, OK?'

But the brigadier was speaking rapidly to Tonya. 'He wishes you to pay him the honour of inspecting his soldiers first,' she said.

'This lot?' asked Jack. Tonya nodded. 'Very well. Good idea. Whoopsadaisy, Varya.' And Jack put the little girl down. 'I'm wanted on parade, my dear. See you later.' He ruffled her hair again. It was so soft. Just as his daughter's must be. She would be much the same age, he supposed. He went to inspect Bakturov's men.

TWO

Years later, Tonya Parvic wrote in her almost perfect English:

Of course I had hoped for too much from my assignment as an interpreter to the occupying British in Austria. Because, to make no bones about it, I had regarded them as a means of escape for me from the unchosen and unwanted loyalties I had been born with. I was at that time, it would be fair to say, a girl on the make.

I was therefore surprised on that first morning in May 1945 to find myself disliking Major Kempe quite so much. But the fact was he struck me as too foreign. It was a shock. I had expected him to be familiar to me. Had I not studied his language and literature for years on end?

But as we drove up to Grubenfeld everything he said, every gesture and grimace he made, caused me to wonder if perhaps England was not, after all, a well-known island close to Holland and Germany. Perhaps my education in Belgrade, Vienna and Trieste had misled me? Perhaps his country was another planet spinning in different dimensions of space and time, thoughts and feelings? Listening to him, watching him, it certainly seemed so. How could this man who said nothing so relentlessly be the heir of

Shakespeare, Byron and the magnificent William Godwin? It seemed impossible. Everything he said was a cliché while his eyes apologised and his mouth half-smiled. Was I meeting the famous English stiff-upper-lip for the first time? Was this his way of hiding his true feelings? Or was he saying between the lines: 'I have no feelings – none – that is why the British Empire is still mightier than any dreamed of by Adolf Hitler'?

Jack Kempe was not alone in this behaviour, of course. Many of the other British officers I met were much the same. By appearing so cheerfully heartless they seemed to imply to you that some things were too deeply felt to be put into words. Their sympathies lay, in their poet Wordsworth's phrase, 'too deep for tears'. This way they became superior to all foreigners by being just as sensitive but far more in control. They exuded heroic pride through boyish diffidence.

Do I sound bitter? I'm sure I do. But then I have my reasons, as will become apparent. I suppose I could say in mitigation that these Englishmen had been through a long war, were battle-hardened and all that, but then we were too. We had endured hardships equal to theirs, perhaps worse. But Brigadier Bakturov and his men, though as proud, were not like this. No. They showed their feelings, did not conceal them behind wry jokes and schoolboy banter. But suppose, as I've said, the English weren't concealing anything? What if they joked because they simply didn't care – were incapable of caring? What then? Could it be that they truly did not see us as quite so human as they were? Did they, like the Nazis, think of themselves as genetically better than everyone else? A superior race?

Oh, so many thoughts went through my head during that first drive up to Grubenfeld because I had desperately wanted to like the English, and Jack Kempe in particular, since I had been selected to work with him.

But then the way he picked up little Varya gave me hope. Suddenly he seemed generous and confident, almost lazily competent. In movements like these he looked a proper man. A sportsman perhaps? I knew the English were sports-mad. Especially for a game of their own which only they and their colonies could understand. The one called 'cricket' is what I mean, of course. I was soon to discover that many of the incomprehensible things Jack said were cricket metaphors. I learned that such phrases as 'a sticky wicket', 'a sound knock' or 'I'm afraid you've stumped me with that one' came from this exclusive national game.

Later on I saw him play cricket and though it remained a mystery to me the easy sureness of his movements was confirmed. It was like, again I must use an English simile, watching an old teddy bear come to life. This rather short, thick-set, sandy sort of man became almost beautiful. He would take the ball, which was made of leather bright as blood and hard as iron, throw it high in the air, catch it without hurting his fingers, then rub it on his trousers and run to hurl it in a very special way at his opponent, who had to hit the ball with a bat like a thick paddle. The manner in which Jack did this was wonderful to watch. Quite special. His arm came up high over his shoulder in an almost liquid motion, his body stretched – no, it is impossible to describe Jack bowling the cricket ball. That was what it was called. Bowling. And when he was doing that he became another being. Someone free. Someone true.

But all this was later that month. First he had to inspect Brigadier Bakturov's troops and then the camp. I looked to see if he would keep a straight face as he gazed up and down at each man standing to attention beside his horse. Even I could see they were a ragtail army really. They wore such a *mélange*, I mean mixture, of uniform, much of it German in origin but always with the Cossacks' crossed sabres embroidered on their collars. Patched baggy trousers, old unpolished boots, wide-shouldered capes, some black, some brown, and fur hats. Brigadier Bakturov and several of his officers carried beautiful jewelled swords. These, I explained, were heirlooms of great antiquity and value that had had to be concealed from the Germans but need not be from the honest British. As for the men's other weapons, their rifles and pistols, well, seeing them through Jack's eyes for a moment I could not help smiling at such an assortment of old and new, from the latest German sub-machine gun to the oldest of Romanian rifles. But he did not smile, oh no, not Major Kempe. He kept a perfectly straight face, paying Bakturov and his officers the compliment of an absolute seriousness. Was this the highest form of condescension or another example of famous English politeness? Again I couldn't tell. I had no way of measuring this man. He was as outlandish to me as the Cossacks were to him.

Oh yes, I even had to explain to him who the Cossacks actually were! He had only the vaguest idea and was reluctant to reveal his ignorance. He was aware they were remarkable horsemen but he knew little else. He did not know that they came originally from between the Black Sea and the Caspian Sea. Or that they'd fought with great bravery against the Germans in the First World War. Or even that they had opposed the Bolshevik revolution. And held out against it ever since. His ignorance, I told him, was lamentable. Most important of all he did not seem to realise that they were not, in their eyes, Soviet citizens at all, nor would they ever be. They would rather die or live in exile than accept that classification.

After inspecting Bakturov's men we showed the major the camp. Forgive me if I use sometimes his rank, then his Christian name. I think of him in both ways: the army officer and the private man. Both have remained real to me. We walked over in a group, Jack, myself, Bakturov with his soldiers leading their horses, followed by all the children, whom some of the goats and sheep had now joined. Jack said he felt like the Pied Piper of Hamelin! Varya, the little girl, insisted on staying close to us, trying to catch hold of his hand. In the end he let her take it despite my having explained to her that this important British soldier was on duty and had no time for four-year-olds. Of course at such an age she could not understand any of that.

He said he thought the tents looked very comfortable and seemed surprised to find how clean they were. He did not know what subterfuges, what sacrifice and what bravery had been required to preserve the rugs, the cushions and the curtains which made these tents into homes. I remember thinking: One day I will tell you what savage compromises displaced persons must make to preserve their identity in places they have no wish to be.

Jack felt one of the rugs and found it damp. He told me to start making a list of things required. The first item was: *groundsheets*. When we reached the bakehouse he asked about the flour, sifted it, sniffed it, wrinkled his nose. I told him the people had to make do with what they could scrounge. He said the flour was mildewed, sour. He was right. He said people would get ill, start dancing all over the place, if they continued eating it. I didn't understand, until he mentioned St Vitus's dance. When I laughed, remembering how my father always danced on St Vitus's Day, he said curtly: 'Write down *flour*.'

By contrast the school delighted him. But first he admired the flagpole that stood in front of it. And the flag. When we went inside, the older children were chanting their lessons. The teachers had put up pictures they had made with leaves and flowers – mostly simple patterns made into images of animals and birds. I explained that all the children were taught to read and write, to do simple arithmetic and to sing. These were the most important subjects. Then came history. He asked about religion. I told him that went without saying, really, like breathing. The church was next door and everyone attended.

So we showed him the church in that other stone barn, which stood at a right angle to the school, thus forming the rudimentary half of what was becoming the central square – the natural public place of the Grubenfeld encampment. Already most of the grass was worn to death. If people lived here much longer it would soon need to be paved, I said. He nodded as if accepting this eventuality.

If the school had pleased him, the church impressed

him. It was dim after the brightness outside. The sacrament glowed gold above red. The light from the open door caught the soft silver facets of the icons, the worn agony on the cross. He asked why there were no chairs. Again, such ignorance! I explained to him that no one sat in our church except the old and infirm. Unfortunately, for them we had none, so people brought their own – well, cushions, mostly, or stools, even saddles sometimes.

'Really? No need for that. We'll organise some. Folding variety. Write down *chairs*,' he said.

By now our priests had joined us and I introduced the pair of them: Father Sacha, who was older than he looked, and the truly younger one, Father Ivan. Major Kempe immediately displayed more ignorance. He said something he thought was polite, making small talk, about it being a pity there was no organ, not even a harmonium. If I had translated this our patriarch would have exploded, so I had to explain quickly that we sang. We always sang. We needed no accompaniment. To most of us, even a tuning fork was an insult. Have you never heard true Russian singing? I asked.

'Only the Red Army choir, and the Volga Boat Song,' he said.

'Well, you must come to hear a mass.'

'Right you are. Good idea. Will do.'

And he did. He kept his promise for two Sundays running. But now Father Sacha asked Father Ivan to fetch the icons – the ones they kept hidden, that is. The truly old and precious ones. I explained to Jack about them. About how old they were, how the Virgin and Child he was holding had come from Byzantium itself. As he inspected the icons their profound simplicity, which is so inexplicable as to be almost – how can one say? – not to be suffered, their terrible liaison between what is and what ought to be, seemed to disturb him, even offend him. He murmured something about their admirable workmanship and how they were clearly the most wonderful sacred objects, but his heart was not in his words. I made a mental note to question him later about this if I could.

'For centuries the Cossack nation has been Orthodox Christian,' I said – rather too obviously, I thought, except I felt I suddenly needed to stress everything with him in case he had not fully understood. I did this not because I considered him stupid but because he sometimes appeared not to listen, as if protective of his own insularity, as if there were many things he simply did not wish to know. Perhaps it was the preoccupied pose of a busy and responsible English officer? Except he was not so very busy. The war was over, it was peacetime suddenly, and his responsibilities were in fact few, even if he had been placed in charge of public order and health here in one of the sweetest, cleanest, healthiest countrysides imaginable. And anyway, as a nomadic nation, the Cossacks had cared for their own welfare for as long as any people in the world. Which is not to say that the camp did not need many essentials such as soap, clothing, medicines, exercise books for the children.

As we left the church, Bakturov was waiting. Jack commented again on the neat alignment of the tents and the brigadier said that he believed in discipline and that this was an army camp. Jack agreed it was, although he must have been thinking that it didn't really look like the sort he was used to.

'Right. Now to matters sanitary. The camp latrines. Where do you keep those? Must inspect the latrines,' he said.

When I translated this, Bakturov looked blank. As I knew he would. He gestured superbly, with a wide sweep of his arm, indicating the woods to the north and east of the camp.

'He says there are the woods,' I told Major Kempe. And I smiled. But he wasn't at all amused.

'They just go in the woods?' he asked. I nodded. 'No trenches, no earth closets, no separate facilities for males and females?'

'Oh, no.'

'Oh dear. This won't do. Good heavens. Basic hygiene. They'll give themselves cholera. Typhus. Right. Kindly inform Brigadier Bakturov that things have got to change on this front.' Again he surprised me. This time by pronouncing the brigadier's name quite accurately. 'We're going to have British standards of hygiene established here from now on. A matter of urgency,' he added. He seemed genuinely exercised in his mind about this.

I did my best to explain to Bakturov, who looked at me as if I had gone crazy. He huffed and puffed, saying it was quite unnecessary because the woods were very extensive. They went on forever and the earth was soft under leaves that had fallen for as long as the trees had been there. But if the mad major insisted, then he would agree – just to humour him. I took care as I translated this. As you may imagine, the work of an interpreter can require a certain tact. It is sometimes necessary to edit judiciously.

Just before we left Grubenfeld, the brigadier sprang his surprise. A bugle was heard, hiccuping urgently, and then a squadron of at least a hundred horsemen appeared at full pelt, galloping down towards us between the tents, with the chickens, children and dogs scattering before them. Their leader, a young captain, held a huge Union Jack on a lance, followed by another with a blond horse's mane skewered on its point and flowing in the wind, and then another, with the skull and crossbones this time, and, last of all, the imperial eagle, which, unfortunately, streamed in the wind beside a huge Nazi swastika. And, of course, they were firing their rifles into the air as they came. When they reached us, all the riders leapt up on to their saddles to ride around us standing up and saluting Jack. They rode round and round. Jack laughed in delight and clapped his hands, whereupon everyone clapped him back and Brigadier Bakturov said: 'We like you, English Major.'

Jack said to me: 'Tell him I like them, too.' Then added, 'But between ourselves, Tonya, I'm not too keen on that swastika, OK?' I smiled and said I'd tell them about that later. He nodded in agreement. Smiles blossomed everywhere.

A tray with bread and salt was brought with another full of tiny glasses and a flask of vodka. I showed Jack how to accept these tokens of hospitality: to sprinkle the salt on the bread; to eat it and then drink the vodka in one gulp.

After we had all drunk three glasses in a row he said, 'Talk about hair of the dog! After last night. Goodness me.'

'What's that phrase?' I said. 'The dog's hair?'

'I can see I'm going to have to teach you real English, Tonya,' he answered, his eyes bright with the strong spirit.

I laughed. I said, 'Yes, please. All the ways of saying things. The good, the bad, everything. I want to know all the English I can.' He grinned and suddenly he looked years younger, warm and human, and I realised I could like him after all.

THREE

As they were loading the thunderbox into the 15-cwt. Colonel Billy and the adjutant, Tom Surtees, walked over from the farmhouse.

' 'Morning, Jack. What's the idea? Thought we kept that lavatory for the top brass. Sacred seat, really. General Alexander, no less, sat there.'

The regimental quartermaster sergeant, quick to cover himself, stepped in smartly. 'Sample, sir. Major Kempe's orders. For his Bolshies up the valley, sir.'

'How many times, RQ? I've told you, they aren't Bolshies,' Jack said.

'Very well, sir. Bloody brigands, then.' The RQMS went back into the barn to organise more stores.

'I've been trying to get it across to the blokes, sir, that these people are in fact an armed nation in exile,' said Jack. Billy and Tom grinned.

'Message not getting through, Grandad?'

'Not really.'

'Can't say I'm surprised. Apparently a whole corps of these characters handed themselves over to 46th Div. yesterday. They all claim to a man to be Cossacks, but it seems they're rather a job lot really. Lots of Serbs and Croats mixed in.'

'My lot are the genuine article, sir. Or so my interpreter assures me.'

'Ah, yes. How's she making out? Didn't I say she was a peach?'

'When she isn't a schoolmarm, sir.'

'Mind of her own, has she?'

'I'll say. Very much so.'

Again they laughed as the RQMS shepherded a fatigue party out of the barn. The men carried sacks of flour and sugar together with three crates of oranges. These were loaded into the lorry beside and around the thunderbox.

'One small thing,' Colonel Billy said. It was often like this in the Bucks: the most important point would be made as if it were merely by the way, so minor a matter that on no account must it ruffle the surface of the small talk. 'Brigade tells me we really ought to persuade the stragglers in the hills to come in. Into the fold, as the Brigade Major put it.'

'A round-up?' Jack said.

'No. A patrol. A show-the-flag type exercise. After all, there must be quite a number of people out there who don't yet realise they're in the British zone.'

'Perfectly possible, given the terrain, sir.'

'Quite so. You can tell 'em it's for their own safety and comfort. As indeed it is. Our job is to tidy things up adminwise. Those you do persuade to come in, Jack, to be accommodated at Grubenfeld, all right?'

'Right, sir. Have to square it with the ataman, of course.'

'Naturally. What did you say his name was?'

'Bakturov, sir. Terrific chap. Admires us this side

idolatry. He may not welcome a whole intake of newcomers, however.'

'Understood. But, that accepted, you're in charge, aren't you? See you at lunch.'

'No, sir. I'm going back up with this stuff. Got to supervise the distribution. And show them the thunder-box so they can knock up a few of their own.'

'Glad to know we're getting it back. Historic item. Cheerio.'

Colonel Billy left them but Captain Surtees remained. The RQMS announced the loading was complete, handing Jack an inventory which he clipped to his millboard. A squad of riflemen trotted across the farmyard, past a couple of three-tonners and the colonel's Jeep making for the field on the other side of the barn which was now the quartermaster's stores. The leading soldier bounced a well-worn football.

'HQ company playing football?' Jack said to Tom Surtees.

'Keeps them occupied, Grandad. Damn-all else for them to do just now.'

'They ought to be playing cricket. It's the season.'

'Ah yes. But, if anything, the chaps prefer soccer.'

'Blow that, Tom. Get on to Brigade. Ask them to rustle up some cricket gear if at all possible.'

'Wilco.' Tom nodded co-operatively.

'Thanks. See you later.'

Jack jumped into his Jeep and waved to the 15-cwt. to follow. They drove out of the farmyard, then up through the village, and soon were climbing the mountain road. Once clear of Selsen, Jack's spirits soared. He realised – it was a shock – he was almost completely happy. This liaison job – well, it was more than that really, it was more one of welfare officer cum village bobby – was quite the best he'd had in years. Soldiering with a difference. He'd really taken to these people he was responsible for. Outlandish they might seem, but, by heaven, they were his sort. The way they looked you in the eye and the way they rode told you everything. After five minutes in their company you could tell they would keep their word whatever the cost. Too damn proud not to. And the air you breathed up there at Grubenfeld made you feel younger, more alive, alert. Jack changed down and began to push the Jeep rather harder through the bends. The lumbering stores truck dropped behind.

Coming out of the last hairpin to reach the high pastures, Jack saw someone walking up the road ahead of him. From the look of her and the headscarf it had to be Tonya. Though, mind you, almost every woman here wore a headscarf – it was pretty well national dress. The walker heard the Jeep and stopped, turning. It was Tonya all right. She waved. Jack found himself smiling inordinately as he pulled up.

'Top of the morning to you,' he called.

'Hello. Top? Top of the morning?'

His smile widened. 'What the Irish say. Very elegant, the Irish. Jump in.' Tonya got in beside Jack. 'You haven't walked all the way from Selsen, have you?'

'It isn't so far. And, walking, you can make short cuts without following the road.'

'Stiffish climb, though.'

'I'm young, Major.' She grinned. Was she teasing him?

Billeted in the village, Tonya had now met some of Jack's fellow officers – Tom Surtees in particular – and she knew they teased him about his age. He stared at her, trying to gauge the depth of her derision. 'Hadn't you better drive on?' she said. Jack grunted and did as he was told.

'Got some stores coming up behind in the 15-cwt.,' he said.

'That is a lorry, yes?'

'Correct. Refers to its unladen weight. Army workhorse, really.'

'Fifteen hundreds of weight?'

'No. Hundredweights.'

'What is the difference, please?'

'A hundredweight is a unit of measurement. A sack of flour, or coal or what-have-you, can weigh a hundredweight. It's about the most a healthy young fellow can carry, really. It's a hundred and twelve pounds, in actual fact.'

'Not a hundred?'

'Oh, no. Hundred and twelve.'

'So, being English, you call one hundred and twelve a hundred?'

Jack smiled. 'Of course. To confuse the foreigner, what else?'

Tonya laughed. 'It sounds as difficult as your pounds, shillings and pence.'

'Very much so. We English have always operated on two scales of value, as you might say – we use twelve as well as ten, unlike you backward continentals who've never got beyond ten. Twelve is a very useful number, actually; divides more ways than ten, for a start. Take for example –'

'Please, Major Kempe, you talk too quickly. I can't follow you.'

'Sorry. It's the mountain air, I expect. Anyway, that's enough nonsense about numbers and measurements, isn't it? How are *you* this morning?'

'Me? Oh, I'm fine, as you say.'

'I was thinking – on the way up, before I met you – just how lucky I've been getting detailed to do this job. But one thing puzzles me rather. You sometimes refer to the Cossacks as *them*; at other times you say *us*, as if you belonged to them. I think what I really mean is I'd like to know a bit of your history, Tonya. How do you fit in with all of this?' When she did not reply, he added, 'This Jeep's bloody noisy. Shall we stop?' She nodded. Jack pulled up and off the road. 'That's better. We don't have to shout any more.'

Tonya swung out of the Jeep. Beyond them, a meadow's breadth away, a craggy granite outcrop flanked by cypresses and young aspens basked in the sun. 'Why don't we walk over there?' she said as Jack gazed across. He nodded and they started off through a meadow which flickered with tiny tortoiseshell butterflies.

The outcrop when they reached it had an almost antique air. There was something classical about it, as though the light upon the rocks refined them in a different way from elsewhere. Their fissures and shadows, the embossed foliage of the cypresses, the etched clarity of saxifrages blossoming out of pockets and crevices created a particular world that engraved itself on Jack's consciousness and reminded him of, yes, Illyria again. His absurd Utopia. He tried to convey to Tonya how that line from Shakespeare had struck him when a child, how he had treasured that dream place, but she didn't understand. She was much more concerned to assure him that Illyria was indeed the Latin name for her father's country. And there was a catch in her throat as she mentioned her father.

'Yes, he came from there,' she said.

'Your father's a Yugoslav?'

'If you like. But first he was a Serbian. And then became a Cetnik, too. Only then Yugoslav.'

'You say *was*?'

Tonya nodded and sat down on a jut of rock. 'Oh, yes, he's dead. Tito tied his hands with wire and marched him till he died. The partisans do that, you know. They said he was a collaborator, but he wasn't.'

'I'm sorry.'

She remained silent. Jack wished he knew more of the infernal politics of middle Europe.

He said, 'Am I right in thinking the Cetniks support your King Peter?'

'That's right. They are royalists. King Peter fled to London; you gave him refuge. And all through the war the Cetniks fight for him but also some fight against Tito, who is a communist. They did terrible things, but so does Tito.' That, at least, Jack knew. 'But now you British help Tito.'

'Do we? Don't know.'

'I think so, yes. Your Mr Churchill is now supporting him. Everybody knows that.'

'More than I did. And your mother?'

Tonya smiled bleakly. 'It was she who was a Kazak. From Kuban.'

'So you're half and half? Half Yugoslav, half Russian?'

'No! You must understand, Major, it is more complicated than you think.' She was blushing with anger.

'Oh dear. Put my foot in it, have I?'

'If that means what I expect it must, yes. Yes. My father – I said – was Serbian and Cetnik first and only then what you English call a Jug. My mother was a White Russian, oh, yes, that is certain, but before that, always before that, Kazak, her family coming from beyond the Black Sea.' She stared fiercely at Jack. The sun caught her tear-filled eyes and they flashed blindingly. She scraped her cuff across them.

Jack dived his hand into his pocket for a handkerchief. 'There. I'm sorry.' He handed it to her.

'I'm sorry, too. I do not have one of these. Thank you.' She wiped her eyes. 'But people mind very much that you understand where they come from, yes? It is part of their inside being, isn't it?'

Jack agreed. After all he had always known precisely who he was. And even if there had been some early doubts – could he recall any? – then school, the royal military academy and a regular commission had long since vanquished them. As had the church at home, St Luke-in-the-Wold. His inner eye could see it now as it always was and, pray God, always would be, bunkered there among the elms, dug-in, watchful, lichen-stained, waiting. In that house – the bright vision was gone – the Kempes had confirmed their successive identities for well nigh seven centuries. Ranks of memorial tablets and squads of tombstones stood everywhere. There was even a nameless, faceless crusader who was claimed as ancestor to them all. And Kempe's First Company of Foot, precursor of the Bucks Rifles, had been raised in the south porch one Saturday in June 1740.

Jack said, 'I could get you some handkerchiefs. They'd be khaki, of course, but I know for a fact our quartermaster's got a box or two.'

Tonya tried to smile. She said, 'You think you may make me cry a lot, do you?'

'Of course I won't. Why should I? How could I? By George, it's lovely here.' Jack leant back against a rock, staring up into the blue. He could swear there was a lark singing high above them, beyond sight. 'But how is it you come to be here, assigned to us? Well, to me, as it turns out.'

Tonya said nothing. Jack began to wish he hadn't asked. Clearly he'd intruded again. When she did reply, her voice sounded older still.

'After my father was captured by Tito I ran away to Trieste. I had a great-aunt living there. She let me stay with her.'

'What about your mother?'

'I don't know. Most likely she is dead. The Nazis took her to a labour camp. When the British forces came to Trieste I tell them, I mean I *told* them, I speak English, Russian, Serbo-Croat, German, Italian and bits and bobs – is that right? – of French.'

'And they snapped you up as an interpreter?'

'Yes. Also, being well-known as gentlemen, they did not rape me.' Jack blinked at such a thought. 'No. Instead they say, "righto, just the ticket, you are now official interpreter – field officers and above for the use of." What is this other way round of words doing? I often hear it.'

'It's just military jargon.'

'It is not standard English?'

'Oh, no. It's how equipment and stores get listed and described. Typical admin approach. Efficiency gone berserk.'

'It is bureaucracy speech?'

'Yes. Army-style. It's become a running joke. "Handkerchiefs cotton girls brave for the receipt of." ' Jack smiled, rather pleased with his own small joke. He felt it had brightened things between them. Certainly Tonya appeared to have relaxed to some extent. 'So there we are, then,' he said. 'Now I know how you got here. Thank you. Shan't ask again.'

'Right you are, Major.'

Was she mocking him, imitating him? For a moment she'd sounded just like he did. Except for one thing. He said, 'As a matter of proper English, Tonya, I think you should either address me as "Major Kempe" or as "sir" but not just as "major", which sounds rather American or lower class.'

'You mean the working class?'

'Among others. In England we have the upper classes, of course, but then there's the middle class, which can be upper middle, middle middle or lower middle, and only after that the lower classes.'

'Oh, I see. Aristocracy, bourgeoisie, proletariat?'

'Mm. Except it doesn't seem like that with us and we don't use those words. But ways of saying and doing things are very much divided off. You reveal who you are in England by the words you use and by the things you do or don't do.'

'Isn't that all a waste of time?'

'Some of it. And I expect it'll all change now, once we get home. People are saying things are bound to change.'

'And what class do I show myself to be? To you, sir?'

She was definitely laughing at him this time. 'Oh, as a foreigner I'm afraid you don't count. You're *hors de combat*, as we say.'

'But that is French?'

'The English use a lot of French. Shows you've had a reasonable education – it's not that we care for the French especially. Historically we have a love-hate relationship with the Frogs.'

'You call them Frogs?'

'Of course, because they eat frogs. And they call us Rosbif because they think we eat roast beef all the time. Wish we did. Haven't had a decent bit of sirloin in years. But what I was really getting round to, Tonya, before you sidetracked me – oh, yes, you did – was to say perhaps you ought to call me Jack from now on.'

'Jack?'

'Yes. I was christened John, but I've always been called Jack – since nursery days.'

'Very well. It's a plain name. But good. Yes.'

'When we're off duty, I mean. Not on parade.'

'Perhaps it is time we went on parade again?'

'Suppose it is. Duty certainly beckons, if not calls.'

Neither moved. They saw the stores truck appear in the distance and approach along the road. When it reached the

Tonya's Story

Jeep, it slowed up for a moment before continuing on its way. Corporal Gibson had glimpsed Jack and Tonya. He winked at the driver, Rifleman Seymour, and began to sing his latest, lewdest version of 'Roll me over in the clover'.

'Yes, you're right. We must go,' Jack said and stood up, holding out his hand to help Tonya to her feet. She took it, but the minute she was upright Jack let her hand go. It had felt so cool in his, which had seemed embarrassingly hot.

Tonya stared at him. She wanted to pummel him, to hug him. Instead she said: 'Oh, you English! You are so – so correct. So kind.' And she turned and ran, half-laughing, half-sobbing, across the meadow amid clouds of butterflies.

Mystified by such behaviour Jack ran after her. 'Hey! Tonya! Stop.'

'So English! So gentle! So awful! So polite! So awfully nice!' Her voice rose and fell.

'For heaven's sake, girl, wait for me!'

When Jack reached the Jeep Tonya was sitting hunched, her face in her hands.

'What was that all about?'

'I think we must keep being on parade, Major Kempe, don't you?'

'Very well. Whatever you wish.'

Stony-faced, cursing himself for his inability to manage someone so volatile, so highly-strung, Jack drove on.

We had many good times at the camp in those early days. But now as I write I find them difficult to disentangle one from another. I see so many pictures on top of each other and I hear so many voices overlapping but mostly I see and hear Jack Kempe. And all the time he is smiling and laughing and becoming more what he would call 'good fun' and I would have called then 'his real self'.

Among the first of these mental snaps is one of the children at Grubenfeld eating the Cadbury's chocolate he brought them. The smallest ones' faces are thick with it. They cannot believe the delight they are tasting. What is this sweetness? Their ecstasy is solemn, big-eyed.

Next I see those adults who cannot quite accept that here they are smoking again, with more cigarettes to come because in front of them are tins of Players Navy Cut but with fifty pungently fresh, neither moist nor damp, but perfectly kept blond Virginia cigarettes in each. And there are cartons full of more all round them. It is quite incredible. Enough for everybody for months. After making do with herbs and grasses, which burn fragrantly but give no satisfaction, this is heavenly. You can see a person's whole body relax as he inhales and feels again that unique pleasure invading his lungs and stomach.

But it was the oranges that were the greatest surprise and gave the greatest joy. While our soldiers helped Jack's men unload the truck, he opened a crate and began as a joke to throw them up in the air for the children to catch. But at once everyone joined in! Jack had to flick the oranges into the air faster and faster. He became a marvellous machine, throwing them up and out at every angle, from behind his back, from above his head, from under his arm, while we all jumped and dived to catch them. In the air they shone as if made of polished gold, but once in our hands they glowed as if lit from inside. And their smell!

But who can describe smells? No one. You can only remember them. And the sensation of dancing, all of us dancing, us on the ground, the oranges in the air. Everyone joined together by Jack's quick-fire generosity.

Other joys followed, but many of these I remember simply as matters of fact rather than in actual pictures. For example, I had to explain what Jeyes' Fluid was. Once our people understood it to be disinfectant they were happy. The same with bottles of aspirin. But there was no need to say what the soap was – the green blocks of Fairy soap from Liverpool – everyone immediately recognised soap. The sacks of flour – each weighed a hundredweight, a measurement Jack had already tried to explain to me – were greeted more soberly, until it was discovered that they contained white flour. White! Now the camp could bake white bread instead of grey. And the first batch baked that day disappeared like nobody's business, which was a phrase I learned from Jack.

Next came the folding chairs for the old people at church, followed by the contraption known as the thunderbox. It was certainly a box made of wood, but it had no bottom to it and in the lid was an oval hole reminiscent of a WC. I said as much to Jack.

'Exactly. But without the water,' he said. 'Has the pit I ordered been dug?'

I asked Bakturov, who nodded once. He had little enthusiasm for the finer points of Jack's new sanitary regime, considering it not only unnecessary but also of the town, too urban, so therefore soft, unmanly, certainly not Cossack.

'Yes,' I said. 'It's been dug.'

'Then lead me to it. Corporal Gibson, you bring the box. You, Seymour, those two planks, OK?'

So off we marched to a spot away from the tents, close to the woods. Here we found a huge pile of earth and a young man still digging at the bottom of a pit at least three metres deep. He had a bucket on a rope, which his companion hauled up when it was full. The pair of them had committed some infringement of camp discipline, I cannot remember what, and been given this task to satisfy the whim of the eccentric English major.

We all peered down. The young man digging looked up, astonished to see so many faces at the rim of the hole. Even Father Sacha had joined us. In his surprise the poor fellow below crossed himself.

'Not at all bad. A decent depth. Jolly good,' Jack said. 'Right, Seymour, put the planks – no, hold on. We'd better get this chap up first, hadn't we?' His two soldiers laughed. I called down to ours, telling him to come up. He did, thankfully, using the bucket-rope firmly held by his companion as his means of escape. He climbed up, legs tensed against the earth wall, as neatly as any mountaineer.

The planks were put across the pit about twenty-five centimetres apart and the box placed upon them. 'And there you are,' said Jack. 'Bob's your uncle.' But there was puzzlement all round. No one could associate this arrangement with the simple natural function it was designed to accommodate.

'You had better explain how it works, sir,' I said, enjoying calling Jack 'sir' for the first time in such circumstances.

'No. That's your job. As interpreter.'

'I know! You must show them. Demonstrate how to use it.'

'Oh, I'm not sure that's quite on, is it? No. Just say in so many words, Tonya. Come along.'

But I knew it would be a waste of breath and take too long. Some actions speak louder than words. I marched forward, pulled down my trousers and knickers and sat on the box. And from this position I said, in Russian, of course, I said: 'There – do you see? It is easy, convenient and hygienic.'

Everybody laughed and clapped. I clapped back. Jack was laughing too, although I think he was a little shocked by my explicitness. 'What are you telling them?' he asked.

'That this is how the English do it, of course.' I got off the box, pulled up my clothes and returned to terra firma.

'And of course the earth here is used to cover things up as you go along,' he said. I explained this and everyone nodded solemnly. As we moved away, a queue formed to initiate the new latrine.

Jack stayed all that day, which ended with Brigadier Bakturov inviting us to eat with him that evening. We sat outside his tent in front of an enormous camp fire. It was hard work for me translating Bakturov's military exploits to Jack. But not the other way round. Jack told no tales of his experiences. All I managed to get out of him then and later was that he had been in the desert war against the Germans before crossing over into Sicily and Italy. Also that he and his fellow officers revered one particular general called Alexander. I said that was a name of classical renown. He agreed that the one was worthily commemorated in the other. But his reticence continued to puzzle me. I couldn't quite accept it. Something obtuse in me refused to. I wanted to make him react more spontaneously, more openly. I wanted, I suppose, to discover that underneath, as we say, he was more like me than he at first appeared.

I also wondered if this reserve of his stemmed from some trauma, some formative experience that he could not bear to contemplate. I was a child of my time and naturally I knew of Freud and his theories. Who doesn't? But when I mentioned that name, Jack just snorted and muttered something about not caring overmuch for the psychology lark. I found out later that this was literally true. He considered all normal people – as he called them – to be entirely responsible for their actions and would allow no excuses or explanations that might exonerate them for behaving badly or strangely. This made him truly foreign to me again and I determined to test this self-control which, although he never admitted it, was clearly for him a moral obligation. But I do remember asking him how he squared all this with being a professional soldier.

'You make me sound like a mercenary,' he said, clearly irritated, which was a start.

'Well, aren't you?'

'Certainly not! As a regular, I serve my king and my country. Nothing mercenary about that. We're hardly overpaid, you know. Besides, it's a tradition in my family. The army. An honourable profession. None more so.'

'But the killing of people?'

'One's got to have right on one's side, of course. As

we've had with Hitler. What's known as a just cause, I suppose.'

After that he wouldn't discuss it further. He didn't like talking in the abstract, he said.

Once we had finished eating, the vodka went round again and the songs began. Jack asked me to tell him the meaning of one in particular, which had an insistent, plaintive tune; the sort of folksong that has centuries of sadness locked inside it. I began to translate without thinking and then summarised it: 'Oh, it's very ordinary,' I heard myself saying – which wasn't true. 'It's about a girl a long way from home who wishes to find and to love a good man.' His eyes were on me and mine on his. I looked away quickly, only to regret at once my cowardice. I should have held his look, made my feelings command a response from him. But it was too late. The song had ended and Bakturov was saying for the hundredth time that he and his men had fought with the Germans from political necessity not because they admired Hitler. Jack agreed that this sort of thing happened in war – after all, who would have thought that Churchill would ever have made an alliance with Stalin? But in 1941 he had. And Britain had rejoiced. I was sorry they had gone back to this subject. It was late and suddenly I felt tired of powers and of politics.

Some time later I walked back with him under the stars to his Jeep. Brigadier Bakturov had invited Jack to stay at the camp. A tent could with no trouble be put at his disposal, he said. But Jack had refused even though he had arranged to return at dawn. I said good night but forgot to call him by his first name. He reminded me of our agreement.

'Don't become too English, Tonya,' he said and grinned.

'You mustn't tease me,' I said.

'Good night.' He snapped to attention and saluted me. I laughed.

'Do you always salute women?'

'Rather! Pleasant habit. Cheerio.'

He drove away under the moon. I watched his Jeep bump along the track to the road. At the turn, he waved and I waved back. But I still felt cross with myself for not holding his look by the fire.

FOUR

In the event the round-up patrol that the colonel had ordered proved something of a waste of effort. The fact was, or so it seemed to Jack, the people holed up in the mountains had somehow got wind of the operation and promptly faded away like banshees amid the rocks and snow. Not that he was entirely displeased. He had not been looking forward to billeting too many displaced persons on Bakturov. The old boy had been distantly sniffy about the idea from the start but had eventually agreed to co-operate. Jack had no wish to test their working partnership any further, let alone be obliged to overrule him. The famous Cossack pride would have got itself severely dented. Why, only yesterday Brigadier Bakturov had invited Jack to address him as Kolya – a signal honour for a foreigner, Tonya said.

The patrol was headed by one of the Cossack lieutenants flying the Union Jack, the flag Jack had been surprised to see on his first visit to the camp. It had been found in the baggage of a British honorary consul murdered in the coastal town of Split, Tonya told him. Jack wondered who this man might have been. Also who had murdered him. Tonya couldn't say. She had answered instead, glancing at

Brigadier Kolya, who rode on the other side of her, that he wanted to know why Jack had deceived him.

'What about?' Jack was immediately indignant.

'He says you told him you only ride a little.'

'Perfectly true.'

'But now he sees you are as good on a horse as any Cossack.'

The brigadier grinned.

Jack laughed. 'Oh, I see. Well, I wouldn't say so.'

'I tell him it is typical English modesty. Never reveal what you can really do until you do it, yes?' Tonya laughed too.

'I suppose so.'

The brigadier said something and Tonya translated: 'He says he likes this, it is not good to boast and brag. Too many people do that. Also he is going to give you a horse.'

'Oh, no, he mustn't!'

'You cannot refuse.'

'I shall have to. Can't start receiving gifts, Tonya. Against King's Regs.'

'What are they?'

'The rules we soldiers live by. There's a whole book of them. You'll have to be very diplomatic about this one. You mustn't let him give me a horse.'

Tonya nodded and they rode on in silence. Higher up, they came to a saddle between hills which took them up and over into a desolate area of threadbare grass giving way to permanent scree below the snow line. Amongst this unwelcoming vastness a huddle of shepherds' huts with a thin wisp of smoke issuing from the roof of the largest one suggested habitation.

Riding towards it, Jack saw first some children and then several women and three men come out of the huts and stand in a frightened group as if hypnotised by their approach. As well they might have been. The patrol made an outlandish and forbidding sight. Twenty glossy horses, the huge flag, the fur caps and wide-shouldered capes of the Cossacks, not to mention himself in battledress ironed and pressed by Corporal Gibson to within an inch of its life. You could cut a finger on the pockets' pleats, he'd told him. Gibson had taken this as a compliment and asked Jack if there was any news of demob yet. There hadn't been. But it would come soon, he'd assured him. Gibson had absorbed this in silence, but the look in his eyes had been, so Jack fancied, rather more civilian than soldierly. It was as if young Gibson, who had been pretty keen for a conscripted man, was already demobilising himself – in spirit certainly.

As they drew closer, it became clear that these poor souls were frightened silly. Their faces were blank with fear. They were half-starved, too. And filthy. Jack's heart went out to them. One of the men, the tallest if not the strongest, was grasping a rifle with bellicose uncertainty. One of the children, a trouserless small boy, began to cry, but a woman grabbed him and held him against her.

Brigadier Kolya addressed them first in Russian. No one replied. He spoke again, this time in German, and the man holding the rifle answered, but in neither of these languages. Tonya smiled and said a number of things very quickly which he understood at once. She turned to Jack.

'He speaks Serbian. They are Cetniks not Cossacks.'
'Your lot?'

'On my father's side, yes.'

'Well, kindly inform him they've no need to be frightened. We're here to help. Say that as the British officer in command of this area I advise them to come down from here so they can be fed, quartered and properly looked after. And that Brigadier Bakturov has agreed to accommodate them at Grubenfeld. It's for their own good, tell him.'

Tonya did so and the tall man replied that he trusted the British officer but not the Cossacks. She added that for obvious reasons she would not translate this last part into Russian.

'Tell him they can trust the Cossacks. That they've got my word they'll be OK. And that I can answer for our friends here. They'll be well-treated, I promise.'

But the man and his companions were not so easily satisfied. They were very afraid of Tito, Tonya said. Jack told her to remind them that they were in Austria not Yugoslavia and that Tito's partisans did not, and would not be allowed to, operate here. So long as they were in the British zone they were safe. And the only reason for persuading them to come down from the hills was in order to organise their welfare more effectively – especially the children, who looked badly in need of milk and fresh vegetables, wasn't that correct?

As Tonya translated this, a rustle of interest, a leavening of hope, spread throughout the group. Finally the tall man nodded, with his mouth crooked into an unaccustomed smile. He spoke briefly.

'He says they will come,' said Tonya.

'Good. Ask if they know of any more people like them living up here.'

When Tonya asked this the man became almost animated. He shook his head while gesturing towards the north-west.

'He says everybody else is gone away now. Over to the next valley and beyond, he thinks.'

'Right. In that case they're out of our area. They'll be the King's Own's pigeon. Good. Better ask Brigadier Kolya to detail some of his own blokes to escort this lot back while we press on a bit just in case this character's mistaken, OK?'

The patrol rode on, leaving four Cossacks behind to supervise the Cetniks. But they found no more fugitives of any kind. The man had been right. These hills were deserted, they concluded, after they had several times scanned them with their field glasses from one ridge to the next. Tonya became expert at the directional clock, but the only other animate things they spotted were crows and a pair of circling buzzards.

By midday they had reached the snow line and were progressing westwards alongside but just below it. They paused to brew up tea and to eat fresh bread from the camp's bakehouse with slices of Spam. The snow-sharpened air made each familiar taste, even the tinned meat, delicious. Jack agreed with Brigadier Kolya that there was little more to be done and they might as well start back. Indeed the brigadier was keen to get going because there was a lot to be done at the camp in readiness for Jack's colonel's inspection the following day. Jack, in mock seriousness, told Tonya to tell him that much would be expected: stones must be whitewashed, boots polished to a glasslike finish, rifles boiled out. Tonya in her turn, surprised Jack by already knowing the term *bull*.

As the brigadier and his men mounted, Jack remained where he was, gazing into the distance.

'Aren't you coming?' Tonya said.

'In a bit. I rather like it up here.'

'And me? Must I go or stay?'

'Just as you wish, Tonya.'

'You are saying you don't mind which way?'

' "Either way" would be more correct.'

'Very well. You don't mind either way?'

'I'd prefer you to stay, actually.'

'Then I shall. Good. But why didn't you say so in the first place?'

'I didn't want to put you under any obligation.'

'I see.'

'Does your heart good, doesn't it? Well, it does mine.' Jack turned slowly, taking in the entire shining panorama. 'I love mountains,' he said.

'The mountains of Cossackia.'

'What?'

'That's what the ataman calls them. He says the Germans before they left gave the Cossacks this part of Austria to live in for their own.'

'Really?'

'Yes. For ever, he says. It is our new country – Cossackia.'

'Oh, dear me. Does he *really* think that?'

'Oh, yes. And most of the people at Grubenfeld believe him too.'

'Do you, Tonya?'

'No, I think it was a joke someone made. But when you live in fear of your future you can easily believe silly things, false things, can't you?'

'Any idea where he got this story from?'

'Some other Cossack commander, he said. I don't know which one. But there are so many rumours going round and, besides, our people are always speaking of how one day they will find a country they can call their own. It is common talk in the camps. Not just here. A persistent hope. But that is typical of exiled persons who can't go home, wouldn't you say?'

'I'm sure you're right. Yes.'

'But in the end something will have to be done about us. You British will go back to Blighty, yes? But us, where will we belong? Here? Or where?'

'You're still saying "us", aren't you?'

'I've told you why – I'm half and half. A half-caste, do you say?'

'No, that is when one parent is black. Both yours were white. But, if you ask me, you're really a Serb, Tonya. Your father's nationality makes you that – legally – I'd say. Of course I can quite understand you feel rather Cossack too, given your mother. One would.'

Tonya did not reply. Instead she said, 'I think those are lilies over there.'

'Lilies?'

'Those yellow flowers – beyond the rocks. Let's see, shall we?'

'Why've you changed the subject?'

But again Tonya did not answer. She went towards the

flowers she had spotted. Jack followed. Wild daffodils had pierced the snow and were blooming with their heads an inch or so above the dazzling surface.

'These are daffodils, Tonya.'

The word sounded strange to her. 'Daffodils!' She repeated it several times, laughing.

'Pretty word, really.'

'It sounds – well, it makes me laugh.'

'But when they grow wild they are also known as Lent lilies.'

'Ah! So I was right. They *are* lilies.'

'If you insist. Yes. We're both right.'

'That's good! I like that. I like us both to be right, Jack.'

She was looking at him and her eyes were dancing with pleasure. She began to pick the daffodils. Jack sat on a rock, delighting in her delight. Watching Tonya, he felt for the first time that this was truly peace at last. This instant was what peace was. You sat with your feet in the snow, your backside on a sun-warmed rock, your face tingling in the crystal air, your eyes drinking in the sight of a girl you couldn't quite fathom. Someone genuinely beautiful, as he now realised. Or would it be better to think of her as gravely handsome? Perhaps. Formidable, too. There was nothing flashy about her, except, as he'd registered from the first, she did move with a physical frankness you could've been mistaken about. He supposed it boiled down to her being, well, foreign. But this last thought irritated him. Suddenly he found himself annoyed with himself. What a stupid thing to think. Even to entertain. If all he could say to explain Tonya's difference from other women, from Betty, his wife, for instance, was that she was foreign, well, that proved he was a dunce, a dullard. Tonya deserved a better response.

She had come back to him, a huge bunch of the delicate daffodils in her hands. She held them out to him.

'For you, Jack. They are for you.'

'For me?'

'I have no one else to give them to. Smell. They smell of springtime, yes?' Jack buried his nose in the bunch. She was right. That was exactly what they did smell of, a freshness like hope, like their own growth through the snow. It was more a sensation than actual scent, yet it existed. To infiltrate your senses, invade your head. He looked up. She was smiling.

'As a child I was taught when you receive a gift you must always give one back. Were you taught that, Jack?'

'No. Just to say thank you.'

'Well with us, us foreigners, you have to be a bit more than polite. If people are only polite we think they are rude.'

'Really?'

'Oh, yes. Very rude.'

'But I haven't got anything to give you in return, Tonya. Only wish I had.'

'Of course you have. A kiss is a gift.'

She held his look. He stared into her eyes, fearful but reluctant to turn aside. He took breath . . . 'Well, that isn't quite on, is it?' he said. 'Not really possible, I'm afraid.'

'Why not?'

'Because, as you know, there is Betty, my wife.'

'Of course. You told me.'

'Well then.'

Jack stood up and, oblivious to the intrinsic contradiction, told himself it was best to call a halt straightaway and at the same time to get a move on back to base. But Tonya stood her ground.

'Here,' she said. She laid a finger to her cheek to indicate the place. 'Your Betty could not object to that, I am sure.'

'Well, no. Of course not. No.'

'Good. Then just here, please.'

Not trusting himself at all Jack kissed her carefully, precisely, on the cheek. But by chance, by a whim of the breeze, a tendril of Tonya's hair teased his forehead. At this, all compunction fled. He hugged her convulsively, crushing the daffodils against her back, pressing her head into the crook of his neck and shoulder. And heard then felt his breathing gather itself into a single held entity that burned in him, in his chest, until he had to release it in an absurd, shaming groan. Embarrassed at this display of feeling, Jack murmured Tonya's name as a feint, a false manoeuvre across terrain held by the enemy – or so he imagined. Yet here was no enemy. Enemy? She? Someone like this? He dropped the daffodils behind her, simply let them go, freeing both his hands to hold her head, oh, the softness of her hair between his fingers, and drew her face back and up to his. Their kiss was long, felt, chaste. Neither moved; neither dared express himself or herself further. Both were equally afraid. Tonya knew she had only to intimate with a simple relaxation of her lips her compliance for Jack to march in upon her as a conqueror. Jack knew he had only to insist for her to give way. Each held the other in desperate abeyance, balanced precariously upon a fulcrum of desire and scruple.

Tonya pulled her mouth from Jack's and buried her face against him. She, too, now murmured his name just as he had used hers – defensively. After a while he realised she was sobbing. He wanted to hold her head again and to kiss her tears away. Instead, like a fool, he said he was sorry.

'Sorry?' In the instant, Tonya was angry. 'Sorry?' she said. 'Oh, how can you? How can you say that?'

Jack was at a loss. He had no means of reply. He hadn't actually literally meant he was sorry. No, it was one of those general expressions, an attempt to encompass the awkward position he found himself in, to convey to her, to this girl, this not any longer unimportant girl, the sudden division of his loyalties. But he couldn't go on about such things. His sort didn't. What you did was to say you were sorry and other people understood everything from the way you said it, didn't they?

He said: 'Well, you must know what I mean?' He wanted to add: *please say you do, please, it's vital you understand.*

'I don't!' she said, still furious. 'How can I know? Why should I? You cannot embrace and then say you are ashamed of it. That is to insult the person you kiss. You insult me!'

'I didn't mean that.'

'Then what?'

'Play fair, Tonya. It was you who suggested I – well – look, you can't hold me responsible, no! It was your doing just as much as mine.'

'But what have we done that is so wrong?'

'You know perfectly well! Of course you do.'

'I don't! It was nothing, in fact. Nothing at all.'

'It wasn't.'

'Very well, it was a nothing which could have become something.'

'Exactly. That's why we had to stop.'

'Oh, how stupid! Stupid, stupid, stupid.'

She sat where he had sat, hunched with anger. Jack stood alongside, amid the fallen daffodils.

'There are standards,' he said. 'I told you, I warned you when you insisted on claiming your reward ... I said then –'

'You're afraid of me, aren't you?' She looked up at him, her eyes full of the glittering sky and jagged skyline.

'No,' he said. And meant it. 'No, I'm quite clear about that. It's me, Tonya. I'm afraid of me. Me.'

'Oh, I see.' Her contempt was complete. 'Inside yourself you say: "No, I am married English gentleman officer, therefore I must not touch wicked foreign girls"?'

'Who says you're wicked? I don't! But I must be loyal. Please, Tonya, please understand me. I'm sure you do really?'

'Perhaps I'm hurt too?'

'I'm sure – yes – of course. We both are.'

'Well, at least that is something.'

'What?'

'We can hurt each other.'

'That's a dreadful thing to say.'

Neither spoke. Tonya got up from the rock and stood directly in front of him. Her body, thick-clad, rocked on her heels in front of him.

'When did you last see your wife?' she said.

'It was Christmas. 1941.'

'More than three years ago? Oh, Jack. As long as that?' He nodded. 'And you've been, you know, loyal, all this time?'

'We say "faithful", in point of fact.'

'All right. Faithful. You've been that, have you?'

'Yes. Haven't ever seen my daughter. Not to hold her, that is. I've got a snapshot, though.'

'And your Betty? What is she like?'

'Difficult to describe. I remember her how she was. Good at tennis. Fair hair. No, I can't really say exactly.'

'Do you think she will have changed in this time?'

'I shouldn't think so. No. Not Betty.'

'But perhaps you have?'

'Hope not.'

'What do you remember best about her?'

'Well . . . No, I'm sorry, Tonya. No. Please don't quiz me.'

'Quiz? What is that?'

'It means "ask questions".'

'But sometimes we must ask questions.'

'I disagree.'

'Why? Isn't it good to reach the truth? I think it is.'

Tonya moved to him and kissed him on the mouth. His surprise was comic. His eyes widened. He felt again he must respond or at once repulse this moment – either seize it or reject it. Which? His torment was complete. But no, it was Tonya who released him. She drew back.

'Forgive me,' she said.

'Is that the same as saying you are sorry?'

'Perhaps.'

He embraced her now. And there was no further shame

between them. They clung to each other in the snow, standing amidst the saffron stain of the trampled daffodils, holding together like children or displaced persons with nowhere to call their own except, perhaps, Cossackia.

FIVE

In the days which followed I felt increasingly ashamed of myself. A little, I imagine, as Eve might have done if Adam had refused to taste the apple. To ease my uneasiness I mocked Jack inside myself, wondering if he would now write home to his English-rose wife to say that the foreign woman tempted him among the daffodils and he nearly, oh so nearly, fell. 'But at the last I thought of you, old girl, and found the strength to resist her.'

But soon such thoughts seemed to be unworthy of us both and eventually I was obliged to admit that I had been worse than foolish. I had played with fire. Jack's dilemma had been genuine, universal and not simply an *opera buffa* affair of English awkwardness. And I warned myself to remember in future that Jack's word was indeed his bond; that keeping faith was for him the foundation of his being, as it was with all fair-playing Englishmen.

During this period of mutual truce we avoided each other as much as we could and so I did not hear that Jack's colonel had attended a top-brass briefing at Brigade HQ, down in the valley at Mittelthal fifty kilometres away. Not a word of its deliberations reached Jack at Selsen or me at Grubenfeld, so perhaps it is hardly surprising it was never spoken of between us. As a consequence, however, we were, like Ophelia upon another matter, the more deceived.

While I helped out in the school, teaching the middle ones their Bible stories (Joseph and his brothers was the favourite), Jack created a cricket ground at the camp. Somehow he had procured an issue of what he called the 'necessary equipment' of bats, balls and stumps, together with a pair of leg pads like small white mattresses.

At his instruction, twenty puzzled Cossacks went to mow a meadow. They worked in a line, their scythe blades flashing in the sun. It was beautiful, like a scene out of Tolstoi. Jack insisted they teach him the way of it and almost at once was as good a mower as any of them. And quite as untiring. They worked in the sunshine so they stripped to the waist, their shoulders reddening as the sweat poured from them.

Soon they had cleared a space of almost a hectare. Or, rather, they had left long lines of the cut grasses across the field to dry out into hay. Once it had been turned twice, first by the men and then by the children, who threw it everywhere in mock battles with each other, it was gathered together to make a haycock like a big round bun. Someone joked that it would keep his horse happy all through the next winter. But his companion wondered if they would yet be there in Grubenfeld by that season.

Next Jack demanded that the mowers sharpen their scythes more keenly than ever so they could cut what he called the square. This was a patch of extremely short grass in the middle of the mown area about thirty metres by thirty metres. Once it was done Jack said it was full of bumps, but to us it looked as smooth as any famous

English lawn to take tea with muffins on. Oh, by the way, I have read my George Bernard Shaw and I know it is permissible in idiomatic English to end a sentence with a preposition if you wish to.

By this time Jack needed my help as his interpreter to explain the rules of the game. So we came together again, carefully, officially. First he selected Brigadier Kolya as captain of one team, giving him ten Cossacks of his choosing to be his men, while he, Jack, became captain of the other side. It was to be the ataman's eleven heroes against the major's eleven, he said. Then the six stumps were set up, three at one end of the pitch, three at the other. There were meant also to be two little bits of wood to rest on top of these three sticks, but they had not been supplied by Brigade, he said. Instead the children offered Jack beautiful, slim fir cones, which balanced perfectly in place. They were the bails, Jack said. He also announced that when everybody had got the hang of the game he would mark the pitch in front of the stumps with a line of whitewash called the crease and another all round the field for the boundary, but at the moment that wasn't of the essence. Naturally I found much of this sporting vocabulary rather difficult to translate.

Next came the time when words began not to matter quite so much because actions took over. And, as always, they spoke loudly. Jack showed the Cossacks how to hold the cricket bat, explaining that it was used both to guard the stumps and to hit the ball so the two men with bats could run up and down the wicket, which was both the pitch and the stumps. This was confusing, but the more they ran, the more they would be winning, he said. That at least seemed clear. Finally, when Brigadier Kolya had understood and practised what to do with the bat, Jack went to the other end of the pitch and bowled the first ball to him. Very slowly. Kolya hit out at it and the bright red sphere flew high up into the air. So high that it went almost out of sight before it fell to hit one chap on the foot, who cursed profoundly. In cricket the ball is very hard, as I think I have said before. Jack told the man he should have caught it: if he had, he wouldn't have been hurt and Brigadier Kolya would have been out. He bowled again at the ataman, a little more quickly, and this time the stumps were knocked flying. Now Brigadier Kolya was truly out, he said. Clean bowled.

As they continued to learn and to practise I found I was needed less and less. Jack could explain everything by demonstration, which he did with great physical eloquence; also, I must say, our people were quick to learn. So I went back to the children's Bible class. By the afternoon it was announced that the two sides were ready to play a proper game and we were all invited to watch. Needless to say, Major Kempe's eleven won.

In the mess that evening Jack described the match to his fellow officers. During the course of his account, which he told with some relish, Colonel Billy was called away to the RT. Another message from Brigade. When he returned, all agreed he'd missed the best of the story.

'Their co-ordination's first class, of course,' Jack had said. 'Hand and eye – superb. As you'd expect of cavalrymen. But as batsmen they're wild in the extreme. Hit out at anything. And as for keeping a straight bat, well, no, that's not in their nature. Goes against the grain. Got a style all their own, somewhere between ice hockey and baseball. Anyway – to start with I was doing most of the bowling and inevitably taking the odd wicket. Could hardly help it. And that's where the problems began. Could I get them to walk? Oh no. Certainly not. Caught or bowled, let alone leg before or run out, they refused to leave the wicket. Seemed to regard it as a matter of principle, personal and national. Cossacks do not admit defeat lightly. *Infra dig*. In the end I had to call on Miss Parvic to explain that it was only a game and that no one thought the worse of a chap for getting himself out. After that, things progressed rather better and then perked up considerably when one of their lads turned out to be a natural medium-pace seamer. He took three in a row and they walked like lambs. It seems they can accept being got out by one of their own but not by strangers such as me.'

'But I understood you were getting along with them like a house on fire?' Tom Surtees said.

'Oh, rather. Great chums. No. Things only get sticky if they think their precious pride's in question. However, I kept this chap on and in no time at all he was bowling a consistent length *and* turning the ball as well! He'd watched my fingers and wrist, you see. Instinctive seamer. Astonishing. Even if he does look like Genghis Khan Minor. Anyway, in the end they were sixty-two all out and it was my side's turn to bat.'

'You won?'

'Well, yes. With three wickets in hand. But I allowed myself to be out for twenty-four, bowled underarm by

Brigadier Bakturov. How's that for international diplomacy?'

It was at this moment that Colonel Billy re-entered the mess tent. His smile made it clear they could all carry on as they were.

Jack continued. 'Which reminds me, they've taken to calling me Major Owzat. No aitch, of course. The kiddies started it and all the adults have followed suit. Rather a compliment, I suppose. Anyway they all insist they want to play again and I must say I can't wait. They may look as mad as hatters in their cavalry boots and walrus moustaches, swinging at anything that comes, but, by heaven, when they do connect it's boundary or a six every time.'

All laughed and the conversation became more general. Colonel Billy called Jack to one side. He wished for a quiet word, he said. They went out, into the soft starlit night damp with dew.

Billy said, 'Need you to organise another small thing, Jack. Up at Grubenfeld. Where it's clear you're the man of the hour. A weapons hand-over.'

'Would you say that again, sir, please?'

'Of course. This is a policy applying to all camps in the area. Your chaps to be required to hand over their weapons pending the issue of standard British small arms.'

'We're going to rearm the Cossacks?'

'Exactly.'

'Really?'

'There's talk of utilising them as an auxiliary force to help keep the peace as we withdraw from hereabouts. For this they'll need up-to-date weapons – 303s, Stens, .38

revolvers, Brens. Can't leave 'em with their present hodgepodge, can we?'

'And this order's come down from Brigade?'

'Tonight. But, from what I hear, it's been formulated much higher up the tree.'

'Well, yes, Billy, it would need to be – issuing British arms to foreign nationals, most unusual.'

'Quite. But then, this is an unusual time, isn't it? A period of disengagement, as we might say.'

'They won't take kindly to giving up their guns, sir.'

'I dare say not. But you're in charge, Grandad. And, after all, they respect you and they'll have got your word they are soon to be rearmed more than effectively.'

'Couldn't we synchronise the hand-over with the hand-out of the new weapons, sir? That would surely be the best way for all of us.'

'I agree. Said the same myself to the Brigade Major. But the shipment's still at sea, he says.'

'But surely Ordnance have got dumps full of the stuff from here to Monte Cassino? I can't believe –'

'Nor me, Grandad,' Billy interrupted. 'But such are the facts as far as Brigade is concerned. As usual we, the poor bloody infantry, must do the best we can. And we will, won't we?' Was it Jack's fancy or had Colonel Billy stressed this last point? It would've been most unlike him if he had. Jack decided he hadn't. It wasn't the Bucks' way of doing things.

He said, 'So my Cossacks have really got to take my word for it, sir?'

'They have. Tell them they'll be getting the new issue as

soon as maybe.' As Jack considered this, Billy added: 'I'm sure you'll cope magnificently, Grandad.'

'It would seem I'll damn well have to.'

'Quite so.'

Both laughed. They weren't sure why. Unless it was as comrades-in-arms. They wished each other good night and went to their sleeping quarters. Alone, neither the giver nor the receiver of the order was entirely satisfied with it. While Billy wondered if Brigade had given him the full picture, Jack hoped Billy hadn't left something unsaid. But since both had no further information to reflect upon they were obliged to accept what they knew at face value. Each slept reasonably well.

I thought I would never forget the confiscation of weapons at Grubenfeld and I haven't. Nor the long explanations beforehand, which I had to translate over and over again to convince Brigadier Bakturov to order our men to obey the English major. When at last they were persuaded to do so, well, that was our crossing of the Rubicon, though it looked and sounded more like a circus. Or, to change the metaphor, on that day the infernal machine was set to work. Oh, yes, I think our tragedy may justly be called a classic one in which we all became sport for the President of the Immortals, as the fine English ironist Thomas Hardy has written.

Everything depended upon our belief in Jack. In Major Owzat. For it was my use of this nickname, which I used without Jack's permission, that finally made Bakturov smile and accept the promise. It did the trick, as Jack acknowledged later.

At once the ataman instructed his men and the hand-over began. But not without ceremony. First every man loaded his gun, then mounted his horse. Next they galloped all round the cricket pitch in a great circle, firing off their weapons into the air, standing up on their saddles to shoot at the sky. Jack, overwhelmed by their display, asked for a horse and joined them, though he did not fire his pistol, nor stand on his saddle. Even so, his presence amongst them did much to dispel any doubt that may have lingered in the breasts of Brigadier Kolya and his fellow officers.

The firing-off lasted almost an hour and one man was hurt when his ancient carbine burst with overheat in his hand. But even this incident did not spoil the joy and laughter of the women and children as they watched their men perform ever more daring feats of horsemanship: riding in formation, charging at an imagined enemy, making their horses kneel while another jumped clean over them, and all the while maintaining a continuous rattle of gunfire. The noise and the smell of gunpowder in the air made the horses neigh as if it were a real battle.

Finally a place beside the 15-cwt. was marked out with sticks so the Cossack cavalry could ride by and fling their weapons and belts of ammunition on to the spot in public view. Corporal Gibson and two other soldiers Jack had brought with him that morning stood guard beside it. Soon – as the men galloped madly past – a huge pile of discarded weapons lay higgledy-piggledy on the ground, interlaced with belts of still-unused bullets. Hand grenades too were flung on to the pile. When all was done, the horses were ridden away to be rubbed down and corralled. A silence fell over the camp.

Kolya said (and I translated), 'Can we expect our fine new weapons very soon? I don't think my men will like being without for long. Not now their excitement is dying down. It is like taking their manhood away.'

Jack smiled and spoke confidently. 'Oh, it should be any day now. And once they arrive I shall lay on weapons instruction – we'll set up a firing range. Your chaps'll be amazed at the difference modern small arms can make to their marksmanship.'

'They are all eager to bear British arms.'

'And they will, sir, they will.'

It was at this moment that two of our senior officers brought forward a young captain and forced him to his knees in front of the ataman. Jack asked me what was the problem.

'He has hidden his pistol somewhere,' I answered. 'And he is refusing to say where it is. He does not wish to give it up.'

'But everyone else has been happy to do so. Where's he been? Look at this lot.' Jack turned to the heap of carbines, rifles and shotguns Corporal Gibson and the other two soldiers were now loading into the 15-cwt.

The young captain said something directly to me. It was embarrassing to translate. I said, 'He also says he does not –' I hesitated '– he does not trust you, Major Kempe, despite your fine words. That is a precise translation. I'm sorry.'

I saw Jack's anger. 'Doesn't trust me? I see. Well, just you remind him that Brigadier Kolya and all his officers bloody well do and –'

But before Jack could finish, Bakturov had broken into the argument and a fierce altercation between him and the captain ensued. I translated briefly, telling Jack that in essence the brigadier was saying what had been said many times now. That he trusted the British officer, etcetera, etcetera, and so his subordinate could too and they should all look forward to bearing British arms very soon, perhaps even tomorrow, which would be better than all this old rubbish they had given up.

Jack said: 'Quite right. Tell him what I've just said. They'll get them just as soon as Ordnance get their fingers out.'

'Please, I do not understand that last part . . .' I replied. Since I didn't, not then.

'Just a phrase. Means "get a move on", "get down to it" sort of thing.' Jack, I think, was genuinely unaware of its ribald connotation. The captain muttered something that sounded contemptuous.

'What was that?'

'He's saying the Germans also made many false promises.'

'Well, he's dealing with us now, not the Germans. Remind him an Englishman's word is his bond. And repeat that our aim is to transform this Cossack unit into a modern fighting force compatible with ourselves.'

I explained at length, with Bakturov joining in. Eventually the young captain nodded and almost smiled in Jack's direction.

'He says he's believing you now, sir. He accepts your oath which is more precious than life to an Englishman.'

'Quite right. Just so.'

Jack grinned and stepped forward, holding out his hand. The captain took it. They shook hands vigorously – all smiles at last.

'He will go and fetch his pistol now,' I said.

'Good man,' Jack answered and clapped him on the shoulder.

Five minutes later he returned and made a formal point of handing over his pistol – a Luger – to Jack, saying he hoped Jack would not hold any grudge against him.

'Of course not. Water under the bridge as of this instant,' Jack said, tossing the pistol into the truck.

And that was that. The hand-over was complete. An hour later, Jack escorted the 15-cwt. down to Selsen. I went with him in the Jeep. The loaded truck was placed under guard in a barn before continuing its journey the next day to a depot in Mittelthal that served as the collection point for all the Cossack weaponry the British had tricked us into relinquishing.

The next evening Jack and Tonya were seated at the ataman's hearth again. It was oddly impressive, Jack reflected – not for the first time – the way Bakturov operated in two capacities: first as a very much on-the-ball, modernish military commander, then, as at this moment in the firelight, as a patriarch of his people going back in time to somewhere well before the Old Testament.

The camp fire glinted and glowed just as their faces did after the wine and the stewed mutton with dumplings.

Tonya's Story

Now there was vodka and the ataman was finishing a slow, loose-limbed story about his old fur cap, which he had treasured since his youth. It boasted a distinctive bald patch somewhat kidney-shaped. Apparently the husband of some young lady from Baku had gone for him with a meat-chopper, he had dodged, the fur had flown and the result had been this bald patch. But, the joke was that he hadn't actually been wearing anything else at the time, not even his boots, and had only escaped the jealous husband's murderous intentions by leaping stark-naked (save for the cap) through the bedroom window, to land head over heels in the open drain outside.

Tonya giggled a lot while translating this. Jack was handed the cap for examination and veneration. It had clearly been a close-run thing. He told Kolya the patch reminded him of the Caspian Sea. This observation pleased the old ataman because Baku was a town on the Caspian Sea, he said, and whenever he saw that patch he remembered the beautiful girl – 'what a girl!' – before her stupid husband burst in. They all laughed, the ataman especially.

Now it was Jack's turn to contribute to the occasion. He had already tried to get out of it once, but no, protocol and good manners now obliged him to struggle through a poem, which, thanks to the vodka, he solemnly announced to be (a) superb, (b) famous and (c) typically English. Nothing, he averred, could be more English than these nonsense verses of Lewis Carroll.

Tonya translated his foolhardiness with commendable accuracy, thus assuring him keen attention from an audience almost entirely composed of eyes shining out of the surrounding dark. He felt as though he was being watched by hungry owls imbued with ancient, unforgiving wisdom. And the horrid truth was he'd forgotten far more of the poem than he'd thought he had. Not only that, what was worse, the Walrus and the Carpenter wasn't proving all that easy for Tonya to translate. Sealing-wax and pigs with wings? Oh dear, oh dear. The charm and the jokes weren't getting across. And she kept asking him to repeat lines he wasn't too sure of in the first place. Still, he was battling on – he'd reached the last verse but one – the end was in sight.

> ' "I weep for you," the Walrus said:
>   "I deeply sympathise."
> With sobs and tears – he um, yes – sorted out
>   Those oysters of the largest size,
> Something, something, handkerchief
>   Before his streaming eyes.'

Jack waited while Tonya translated, hoping someone might laugh or just smile, for heaven's sake. No one did. He couldn't tell if they had even followed the gist of it. He took breath again.

'Last verse coming up,' he said. At this they all nodded. Probably with relief, if the truth were known.

> ' "Oh, oysters," said the Carpenter,
>   "You've had a pleasant run!
> Shall we be trotting home again?"
>   But answer came there none –
> And this was scarcely odd, because
>   They'd eaten every one.'

Tonya led the applause. He clapped back, pleased at remembering the last verse in its entirety.

'I was word-perfect on that last one,' he said. 'But I don't think it was really their cup of tea, do you?' Tonya said many English ideas were difficult, not only to translate but to understand in the first place. Besides, the audience hadn't understood what a walrus was.

'But I thought you'd explained?'

'Oh, I did, yes. But a sea animal with a moustache did not appear so very funny to them because nearly all their men have moustaches, don't they?'

'Oh, I see. Got you. What else would a self-respecting walrus wear but a Cossack moustache? Of course. Quite. Most natural thing in the world.'

They smiled and gazed together into the fire. Tonya was tempted to put her arm through his, but instead he took her hand. They didn't look at each other. A balalaika struck up and singing began. Soon they heard the song Tonya had explained to Jack before. Despite herself, she felt a tremor run through her. Had Jack felt it?

He had. He said, 'Here comes the girl who's on the lookout for a good man.' And he turned to look at her. Tonya continued to gaze at the fire. She could feel tears welling up in her eyes.

She said, 'I should have made up different words for it. Then you wouldn't have been any the wiser.'

As they walked to Jack's Jeep he offered her a lift down to Selsen.

'No, thank you. I think I'll stay up here from now on.'

'Oh? Right. Right you are.'

'I feel better up here with my own people.'

'Only half yours, Tonya.'

'It's enough. My mother was very strong. Perhaps stronger than my father really.'

'Often the case with the ladies. Known some as tough as old boots.' Jack laughed, making light of his disappointment. He had wanted Tonya to accompany him back to HQ. He'd got things he wanted to explain. About himself, about Betty and about, well, what had happened, or, rather, hadn't, up in the mountains. He'd planned in his mind a stop and a chat halfway down, under the moon, which was just rising.

'Well, if you want to stay here ... well, that's your decision, naturally. I can see the attractions.' He smiled determinedly.

'Yes, the tent I have is very comfortable and not at all damp.'

'Well, that's thanks to the groundsheets we've supplied.'

'Yes.'

Neither spoke until Jack said, 'Well I'd better be getting along, hadn't I? Good night, my dear.' And he saluted her. But the clipped endearment had entered Tonya like a bullet.

She said, 'You could stay too, Jack. If you want. Tonight.' Her throat was dry, her breath short, her words scarcely voiced.

'No. We agreed, didn't we? Up in the snow. Never to allow our feelings to run away with us, not again. Correct?'

'You make it seem far worse than it was, Jack. We did nothing so bad. We were like ... children.'

'Possibly. But now we're not, are we?'

'Please stay.'

'Oh, Tonya, I want to.'

'I know. So please say yes.' Tonya held out her hand, thinking Jack would surely take it. He didn't. In the instant, she was angry. Her English stumbled. 'Always, always, you humble me! Do I ask a man easily, you think? Like some street woman?'

'Of course not! Oh, no, Tonya. Please, I'm sorry, truly sorry –'

'Don't say you're sorry! It's like before! I hate it when you say you're sorry! Don't say it! Not again! Sorry, sorry! It's all you Englishmen ever say!'

'Very well, then! Very well. I apologise instead. How's that?'

But to his irritation and incomprehension Tonya collapsed into hysterical laughter. It was like, but worse than, that earlier occasion, when they'd stopped on their way up to the camp. She, who could seem so grave, so sensible, was staggering all round him, doubled up with a laughter so painful it sounded forced, somehow put on. Surely she was exaggerating deliberately? She must be! It made him want to grab hold of her, shake her. Just to stop it. Before it got even more out of hand. He lunged at her, but she evaded him. He stumbled, recovered. Then he was ashamed at thinking so ill of her and stood quite still, simply murmuring her name like an incantation, imploring her to stop. Finally Tonya did. She straightened up, her tear-stained cheeks shining in the moonlight, took breath and said: 'Goodnight, Major Owzat.' He shook his head as if she had cursed him.

Jack watched her walk away, shrugged uneasily and

then got into the Jeep. But his foot would not, could not, press the starter. And he seemed to be holding his breath – or was his breath holding him? Finally, after ten minutes or so, he swung out of the Jeep and ran in the direction Tonya had taken. He knew which tent had been allotted to her. It was just behind the church. Why, only the day before she had asked him to admire its rugs, its cushions, its meagre furnishings. She had offered him tea, which he'd accepted. And she had smiled at him over the modest samovar and he'd almost expressed what he really felt, had almost said: 'I love you.'

Approaching the church, Jack spotted a Cossack on picket duty. For lack of a rifle the man carried a pickaxe. Jack stopped running, took breath, and proceeded to Tonya's tent by another route.

There was a glow of candlelight within and a long chink of it, bright as a scimitar, hung in the rug-draped entrance. Seeing this, Jack found he was smiling, then laughing, because he was wondering whether to knock. But how the hell did you knock on a couple of hanging carpets? The absurd thought was a balm, a blessing. It vanquished any further doubt, any remaining guilt. What had been said in denial, hesitation and anger beside the Jeep was no longer important. Only this moment and its consequence mattered. Jack spoke her name.

Tonya's face appeared in the chink of light. She was asking in a whisper if he were he. Jack realised he was merely a dim figure standing within the moonshadow of the little church. He stepped two paces to the entrance of the tent and crouched in front of her. And at once he was telling her without compunction, with no reservations at all, that he was a blind fool and had come to make his peace with her. Would she accept him or had he blotted his copybook for ever? She didn't know this phrase, asked what it meant, but as he began to explain she held out her hand and led him in.

Once inside the tent it was just about possible for Jack to stand up near the middle. But it was easier to sit down on the rug, among three cushions beside the low camp bed. Two candles in wax-encrusted cigarette tins were the only sources of light. Tonya drew glasses of tea from the samovar. They sipped them without once breaking the look that had grown between them. They were becoming each other's eyes. Then, almost in unison, they set their glasses aside and leant forward, one to the other.

SIX

After that night I didn't see Jack for several days. I kept my hurt to myself, wondering what could have happened. Brigadier Bakturov was equally anxious, though of course for less personal – or should I say sentimental? – reasons. Where were the new guns Jack had promised him? His men were beginning to murmur. And naturally he expected me to be able to answer for Jack. Twice I walked down to Selsen to try to speak to him first – on my own behalf, I admit, but also on Bakturov's. Each time I had just missed him, they said. He was very busy just then – up to his ears in admin. In that case, should they not appoint another liaison officer to us? I said. They told me not to worry. The walk back to Grubenfeld seemed very long.

Was the truth really that Jack could not face me? I wondered. Could he not bear to be loved by me now we had surrendered to each other? Was he as childish as that? I feared he was. I told myself, while praying, that I was wrong and wrong again, that Englishmen were all the same – sunny faces but dark inside.

The next morning he arrived, looking pale, almost ill. He refused to speak to Bakturov and insisted I come with him for what he called 'a quiet word'.

We walked into the woods beyond the latrine area he'd

encouraged us to make. Foolishly I thought the change in him was due to me. But it wasn't. I had flattered myself. In those days I was in many aspects a stupid girl. Even though I had seen many terrible things I still refused to believe they were all there was to life. Or indeed that the world, that human beings, were necessarily, inevitably, invariably cruel. Against all the brutal evidence of my short existence I remained the youthful optimist!

First Jack informed me our affair was at an end. I did not get angry. I didn't say that 'affair' was too grand a word for so short-lived, so incomplete a business. Why, we had only known each other for three weeks, spent just one night together. I didn't say I thought my love had been misplaced, or that I had been infatuated and then deceived by his apparent scruples and his sense of honour. No, I'm afraid I became just like him.

I said – it's difficult to believe this now, the times are so different – I said, 'Yes, Jack, I understand.' Though I didn't. Not at all. And I added – oh, the fool I was! – 'Yes, we've both been foolish. I especially. I suppose it was because peace seemed to have come at last with the spring and brought so many possibilities of newness – new loves, new generosities, new gratitudes, new worlds.' And I made it worse. I went on to say I realised how deeply he cared for his faraway wife, his unseen daughter, and there had never been any question of my supplanting them in his affections. This was untrue. There was nothing I wanted more, but I couldn't admit that, not any more, not even to myself.

Naturally he agreed with everything I said. And that was that. I needn't relate anything more, I think, I hope. It was so crude, so banal. As are all renunciations of real feelings. After all, how do you dress up the creation of nothingness, the establishment of separation, the making of a void?

'And now you wish to make some sort of boundary for us, Jack?'

'On that side of things, yes, I must.'

'Very well. You have. It's done.'

'But in our official capacities we continue, of course. That is, you as my interpreter.'

'Of course.'

'Good. There's still quite a job to be finished here, you see.'

'Helping the Cossack nation?'

'Quite so.'

'Are you all right? You look rather pale.' I'd learned the use of 'rather', a fine English word, almost as useful as 'sorry'.

'I'm fine. On top form.'

'Poor Jack.'

'What?'

'For a moment I thought you were making fun of yourself. You know, a parody, yes?'

'I'm serious! Never more so!' He was sweating and his eyes were alert as if he feared we might be overheard or interrupted.

I said, 'There's no one here but us.' Still he didn't look directly at me. 'Don't worry. I'll take the blame, Jack. I know I've asked too much of you.'

'Well, there is something in that, yes, actually.'

And suddenly he looked again as he had first looked to

me: dislikable. But, despite this, I didn't recognise his words for quite the lies, the smokescreen, they were. Oh, I was so deluded that day. His pallor, and his nervousness weren't due to me alone. No. Behind him, behind Jack become Major Kempe again, lay things he could not speak of. Yes, literally quite unspeakable things. He was hiding another truth far, far worse than his sentimental notions of propriety concerning him and me.

'Speaking as liaison officer, Tonya, I must ask you to inform Brigadier Bakturov he is to make himself, and all his officers, not the men, just those of commissioned rank, ready to embus tomorrow. It'll be an early start. I'll be here with Tom Surtees, our adjutant – you've met him, of course – yes, we'll be here with transport at 0700 hours.'

'An early start? Where are you going?'

'Mittelthal.'

'Why?'

'Conference. All Cossack officers in the British sector to be addressed by the GOC. Everyone to attend. No exceptions.'

'You sound like a notice board, Jack.'

'Please don't joke.'

'I wasn't.'

'They'll all be back by 1800 hours. So they can come just as they are. They'll get a midday meal, tell them.'

'A day trip?'

'Excellent. Your English is superb.'

'Please, Jack, please. Please talk like you used to.'

'I am.'

'And smile perhaps?' He did not reply to this. So I said, 'But why must all our officers travel to Mittelthal? Apart from those here there must be hundreds, thousands, all around?'

'Possibly. But that isn't my concern. I'm only responsible for this encampment. For Grubenfeld. Understood?'

'Not really, no.'

'Well, that's how it is.'

'I think you must be present when I tell Brigadier Kolya. I'm sure he will have lots of questions, too.'

'No time now. Tell him he can ask me tomorrow morning. At 0700 hours. I'll see the pair of you then.'

He saluted me. I pleaded with him to stay. To explain a little more. It seemed so strange for so many people to have to displace themselves just to be addressed by one man. Couldn't the British general come to Grubenfeld? Wouldn't that be more efficient? I was pleased at producing the word 'efficient'; it seemed so in keeping with Jack's new tone. But he refused to answer my questions however well put, repeating he was busy, he had a lot on his plate, these were his instructions, cheerio. And he went. Only then did I sit down and cry.

Inevitably he was as good as his word. The next morning, with dawn already broken but the sun not yet high enough to dispel the lurking ground mist, he arrived followed by four lorries and with another Jeep bringing up the rear. The first three-tonner contained several soldiers, who jumped out smartly and fell into line commanded by a sergeant carrying a Sten gun.

Jack's Jeep had a bulky radio transmitter occupying the back seat. It was attended by a hunched soldier with earphones round his neck. The radio spat and crackled. It seemed to leak liverish bad temper. As the other vehicles drew up I recognised the driver of the second Jeep as Captain Surtees. He was not only younger than Jack but taller and slimmer. If Jack was what is called Anglo-Saxon in his physique, then Tom Surtees was more Celtic, I suppose.

Jack and he came up to where Brigadier Bakturov and Father Sacha stood waiting. All the other officers were drawn up behind. They stood in a square, a phalanx, hedged about by unruly groups of women and children with goats and geese. Bakturov had insisted his men look soldierly, but they were uneasy, doubtful and seemed diminished, too, without their guns and horses. As always, I was to one side as the interpreter.

Jack and Tom saluted us. It is difficult to describe the way they performed this familiar military greeting. It seemed so casual and yet was calculated, studied. As a recipient of it you were honoured by a kind of careless grace. You felt flattered and found yourself disarmed. Only the officers in the British forces had the knack of it. Their ordinary soldiers saluted just as ours did – like anxious automatons.

We nodded back, smiled carefully.

'Good morning, Brigadier. 'Morning, Tonya. All present and correct, I take it? Good. Let's get moving, shall we?' Jack spoke heartily, in a militaristic manner. The private man had vanished.

At once Bakturov burst out with all the suspicious questions I'd asked the day before. I started to translate, but Jack flushed and interrupted me.

'We've been through this! I said yesterday, I told you, we've all got to attend this conference because the general hasn't the time to come to us. He can't possibly visit every camp in the area. How can he? Nor should we expect him to. His schedule is awfully tight. For him to come up here from Mittelthal would take up a whole morning and Grubenfeld is, as I said and as I say again, just one camp among many. So do make that clear, please, would you, once and for all? It'll save much valuable time. Thank you.' And he sighed with sharp, rhetorical impatience.

Bakturov, who had sensed the gist of what Jack was saying and not mistaken his manner, spoke again, trying to control his anger. He announced he wanted, indeed he demanded, Jack's assurance, his very own word, that he, Bakturov, together with all his officers, would be returned safe and sound that evening. Jack must swear this in front of everyone present . . . and the sweep of Bakturov's arm embraced us all, men and women, children, even the livestock. He spoke as father of his people, he said. Even as I began to translate his words I saw Jack and Captain Surtees grow colder, become more distant. Jack didn't reply immediately. He turned to his brother officer and they conferred in low tones. I couldn't catch what they were saying, but when Jack did face me again he looked peeled. 'Peeled' is the only word. Like a tree that has been struck by lightning and stripped of its bark by time and weather.

'Such a reassurance is not necessary,' he said.

'But we want it, Jack.'

'We agreed, didn't we? On duty you address me as "sir" or "Major Kempe" or am I mistaken?'

'Very well. Forgive me.'

'Of course.'

'Without your sworn word they won't get into the lorries.'

'Nonsense.'

'It isn't. You see, there have been so many rumours. That's why the ataman needs your promise of safe conduct to the conference and back.'

'Rumours? What sort of rumours?'

'About boats from England. And from America too.'

'What on earth's that to do with us?'

'Many Cossacks who have been refugees in those countries are being sent by sea to Odessa.'

'Sounds a tall story to me.'

'But people are jumping overboard, they say. They try to escape or to die – either is better than going back to Russia. Stalin will kill them.'

'Now, don't let's exaggerate. One can always find people only too ready to spread alarm and despondency. But you can take it from me, Tonya, that these rumours are groundless. And nothing to do with us here. They need not affect general morale, all right?'

Tom Surtees said to Jack, 'I do think we should get a move on, sir, don't you?'

I explained to Bakturov what Jack had said, but he simply repeated his demand.

'But surely he trusts us? Up to now I've always understood he did. Respect on both sides?'

'He says he would have trusted you still if you had kept your word concerning the issue of new weapons. You have taken theirs and they have nothing now.'

'But, again, I've said! There was a cock-up. But they'll get them soon, don't worry.'

On learning this, Bakturov nodded and smiled without conviction. He beckoned Father Sacha to come forward. The priest unwrapped a small object from a threadbare velvet cloth. It was our most sacred icon. It measured not more than twenty centimetres square. The faces of the Mother of God and the infant Jesus peeped out at you from beaten silver.

'The Brigadier says if you will not declare your oath to the assembled company you must swear to him on this,' I said.

For the first time I saw open anger in Jack. I had, I realised, completely underestimated the power of his English Protestant feelings. While he respected such sacred things, they were not something he could swear by. For him that would have been idolatrous. Besides, the whole point of Jack's honour was that it had to be taken for granted. For him to put his hand on an icon, however sacred, however precious, however beautiful, and repeat an oath was out of the question.

'Tell the Brigadier he has my word. And tell him too I am insulted. You can put that thing away. He has my word. The word of an Englishman.'

I suspect Jack was even more vehement than he might otherwise have been because Captain Surtees stood beside him. His presence highlighted Jack's dilemma. It wasn't just that he'd been so friendly to us, it was that he'd gone further: in the eyes of his fellow officers he had, to use the English colonialist phrase, 'gone native'. I knew that in the mess at Garten they had teased him about his little Russia up in the valley, and about me too.

It was this natural kindness and warmth of spirit that

had betrayed him. He was in a most terrible fix. I think part of him longed to tell us the truth, to invite us all to escape while there was still time, to fade away into the hills, but he couldn't. Nor did he try to. Quite the opposite.

His anger astonished Brigadier Kolya and me, too, come to that. Bakturov apologised, said he had made a mistake and of course he trusted him. He accepted his word – it was known to be his bond, wasn't it? The English were world famous for their honour, their sense of fair play, their love of freedom. He and his officers would go to the conference to hear what the great British general was going to propose for their future – the future of Cossackia.

Jack remained unmollified. I was surprised he didn't accept Bakturov's capitulation and compliance more graciously. Instead he said, 'I should damn well think so!' and turned away, his anger curdling, I suspected, into shame.

Tom Surtees and the sergeant with the Sten gun counted our men as they clambered up into the lorries. Jack sat in his Jeep. Once everyone was embussed (I learned a lot of soldiers' patois in those days), Tom came over to Jack and gave him the total. The head count. Jack turned to his radio operator and told him to inform Sunray – a code which on the air identified their colonel – that they were on their way with one hundred and fourteen prisoners of war. I could not believe my ears. *Prisoners of war*?

'Why do you call them that?' I said.

'What?'

'Prisoners of war.'

'Because it's true. According to the book. That's their designation.'

'But why haven't you told us?'

'Give us a chance. Only heard myself yesterday. Cheerio,' he said.

I could not speak. I was horrified. Prisoners of war? Us? No. But Jack had already started up, giving me no chance to question him further. He drove away shouting across to Tom unnecessarily – it was just military noise – to bring up the rear. It was then that I noticed that the soldier sitting in the back of Captain Surtees' Jeep was cradling not a rifle but a Bren gun across his knees. They used to call it a light machine gun, but I thought it looked quite heavy and Jack had told me it could fire off twenty rounds in as many seconds.

As the convoy turned on to the road one of the women, Katya Ivanovna, came to me with a baby at her breast and little Varya holding her hand. She said Varya had wanted to say goodbye to her special friend, the English major, but she had told her daughter this wasn't the time for that. He would come back that evening when they all came back, wouldn't he? I nodded and said I was sure he would. She smiled and believed me, telling Varya she would see her major soon. But I knew, not from logic but from an instinctive fear, that my assurance had been false. Without concealing the truth (for I did not know it) I had nevertheless lied.

Jack was taking the bends too fast, leaving the three-tonners far behind. Damn it, he was driving like an idiotic young subaltern issued for the first time with a brand-new Jeep. He slowed down, allowing the convoy to close up behind him. He heard himself mutter an apology to Tom Surtees even though Tom hadn't said a word.

He still felt dreadful. Mind you, it was his own fault. A self-inflicted wound, as it were. He had drunk hard for three days, his binge ending the night before last in a rabid game of Bucks' Ducks after dinner. This particular mess-game was entirely pointless, studiedly fatuous and a regimental favourite. It was a kind of compound leapfrog heavily biased against the more senior officers present. To be played correctly all needed to be thoroughly boiled, preferably incapable. Furthermore, it was imperative not to lose. If you did you paid the final penalty.

The game proceeded in reverse order of seniority: the youngest subaltern bent over to be leapfrogged by the next, who then joined on ahead of him, and so on until you had a sort of swaying caterpillar of ten or so backsides to vault over – lengthwise. If you failed to clear the lot in one elongated leap, if you fell by the wayside, or landed astraddle in the middle, that's when you were obliged to pay the price. And considering what you'd already drunk it was a trifle risky. You had to down a pint of claret from an eighteenth-century punchbowl without drawing breath. In Garten they had made do with a pudding basin and the local plonk. Legend had it that even the claret was an effete substitute for port, which had been the required brew until the Boer War. Apparently the Bucks had lost an honoured guest, a major general no less, who'd downed the port and promptly expired horridly on the carpet.

That night Jack had been the penultimate jumper. Only Colonel Billy was left to follow him. The line of braced backs looked formidably long. Nor was there much of a run-up in the bell tent that did duty as the mess. Ten upside-down, very red faces were all turned to him, yelling: 'Come on, Grandad!' He took a deep breath, ran, leapt and, by some miracle known only to the truly drunk, cleared the lot. He landed flat on his face, but cheers rang in his ears as he staggered to his feet and bent down in the doorway to form the last frog Colonel Billy had to clear. In unison the upside-down line chanted at their colonel: 'Bucks' Ducks one! Bucks' Ducks two! Bucks' Ducks three!' Billy rushed it and his leap got him no further than the middle, where he lay prone for a second or two before rolling off on to the floor. Most of the line collapsed with him.

Everyone straightened up, delighted. The game had ended exactly as had been hoped. Their colonel must pay the price. The basin full of red wine was brought solemnly to him.

'My God,' Billy said. 'The last time I had to do this I thought everything would drop off.' They all laughed, chanted Bucks' Ducks one, two, three again ... and Colonel Billy proceeded to pour the plonk neatly down his throat without a pause for breath. It was a remarkable, open-throated, steady drain which drew admiration from everyone. Not a drop was spilt or dribbled. Jack heard murmurs of appreciation all round him. The basin was drained to the dregs. With a gracious almost hieratic gesture, Colonel Billy returned it to the mess waiter. For a moment you would have thought he had become stone-cold sober; then his eyes rolled heavenwards, his lips just managed to enunciate 'Up the Bucks' and he fell bang forwards, poleaxed. Everyone cheered.

The next morning Jack faced Colonel Billy in the bell tent which was the CO's office. They both agreed, ashen-faced, throb-headed, that the less said about the night before the better. Next Billy explained for the first time what had happened at Brigade and what their latest orders were. When he'd finished, Jack felt as struck down, riven, poleaxed, as Billy had the night before. He couldn't speak. He just stared at his commanding officer, not wanting to believe him.

'I'm sorry, Jack,' Billy said twice. 'But that, I'm afraid, is how it is.'

'You might've told me, sir.'

'I couldn't. The information was restricted. Battalion commanders and above.'

'But these new orders aren't?'

'Still confidential, Jack.'

'We've got to pass these people across to the Russians?'

'So it would appear, yes.'

'And you knew all this last week? When you asked me to organise the weapons' hand-over?'

'Not all of it, no. I certainly hadn't heard of this GOC-to-address-all-Cossacks nonsense. But it was vital to disarm them without raising the alarm. That's all I can say. Surely you can see that? Or they could've turned their weapons on us – on our blokes.'

'But to get me to lie! When you were already aware there was to be no new small-arms issue from us. Oh, Billy.'

'Frankly, I thought you too had seen through that one, Jack. And gone along with it. A nod being no more necessary than a wink.'

'Well, I didn't. I believed you.'

'You astonish me.'

'And they in their turn believed me!'

'Odd. I've always thought of you as, well, rather more experienced than this, Grandad.'

'Not in lying, sir! Sorry!' He had really snapped then.

'Well, put it this way, at least you lied in good faith.' Jack was lost for words. Billy continued, 'And anyway what else could I have done? Do try to see my side of it, Jack. It was still hush-hush.'

'And I still feel tricked!'

'I was obliged to deceive you but comforted myself by thinking you'd seen through the whole thing and were prepared to carry it out.'

'Very well, I was naïve.'

'And I'm very sorry, too. Personally, really so. But there you are.'

They fell silent. Both knew something was irrevocably lost between them. It was as well the war was over. They could not have entrusted their lives to each other any longer. Billy avoided Jack's eye.

'It was a shabby thing,' Jack said finally.

'I've apologised as far as I can. I'm not prepared to go further. We both have a job to do.'

'Yes. Best move on. Yes. This next phase, sir? What does it entail?'

'A number of things, actually. Having achieved our first objective – disarming them – we now proceed to the second.' Already Billy was sounding brisker, more his old self. 'And that, of course, is this conference, as it's laughingly described, at Mittelthal.'

'Will the general actually come to address them, do you think?'

'No idea – and, between ourselves, I'm not going to ask.'

'But shouldn't we?'

'Waste of breath, Jack. Now, for the present the aim is to separate the officers from their men, and also from their women and children. You, as our liaison officer, will inform them that they are to embus at 0700 hours –'

'But having let them down over the small arms how can we expect them to swallow this?'

'Jack, please. We haven't let them down to date, have we? Well, not so far as they know. All you've got to do is just keep up the idea of the weaponry being on its way. Put it down to Ordnance or idleness, admin cock-up, vagaries of war –'

'But this is peace now, sir.'

'Not till we've coped with these bloody Cossacks, it isn't! There's twenty-five thousand of them in this sector alone.'

'Hardly surprising. They thought the Austrians had allotted it to them.'

'Well, too bad! They were misinformed.'

'So I've got to lie to them again? Knowingly, this time?'

'Please, Jack, I've said! I feel as badly about it as you do.'

'But *I've* got to do it, Billy.' The CO did not reply. Jack said, 'And what will happen to them at Mittelthal? Or is that still confidential?'

'Yes. A reception area has been prepared. Joint op. – Sappers, Pioneers.'

'An internment camp?'

'Depot, really. They're to stay there until, well, the next move.'

'Mittelthal being the railhead?'

'Exactly. The line connects us to the Russian zone.'

'The logistics speak for themselves, don't they?'

'A glance at the map makes it reasonably clear, I agree.'

Again each found it difficult to speak. Jack remembered the sound of rain on the canvas – a light pattering as of fingertips on your cheek, a caress of Tonya's that had charmed him. He drew breath and made up his mind. Yes, in the circumstances, it was the only thing to do, yes. And he told Colonel Billy, in fact he formally requested it there and then, he wished to be relieved of his duties as liaison officer to the Cossacks in the 5th's area of responsibility. Yes, and that it take effect forthwith, from that very moment that morning – 0813 hours.

'No, Jack,' Colonel Billy said. 'That can't be. It isn't on, I'm afraid.'

Jack was horrified. And angry. 'But why not? I can't lie to them again, sir. Once is bad enough! No, I can't do it. And you can't ask me to. Not again, sir. No.'

'You wouldn't be suggesting you might refuse to obey an order, Jack?'

'No! I'm asking for a posting, Billy! A transfer to somewhere else. Wherever you like. The Far East, if need be. Anywhere but here. And it's a fair request, sir, a reasonable one, an honourable one.'

'Leaving the rest of us to do the dirty work? Generous of you.'

'But I've become their friend, sir! With respect, no one else has. Well, not to the extent I have. They trust me, like me; the kiddies take my hand, expect me to bring them chocolate, and most days I do. Besides, we've supplied them with so much – food, medicines. They bake white bread now thanks to our efforts, sir. Oh, damn it all, Billy!

You can't ask me to lie to them again. Not when I've taught them cricket. You can't. No.'

'But all that was before, Grandad. Before I attended that initial briefing, before we got these orders. And you can believe me when I say Brigade and Division are no happier than we are about this job. The GOC's admitted it's a thoroughly unwelcome one. He's made no bones about that. If you want to blame anyone it'd better be Winston himself – not even the War Office, oh no. Churchill and Roosevelt, they're the prime movers. They made the deal with Uncle Joe. On the Black Sea somewhere, I've heard. And Stalin wants all Soviet citizens at large in the Allied zones sent back home to him, pronto. So it's up to us to post them along.'

'But these aren't Soviet citizens, sir. These people are Cossacks.'

'Yes, I pointed that out at Brigade. It wasn't accepted.'

'But it's true, Billy.'

'The guidelines are: one, the onus is on the individual to prove his claim for exemption. And, two, if in doubt we're to treat any such as a Soviet citizen, OK? Understood?'

'You haven't replied to my request for a posting, sir.'

'I thought it was obvious. No. The answer's no. There can be no question of a posting. You will continue as liaison officer precisely because these people know and trust you.'

'Those are your orders, sir?'

'Yes.'

'I must continue to lie to them?'

'Jack, please. I'm asking you not to allow your personal feelings to interfere with your duties. That's all. The job is the job. Besides, as you will appreciate, if I pull you out now, they'll smell a rat, won't they?'

For the third and last time that morning Jack found it impossible to speak. He simply stared at Colonel Billy, wondering if this was really the younger man he'd been so happy to serve under.

Billy said, 'You must understand, Jack, I've already put those very same objections myself to the GOC. And equally strongly. And I got the same dusty answer I've had to give you.'

Jack still could not reply. Almost pleadingly, Billy added that he was truly sorry, but they must do their duty and get back home.

'I just wish I hadn't got to know them so well,' Jack said at last.

'Can't be helped, Grandad.'

'What's done is done?'

'Precisely.'

'Except it isn't, is it? Not just yet?'

'True. But anyway you'll carry on? As we all must?'

Jack had nodded. Later that day he'd gone up to Grubenfeld to tell Tonya what was expected. It hadn't been easy. He felt now that his drinking bout after that one brief ecstatic night with her had been triggered not merely by personal guilt but by an intuition of public infamy to come. An infamy in which he was now intimately and inextricably embroiled. Was he not even now heading a convoy leading these men to an uncertain destiny?

As the road straightened out, the crowded lorries behind him began to sing. An innocuous, repetitive ballad. Oh, their voices! How they could sing! Every single one of them seemed to have perfect pitch. Jack had heard something to the effect that in Shakespeare's time people could sing as readily and as tunefully. The Cossacks' singing always sounded to him as if it came from such a golden age.

Jack's radio operator said, 'Reckon they've cheered up, sir?' Jack nodded, and felt a little better himself. Perhaps he'd exaggerated, perhaps he'd been mistaken, perhaps all would be well?

But any such emotion evaporated on reaching and passing through Mittelthal. Out from the station in an easterly direction, past a few decrepit factories, grass-grown sidings and a cobbled stockyard, the road crossed over a single rusted railway track and then ran beside a barbed-wire fence until they arrived at a main gateway where a traffic controller from the 1st King's Own called the convoy to a halt while a string of empty three-tonners identical with theirs bumped its way out. This entrance was dominated by a watchtower – the wood of its construction looked noticeably raw and the corrugated-iron roof almost mirrorlike in its newness – while within the high-wire perimeter Jack could see rows of oblong huts. Apart from the traffic marshal there was hardly any military presence – the watchtower did not appear to be manned – but, even so, the place had a forlorn air. And the drivers driving out struck Jack as looking rather sullen.

Having left them to tick over for fifteen minutes, long after the other convoy had gone, the traffic controller summoned them in. Jack led the way, turning to his right as indicated. The convoy followed. No one sang any more.

When they stopped, soldiers in platoon strength were

there to greet them. The subaltern in charge saluted Jack politely. He looked like a pink cherub just tumbled from the scudding cumulus above.

'Good morning, sir. Found your way here OK? No difficulties *en route*?'

'No. We came straight here.'

'Oh, good-oh. The last convoy lost six chaps.'

'Lost them?'

'Jumped out and legged it, they did.'

'Oh, I see.'

'But you're full strength?'

'Yes. Didn't anyone stop them?'

'Apparently not. Rather a poor show really, sir, I'd say.'

Beyond he could see groups of Cossacks in their black capes huddled together, conferring in low voices. Occasionally a face would turn to glance at Jack's convoy.

'How many have arrived so far?'

'Three to four hundred. Plenty more are on their way, though.'

'The general had better have something worthwhile to tell them, hadn't he?' Jack said, trying to test how much this young officer had been told.

'Well, I don't see him actually coming here to spell it out in detail, do you, sir? More than his life's worth, what?' He laughed chummily, uneasily.

'Ah, so down here in Mittelthal you, too, reckon this conference idea is just hot air? We did – up in Selsen.'

'More or less. We'll have to see, won't we, sir?'

'Right,' Jack turned to Tom, 'let's get on with it. Disembus them, Captain Surtees, would you?'

Tom saluted and went to supervise the operation while

Jack, at the subaltern's invitation, walked over to inspect one of the huts. It was clean but bleak. Rows of straw palliasses, each with a single grey blanket folded and squared off on top, graced the concrete floor. At the further end there was a standpipe and two buckets. Trefoil air inlets above eye level had been drilled through the walls. There were no windows.

'My Lord,' Jack said. 'The minute they see this accommodation they're going to twig, aren't they? They'll realise they aren't exactly here for their health.'

'Hence our orders, sir, not to allow them inside the huts just yet.'

'Oh? Wait till they've all been gathered in, then break it to them – is that the idea?'

'I'm inclined to think so, sir.'

'Me too. Not all that pretty, really.'

'No, I can't say I care for it, sir. I don't think any of us do. I've told my blokes it's a job like any other. Just one of those things. They're being rather good about it, considering. They're due for demob, after all. Our platoon joker quoted the old chestnut *dear mother, it's a bastard, dear son, so are you but don't tell your dad*, which helped us get on with it. Goes against the grain, though.'

Jack nodded and they went out into the sun-bright, wind-clean air.

Brigadier Bakturov, with a cluster of his more senior officers around him, was expostulating at Tom. Jack went across, but without Tonya, and although Tom tried his French all they could communicate each to the other was angry doubt and choking distrust. Jack asked the King's Own subaltern if there was an interpreter on hand. There wasn't. So he and Tom were obliged to shrug apologetically at Brigadier Kolya and made good their escape. One officer spat on the ground as they turned away but Jack pretended he hadn't noticed that.

As they drove out of the main gate, with the empty lorries clanking and echoing bumpily behind them, they passed a substantial convoy. Or, rather, a series of convoys like theirs, all stuck nose to tail, waiting to get into the depot. The queue seemed to stretch for almost half a mile. And every lorry was packed with anxious, uniformed Cossacks. Occasionally a face would crane round a canvas canopy, trying to see what the hold-up was really about. Military police now patrolled busily. Neither Tom nor Jack spoke. Their single thought was to get back to Selsen. Without uttering a word each had made it clear he would only – or was it *could* only? – think about this operation later. It wasn't something to be analysed on the spot amid idle engine chug, stinking exhaust fumes and plain bloody, squittering fear. Both could sense it, on the increase, by the minute.

SEVEN

I spent most of that day in the school and at the church. I had promised the teachers (the camp had two teachers just as it had two priests) I would teach some of the older children a bit of English. They were eager to learn but I found it very difficult that day after the officers had gone. Also they always asked me about England and about London because they thought, naturally enough, that I had visited that famous, faraway country. I had told them time and time again I hadn't, but that did not prevent them asking me about Big Ben, the King and Queen and English beer – was it true they drank it hot? On any other day I would have laughed and told them to ask Jack the next time he visited the camp, but that day I couldn't find a smile. I'm afraid I was a very bad teacher to them. Finally one of the boys asked me why I was so sad. That was the last straw. I said I wasn't, just rather busy, and handed them back to the care of their proper teacher. With these wretched fibs depressing my heart, I went to find Father Sacha.

He, too, was upset. He thought he should have insisted that he go with Bakturov and the others. He felt ashamed that he had not insisted. But it is just a military conference, Father, I said. Did I really believe that? he asked. I said I had to, we both had to, everybody must, surely? What else was there? He nodded and said we should go and pray. I was glad to go with him.

The little church was quite crowded. Gradually Father Sacha gathered our private prayers into a concerted service. We even sang a psalm and were all considerably comforted, but then a child came and said soldiers were taking the horses. We couldn't believe it.

But it was true. Soldiers I did not especially recognise but who wore the same regimental shoulder flashes as Jack were leading the horses out of the corrrals and away towards the road. I ran across to them with the other men and women and accosted the leading officer, a major, who seemed familiar and yet not – I must have seen him out and about in Selsen, I suppose. He had an arrow-thin moustache.

'What are you doing?' I said.

'What does it look like?' he answered. 'We're impounding the horses.'

'But these are our horses. I mean, they belong here. To the people here.'

'That may well be, Miss Parvic, but our orders are to take in all the horses. And bring 'em down to Selsen. Directive from Brigade – to be applied throughout the sector. There've been a lot of complaints from local farmers. All these Cossack horses running wild.'

Once again it was difficult for me to believe what I was hearing from the English. 'But these horses aren't running wild,' I said. 'They're never allowed to run wild. They're too precious. That's why they are kept behind fences. Please – you cannot take these horses.'

'Sorry – orders are orders.'

'First you take the guns, now while the ataman and the officers are away at the conference you take the horses.' Behind me some of the men and women were muttering angrily. The soldiers had tensed.

'I'm sure reparation will be made,' the major said. 'It's all taken care of. It'll be in hand. You can assure the people here they're bound to be compensated. Oh, yes. No problem about that.' *He* knew and *I* knew he was lying. The last of the horses were being led out. One of our men shouted and three others ran forward with him trying to seize them by their rope halters, but six of the soldiers intervened and a fight began. It was an unfair encounter because the soldiers used their rifles as clubs.

The major shouted an order to his other soldiers. They fixed bayonets and ran forward to form a line to prevent anyone else coming to help our people. We all watched in hot indignation. The major told me to come with him. And he marched over to where the protestors were being beaten down. Two already lay on the ground with their mouths full of blood. Out of habit I started to go with this major, then I stopped. I hung back. Was I to act as interpreter for *him*? For this? Never! Let him explain as best he could – which wouldn't be at all. He would get nowhere and serve him right! But I was wrong. This major could speak German. When he realised I hadn't accompanied him he shouted in German at the men on the ground. Most if not all Cossacks, having tried to fight as equals beside the Germans against the Stalinists but having been cheated and exploited by them, understood German well enough. So this English major could insult our men as efficiently as any Nazi storm-trooper. And all the while he was snapping and barking, the horses were led further away, with the sun burnishing their backs, creating iridescent rainbows upon their well-groomed haunches.

After they had all gone we gathered in the space between the church and the school. Father Sacha and Father Ivan asked me, in the absence of the ataman, to speak to the people. Of course there was nothing I could say that they didn't already know – since the taking of the horses I was as unsure as they were of the safe return at six o'clock of Brigadier Kolya and all the other officers. Was this perhaps a calculated move by Father Sacha to get me to speak? I had noticed – so maybe he had too – several persons muttering together and looking at me as if they suspected I knew more than in fact I did and surmised I was in some way a collaborator with the now openly hated and distrusted English.

Yes, I think he asked me to speak to make quite sure everybody present recognised me as being on their side. He manoeuvred me into solidarity with their cause. Not of course that I needed so very much persuading. But from that moment I was seen by others – and I saw myself – as no mere go-between any more. Now, through my own words, though saying nothing new and repeating only what we had all experienced, I became at one with the Cossack people of Grubenfeld and also their representative as well. From then on I was their ambassador rather than Major Kempe's interpreter.

After this we dispersed. The afternoon seemed very long. Towards six o'clock, as the sun sank lower, people began to drift like ghosts in the slanting light towards the road to watch for the return of their menfolk. That hour passed, so did seven o'clock, then eight o'clock. The dusk enveloped us. People said little. The children became quieter and quieter. When it was nine o'clock I said I would go down to Selsen to ask the British what had happened. Father Ivan offered to come with me, but I told him I preferred to go alone and he could trust me. He nodded and said he knew I would do everything I could. I said perhaps there was some very obvious, very simple explanation, you never knew, did you? But his eyes said, and I think mine did too, that you always do know really when things are really wrong.

I ran and walked all the way down to Selsen, doing what I had been taught is called in England 'scouts' pace.' You are supposed to preserve your energies even though you are travelling quickly. You run fifty paces, you walk fifty paces. Everybody all over the globe does it quite naturally, of course, but it takes the English to appropriate such a thing and then export it again as their own invention. Jack used to move as if he owned the earth. We have heard a great amount about the Germans determining to be the master race, but in Austria in 1945 the English *were* the master race. At least in their own opinion. Perhaps that's why they did not notice what they were doing? I believe sincerely they did not know, but that does not excuse them. Not in my eyes. They will never be able to say they are sorry to me again. To exonerate some things is to murder the innocent twice.

Tonya's shock at the removal of the horses equalled Jack's when, on his return to Selsen, he saw them hitched in lines to the fence behind the QM stores. Unfortunately Colonel Billy hadn't been there to receive his immediate protest, let alone offer an explanation. The fact of the matter needed no explaining, however: it was only too evident, plain as daylight. Advantage had been taken of Bakturov's absence to remove another piece of the Cossacks' strength. First their weapons, then their most effective personnel, now their mobility.

Militarily speaking, it made good sense. And it would have happened throughout the sector – to all the other Cossack camps. Yes. Except these people hadn't been the enemy, had they? Well, hardly. And he'd been appointed to be their friend. To care for them. Or so he'd thought. Certainly he'd behaved as such. What a mistake. He really should have been more circumspect. Not allowed himself to succumb to such gypsy charm, such farouche nobility, the magical innocence of their encampment. And Tonya, too, she had been part of that golden vision. All gone now. Vanished with the dew. No. Correction. He was deceiving himself. No. Destroyed by order.

Tom had just fetched his bottle of gin. They were in Jack's billet in Selsen – an attic stinking sweetly of bats. Tom lolled in an old wicker chair while Jack sprawled on the bed. Tom was in shirtsleeve order. Jack had his boots off. Their unusual disarray owed something to the fact that, before Tom had gone down to his room to get hold of his ration of Beefeater, they had consumed what had been left of Jack's whisky: a good half, the better half, of a bottle of VAT 69, the Pope's phone number, as the routine pleasantry had it. But however much they drank, the thought of Mittelthal remained. Their shared silence on the drive up had seemed to imply, to carry with it, the hope that once back at HQ they could sort the whole thing out. Resolve each other's doubts. This hadn't happened.

'Me. Me do such a thing,' Jack heard himself saying for the umpteenth time.

'We ought just to demand immediate demobilisation, that's what, bloody pronto, Grandad,' Tom said. This was patent balderdash, which Tom as adjutant, and when sober, knew perfectly well. The blokes were forever coming to him to ask when they would be going home. When, when, when? But no one could actually demand demob. You had to wait for it. Wait and see.

'I asked Colonel Billy for a posting. Anywhere. The Far East. But did he listen? No, Tom, he did not. No.'

'So you said.'

'I did?'

'Lost count how many times, actually.'

'Oh? Sorry. Old ground, too much going over of. Sorry.'

'You told me your popsy thinks we –'

'Popsy?'

'Miss Parvic.'

'I wouldn't call her that, old son. Not my popsy.'

'Wouldn't you? Pretty enough. Good figure.'

'Please!' All of a sudden he was violently angry. He wouldn't – he would not – no – no – no, thank you – he would not have Tonya referred to so lightly. 'Kindly withdraw that . . . that epithet, Tom,' he said. 'At once!'

'What? Popsy?'

'Yes! Bloody Popsy! Withdraw it! Retract it!' he was shouting. He was beside himself with rage.

'Steady on, sir.' Tom was evidently shocked, abashed by Jack's unaccustomed fury.

'Do as I say!'

'Of course. Didn't realise you felt so strongly about your interpreter. Sorry. Just a turn of phrase. Anyway, as you wish – epithet withdrawn.'

'Thank you.'

'Which reminds me. As I was saying, your Miss Parvic, or so you tell me, thinks we apologise too much. Correct?'

'She doesn't.'

'But you told me she did! You bloody did, Grandad!'

'No. She thinks we say *sorry* too often.'

'Same bloody thing.'

'No. Different. Because ... because, Tom, she reckons we don't mean it when we say it.'

'Ah! I am with you now. Yes. I see what you mean, Grandad.'

'What *she* means, Tom.'

'Quite. Point taken. Absorbed. Yes.'

This rejoinder silenced them for some time. Jack now regretted sharing his thoughts with Tom, while Tom looked at Jack with new eyes. Surely Grandad could see what he was getting at? Of course he could grasp it. He might be a typical pre-war regular in some ways but in others he wasn't. He might sound rather thick from time to time but he wasn't really. He was as sensitive as the next man. All of them in the Bucks were. They were cultivated riflemen not boneheaded guardsmen, for God's sake. But these eternal military snobberies did nothing to ameliorate Tom's interior disgust at himself, at Jack, at everything.

The next thing Jack knew, he was pushing himself off

the bed, grabbing his boots and lacing them up with shaking fingers. And his mouth was spewing out fabulously mixed yet determined words about doing the right thing. Yes, he was telling Tom he had to go and face the music.

'Got to tell 'em, got to face 'em, go back up. Must. Least I can do. Only decent thing left. Must be decent, Tom, do you see?'

'But they'll murder you!'

'Have to risk that.'

Tom was genuinely alarmed. 'No, Grandad, you can't! You can't go up there and say their blokes are all behind barbed wire ready for shoving off to Russia in the morning.'

'I can't *not* go, Tom.'

'You bloody can!'

'No, that'd be wrong. Cowardly. That's the coward's way out.' He reached for his belt and holster.

'But you're drunk, Grandad.'

'Night air'll soon sober me up.'

'No! I can't let you go there. No. They'll tear you apart.' And Tom grabbed him by the arm, saying it was for his own good that he was preventing him leaving, thank you very much. Then they were struggling absurdly, half wrestling, with Jack shouting at Tom to let go and Tom calling him 'sir' over and over before elbowing him in the diaphragm so he fell back on the bed winded and utterly furious.

'Please, please,' Tom pleaded. 'Let's go and talk to Colonel Billy –'

'Done that! Been through it all.'

'Well, I'm not letting you go and that's that!'

Jack fought for breath, found it and pulled himself together. He stood up again. Oddly he felt rather steadier. 'You can't stop me, Tom,' he said. 'Don't try to this time or I'll kick up such a to-do you'll find yourself under arrest. I'll use my seniority, Tom, I promise you.'

'Very well. I'll come with you.' Ghost of a smile. 'Your support group, how's that?'

Jack shook his head.

'What's the matter?'

'Nothing – just I could wish you hadn't said that, Tom.'

'Said what?'

' "How's that". My nickname up there. Ever since I taught them cricket. I'm known as Major Howzat. Except they can't pronounce the aitch.'

'Oh, I see.'

'But I don't think you should come. I was the one who did the lying, not you. Twice.'

'But you didn't bloody know you were lying. Well, not the first time.'

'The second, I did. This morning.'

'Well, I was there, too.'

'Yes – but I did the talking. I obliged them to believe me.'

'Look if you insist on going, Jack, then for Christ's sake be vague. Prevaricate somehow. Tell them their chaps'll be back tomorrow or the next day.'

'Lie for a third time?'

'You can't tell them the truth!'

'Must. Yes. Whole point.'

'You can't! Self-preservation, sir!'

'Too late for that.'

Tonya's Story

'No. Please. No.'

They fell silent, staring at each other. Both recognised their quarrel was the more insoluble for being based on mutual well-meaning. Eventually Tom offered another suggestion, blushing as he spoke.

'Suppose we were both to go and tell them, on the quiet, to, well, you know, skedaddle? Push off? Fade gently away? Take to the hills? Before stage three of the operation?'

'There are simply too many of them for that, Tom.'

'But if it saved some?'

'It's a tempting thought.'

'I bet you other units are doing it. May have already. It'd be one way to make some sort of amends, wouldn't it?'

Jack supposed it might, but there was no time to ponder it further because they heard footsteps on the rickety stairs that led up to the attic and then the door juddered open and Tonya stood before them, pale as death.

The little room stank of alcohol and sweat. On my way in I'd been stopped by two sentries but, luckily, one of them recognised me and allowed me through the farmyard, indicating the way up to Jack's quarters. The farmyard was packed with the battalion's vehicles, so it was clear that they at least had returned from Mittelthal. All Jack said was, 'Oh, it's you, is it?'

'Where are they?' I said. Jack blushed. He looked awful. His eyes were inflamed. You might have imagined he'd been crying, but that was unthinkable, knowing him, so perhaps it was the drink or Captain Surtees' cigarette smoke. Whatever it was, he was red-eyed and uneasy. No, worse than uneasy: he was shifty. Jack, of all people. I was mortified. I suppose it was seeing him in such a state, when, earlier on, I had made him into such a hero. A kind of Sir Galahad or Sir Percival. Why, he had come from Albion, had he not? The seat, I had been told as a child, of all chivalry. But now he looked mean and ill-favoured.

'Where are they?' I repeated. 'You swore they'd come back. All of them. By eighteen hundred hours. Everyone's very worried up at the camp. Where are they? What's happened to Brigadier Bakturov? What did the general have to say when he addressed them? Please tell me, Jack! Oh, I'm sorry, I must call you *sir*, mustn't I? I'm sorry, sir, please tell me, sir. Please, sir. What's happened?'

'Well, as a matter of fact, there's been a slight delay –' Tom Surtees had begun to speak but I wasn't going to listen to him, oh, no! I would only attend to Jack.

I said to him, 'After you went they sent some other soldiers to take away the horses. You've taken our horses now!'

'I know. Yes. I've seen the horses, actually,' Jack said. 'When we got back. They're all in the field behind the QM's stores. I was surprised too.'

'You didn't know they were going to take the horses?'

'No.'

I turned to Captain Surtees. 'Did you?' I said. He didn't reply at once, so I asked him again. He muttered something about it having been mooted at one stage. I returned to Jack, who mattered more to me. 'But where are the men?' I asked for the third time.

'Well, as I was saying –' Tom said but Jack interrupted him.

'It's OK, Tom. I can deal with this. You needn't stay.'

'With respect, sir, I think in the circumstances –'

But Jack rode over him. He thanked Captain Surtees in a hard, thankless tone, telling him he could cope with me, with Miss Parvic. He referred to me like that! Surtees stood up swaying and just about managed to take his leave without hitting the doorpost. I hadn't realised just how drunk he was; nor, I suspect, did he until he stood up. Jack shut the flimsy door after him. Then he offered me some gin to drink. I refused. Had he forgotten already, so soon, that I rarely if ever drank alcohol? It seemed so. He helped himself to more, to too much, saying – I couldn't believe it – saying I must excuse Tom. 'He's had a very trying, rather taxing day of it. So have I, if the truth be told,' he added.

When I recovered my breath after this effrontery, I said, 'You gave your solemn word they'd come back. Your sacred word. So sacred to you it was – or so you said – you refused to touch the icon.'

'I don't deny it. Have I denied it?' He sounded querulous. Like a peevish bachelor.

'Everybody says it is all lies. The conference was a lie. Just as with their guns. Especially now the horses have gone. Please! They're all saying to me it will be their turn next time. The private soldiers, the women and the children – they're all going to be sent to Russia so Stalin can kill them!'

Jack gulped at his gin and told me, the drink catching in his throat so that he coughed and choked, that I was hysterical. I told him I wasn't and demanded he treat me as an adult, an intelligent person, someone competent who deserved a proper answer. After all I had been selected as an official interpreter to the British army. In other words, rather pathetically, I tried to assert myself as his equal, but of course no civilian ever can be, not with an occupying power.

Jack listened to me resentfully. Finally he said, 'I'm not in a position to speak further. Suffice it to say my orders were to transport Brigadier Bakturov and his officers to Mittelthal, there to be addressed by the GOC.'

'I know that! But is it true? Is it true?'

He belched, splaying his hand across the base of his throat as if to prevent the bile rising into his mouth. With a grimace – had he failed to halt the sourness? – he said that to the best of his limited knowledge it was true. But I noticed he had spaced out his words like a politician balancing one half-truth against another. He didn't sound human at all.

'Jack, please! Please let me call you Jack again. I can't not be a person with you. Please,' I said.

'It won't make an iota of difference.'

'Please.'

'If you wish.' His voice sounded so cold I actually shivered.

'It's been so terrible at Grubenfeld. Taking the horses has confirmed our worst fears, you see. Are you quite sure you didn't know they were going to do that?'

'I said!'

'Captain Surtees seems to have known.'

'Do you doubt me?'

'No, no,' I said quickly, fearing his anger. It was strange but having won his permission to call him Jack again I found it almost impossible to use his Christian name after all. I had one last question. 'But why did you say they were prisoners of war? I haven't yet dared to tell them at the camp about that. Why did you?'

'Surely you heard? I told you why this morning. That's what they're designated as – officially. That's their status. Technically.'

'But how can they be? No one's defeated them. It isn't as though you have fought the Cossacks and won, is it? You haven't taken them prisoner – well, not until today! And that by trickery!'

'It's a staff decision. Nothing to do with us in the field, Tonya.'

'But you can't call free men prisoners of war! Let alone women and children! It doesn't make sense!'

Jack sighed expressively, making it clear he found my expostulations not only tiresome but childish too.

'Just take it from me, Tonya, I've done my best. But there comes a point where all you get is a dusty answer.'

'Like me – like I'm getting now?'

'Look – I'm a soldier! Or has that escaped your notice? And, as such, I'm obliged to obey orders. OK? Understood? Message received?'

'But there are things above that! Like trust and love and holiness; yes, Jack, the holiness of people, of life.' There, I'd managed to use his first name again and, for an instant, it made me feel a little better. But his reply at once dashed any hope of reciprocal understanding.

'You overstate and your command of English is slipping,' he said. Surely it wasn't? I thought I'd put it very well. In fact I knew I had. Suddenly I saw his motive. He'd only said this to assert his power over me. I became extremely angry. Indeed, I lost my temper.

'You disgust me,' I shouted. 'And so does England, too! So kind, so polite, so full of honour! When you aren't. You're full of lies, of deceitfulness. You're worse than the Nazis! They at least never pretended to be anything other than they were. They didn't go around telling everyone they weren't the ruling race really but just happened to be so, please excuse us, so sorry we have to kill you, but you mustn't complain, we can't help doing this, it hurts us quite as much it hurts you to be sent to the firing squad!'

Jack leapt to his feet and grabbed me by the upper arms. He shook me so hard my head jerked backwards and forwards on my spine. It was a sudden, dreadful pain. He hissed at me to be quiet, did I want to disturb the whole battalion? Yes, I did, I said. He shook me again. That hurt so much it confirmed my hatred of him.

'To think I admired you. Even loved you, perhaps. What a fool I have been. Now let go. I cannot have you touch me. I am not your prisoner of war, Jack.'

He let go, knowing his use of force had brought about his own defeat. I had won and it was sad, and very squalid. He looked at me like a dog, a dog so well trained it remembers the whip. He asked me not to shout my head off again. I knew I would not need to any more. I was the master now.

'You were afraid to come up to the camp tonight, weren't you?' I said.

'To be frank, yes. To start with, I was. Then I persuaded myself I had to. And I was going to, Tonya, only Tom didn't want me to. He thought it too dangerous. We had quite a tussle about it.'

'Captain Surtees was right,' I said. 'If you do come back you'd better bring a lot of soldiers. Good night, Jack.'

'I did do my best, you know.'

'I don't think Brigadier Kolya would agree. You're keeping him and the others at Mittelthal, aren't you? Have you billeted them in a hotel or in private houses?' No reply. I moved towards the door, but Jack intercepted me.

'No,' he said. 'I think in the circumstances you'd better remain here in Selsen. Yes. You must.'

'But I'm a free person, Jack. You cannot keep me here.'

To my horror he drew his revolver from its holster. He was shaking. I could not believe this was the same man I had met only some three weeks before. He pointed the gun at around my middle. He gabbled at me like a sort of dummy talking, a ventriloquist's dummy whose voice comes, just perceptibly, from somewhere else, from a superior authority.

'Your fears are correct,' he said. 'They are held in a reception area. They will be deported in accordance with our international treaty obligations. You cannot blame me. And, anyway, I do not accept your blame. Why should I? I have simply done my duty. You, however, will remain here. I cannot be responsible for your alerting the camp. Do I make myself clear?'

I stepped to him. I took his hand holding the revolver and pulled it towards me until the muzzle was pushed against my left breast.

'To stop me going you must shoot me. Just here, where it will hit my heart, Jack. But you are too much a coward, I think, and also too much a gentleman to shoot a woman you know, whom you have known, face to face, so close, yes?'

He hesitated. My victory was complete. It had taken no courage at all – just a sometime lover's instinct. He stepped back, lowering his revolver. He looked very old. Then he sat on the bed and I could see that he was crying.

I left at once, thinking like a fool that I should not humiliate him further. If I had known what was to come I doubt I should have been so tender towards him.

After quarrelling with Jack I returned to the camp to find everyone, except some of the smaller children and babies, awake and waiting for me. I can't even now describe how ugly a time that was as I tried to explain what had happened. Although innocent, I felt myself to blame and I could tell that many there – not all, but nevertheless a significant number – remained distrustful of me. But all I could say was I also had been deceived. Yes, me too. Just like them. Their eyes were unforgiving. They knew I had loved their persecutor, whereas they had merely liked him. Over and over again I told them they were wrong to blame Major Kempe alone. He had acted in good faith to begin with. His orders had been to look after their welfare, and he had, hadn't he? The terrible fact that his orders had been changed was not his fault, was it? But they refused to accept this explanation. As far as they were concerned the English had deceived them from the start and Jack was the nearest, most appropriate target for their anger, hatred and contempt. Whatever I said, some still thought of me as his collaborator, when I wasn't – well, not in the sense they imagined. Meanwhile many of the women were keening as though their men, incarcerated in Mittelthal, were already dead.

I heard later how the ataman and all the officers in the transit camp had also argued through the night. They convened futile meetings, impromptu conferences, racking their poor brains to find ways of reasoning with their English captors. They'd got up petitions – every man signing for his life – while some, claiming acquaintance with the English top brass, wrote desperate letters pleading for this or that important man's intervention (the idea of a *deus ex machina* dies hard) and others made grey or black banners out of blankets or even a patriarch's cassock to hang on the wire fence. Prayer meetings were held; disciplined was maintained. None of it made an atom of difference. Down in Mittelthal they might just as well have become as hysterical as we did up at Grubenfeld for all the good it did.

Dawn came with nothing resolved. I went back to my tent but, although exhausted, I couldn't sleep. I decided the only thing to do was to go for a walk in the woods. They would refresh me. The woods above the camp were mostly of sweet chestnuts. You walked through centuries of leaf mould and soft husks like tiny sea urchins; some, the older ones, black with decay; those newer, bright green. These trees clothed the lower slopes of formidable foothills to the main alps and were riven by rocky gullies drenched in moss. Until that morning I had loved the woods with an almost painful passion. Like Wordsworth again. They had become for me, it seems a little crazy now, a sort of refuge; no, that isn't the word, more a retreat, yes, that's right – a place to which you can retire to pray because the place itself is a kind of living prayer. Forgive me, but I am not a Marxist materialist despite my re-education in the mines at Vorkuta.

I found little Varya first, the four-year-old who had taken so immediately to Jack. Then I saw Katya, her mother, with the baby boy. Then her father a little further away. He had killed them and then himself rather than allow the family to be sent back to Russia. He had used a hunting knife to cut their throats. It remained clutched hard in his hand. He must have kissed and smoothed their faces afterwards, I think, because all three looked quite peaceful, whereas he did not. His eyes were open. The shock to me was dreadful. My first reaction was anger; how *dared* he! This man had taken too much upon himself! He had presumed too arrogantly to know what was best – he had played God, in fact. But of course I had not then been repatriated, as they called it. Now I can see him as a man possessed of foresight and compassion.

I ran back to the camp to find Father Sacha and Father Ivan. I was sobbing, talking wildly to myself, saying, 'Look what you've done, Jack, look what you've done.'

EIGHT

Before setting out for Grubenfeld Colonel Billy had the entire battalion on parade in order to address the blokes. Most unusually, Billy, who was a fluent fellow, spoke from notes on his millboard, as if he needed to be quite sure he said precisely the right things in an almost legal way. Jack couldn't help feeling the colonel didn't wish to be caught out, that he didn't want anything he said to be quoted back at him later. He spoke like some godawful politico.

Colonel Billy informed the 5th that he had been ordered by Brigade to brief all ranks before that day's operation. It was vital now that everyone was aware of what they were about to do, indeed to achieve, and that it was in accordance, in complete accordance, with a trilateral agreement made by the Allied leaders at Yalta in February last.

Under this agreement, which had the force of international law, all Soviet prisoners of war and Soviet citizens, and that included all personnel of every age and sex in Little Russia up the valley, were to be returned to their country of origin – the USSR.

For the battalion this meant conveying everyone, man, woman and child, from Grubenfeld down to the transit camp at Mittelthal. Just as they had the Cossack officers yesterday. Understood? From there they would be transported by rail to the Russian zone just to the east, but that part of the procedure was not the 5th's immediate concern. Their objective that day was the transit camp. He pointed out they might well meet some resistance at Grubenfeld but, though possibly distressing, it would not be serious, since the Cossacks were no longer a nation-in-arms as such. They had surrendered their weapons, they lacked transport and they had lost their officers and, therefore, any leadership. He suggested, but did not state it categorically, that this had been part of a deliberate strategy to protect all British ranks when the crunch came. As it now had.

As CO, his first duty, he insisted, was to get every single rifleman safely home, back to Blighty, in one piece. This raised a small cheer. Billy added that he could not pretend the operation would be particularly easy, let alone pleasant, but they would just have to do their best and maintain discipline throughout, especially in the face of any protest or provocation. 'Steady the Bucks' was the order of the day. Furthermore they would do well not to feel too sorry for these people. They should at all times remember that the Cossacks took up arms for and with the Germans against our Russian allies, thus prolonging the war. They had been German auxiliaries, was that clear? But once back in the USSR they would – Joe Stalin had promised this to Churchill and Roosevelt – they would be given accommodation and work, helping rebuild their shattered homeland. He was aware there had been rumours to the effect that, once handed over, they might face execution, but there had been no official indication, let alone confirmation, of this most unlikely outcome. The fact was Stalin needed as many living, breathing, healthy Soviet citizens as he could get hold of in order to rebuild Mother Russia.

Summing up, Billy exhorted the battalion to act firmly, to avoid confrontation whenever and wherever possible, but, if the use of force were required, then it should be used promptly and without hesitation. Every man who took reasonable, measured action would have his full support. Lastly, he did not think this was an occasion for questions, it was just a matter of getting on with it, so he wished them luck.

They moved off in silence, except for Jack, who, left in command of nothing at Selsen (for his own safety, Billy had insisted), watched the battalion go. Never had he seen the blokes so quiet. They seemed rather like prisoners of war themselves. Or as if, like Corporal Gibson, they had already reverted to civilian life. Demob fever was now clearly endemic. And who could blame them? Not Jack. They had done a good job, only to get saddled with this final exercise, this unwelcome, bloody sideshow.

There was no mistaking their intention this time. I looked for Jack but saw only Captain Surtees with Colonel Bellgrave. As well as several more empty three-tonners, the convoy now included six caterpillar-tracked troop carriers packed with armed soldiers in what I can only describe as full battledress. Some of the younger children thought these vehicles were a new kind of tank. On arrival, the troop carriers fanned out all round the camp and the soldiers jumped out and spread themselves a few yards apart from each other so they became an encircling, armed human fence.

The colonel and Captain Surtees came up to where I was standing flanked by Father Sacha and Father Ivan. They saluted. Obviously they saw me as a sort of substitute for Brigadier Bakturov. Colonel Bellgrave said good morning as if he had come to inspect the camp rather than to depopulate it. I asked him, without having returned his greeting, to come with me, please, to the church. Perhaps there was something undeniable in my manner? I don't know, but they followed me to where we had laid out the bodies I'd found in the woods. We had covered them with blankets. Father Sacha revealed them one by one. I explained.

The two English officers nodded sympathetically, as if commiserating with us upon an unfortunate road accident that was no one's fault. For answer I told them I no longer regarded myself as an official interpreter to the British army. I considered myself now the representative of the free people of Grubenfeld. Again they nodded as though accepting the fact with heartfelt understanding. They didn't even bother to dispute my careful use of the word 'free'. It was clear there was nothing I could possibly say with which they would dream of disagreeing. I was right, they were right; I was weak, they were strong, but it would be bad manners to demonstrate this any more than was absolutely necessary for the maintenance of public order. Nothing else was required of us than to embrace our disgusting future as decorously as possible, please, and in return the English military would favour us with their invincible courtesy.

'The people are very afraid,' I said.

'I understand, Miss Parvic,' the colonel said. His voice was that of a family doctor beside a deathbed.

'They know very well they have been deceived.'

'That, too, I appreciate.'

His sympathy was armour-plated. How could I pierce it? I said, 'Major Kempe did not dare to come today? He is a coward now?'

He smiled regretfully. 'Not at all. He wanted to be with us. In fact, he felt it was his duty. But, as his CO, I required him for other tasks elsewhere.'

'Many people here would like to kill him, you know?'

'I can well believe that but, if I may say so, their wish is a mistaken one.'

'I have told them so.'

'Quite right, Miss Parvic.' And he smiled as if to suggest I were still on his side after all.

'What happens now, please?' I said, trying not to cry, not to scream, not to shout what I really thought of him, of all of them.

'I would've thought that was pretty obvious really. We're here to conduct everyone down to Mittelthal.'

'We shall all be killed, you know.'

'That I sincerely doubt. And certainly everyone here is perfectly safe in the British zone, believe me. Do tell everyone that, if it helps.'

'I mean if we are sent into the Russian zone. I mean if we go there, Colonel. Quickly or slowly we shall die. We aren't fools. We have good reasons for our fears, you know.'

This time I think I made him uncomfortable. His smile

became less mobile. He half turned to Captain Surtees. He said 'Our adjutant, Captain Surtees, will now put you in the picture. Tom?'

Tom Surtees said, 'Kindly inform the people they are to embus forthwith. One bundle of belongings per person. Anything in excess will be confiscated. No pets. No livestock. And do point out that the more everyone co-operates the easier it will be for everyone.'

'Don't you mean easier for you?'

'No, I don't!' he said and for a second time I heard and saw English anger. 'I was thinking of your people. I need hardly say we, for our part, are equipped to cope, Miss Parvic.' The sweep of his arm invited me to remember – as if I needed reminding – the soldiers who surrounded us.

We all obeyed like sheep. A terrible, dreamlike lethargy had come over us. People packed their most precious things as best they could and, oddly enough, scarcely anyone cried. Not even the children. The men were sullen and silent. In fact the whole place had become very quiet. Only a few dogs barked from time to time. Father Sacha and Father Ivan went from tent to tent trying to comfort people as best they could. When they said God would protect them, all agreed. Finally queues formed as men, women and children waited to climb into the lorries. People told each other that at least in Mittelthal they would see Brigadier Bakturov and his officers. Once they were all together again perhaps things would be better, a solution would no doubt be found; the English might have behaved badly but they weren't bad all through, were they?

It occurred to me that in my anxiety and distress I had let Jack's colonel off too lightly. As the lorries were being loaded I went over to his Jeep. Like Jack's it had a field radio and again the air around it was full of repeated questions. Soldiers never seem capable of hearing each other easily. Over and over they have to enquire: 'Do you receive me? Are you receiving me?' I asked Colonel Bellgrave for permission to speak. Being there in person, I got through at once.

'But of course. Fire away.'

'It seems to me, sir, that you ought to make an announcement, you know, a public address to everyone, telling them what is happening. And what will happen to them.'

'I assumed they already knew.'

'Well, yes, of course they know they are being taken to Mittelthal. But I think in fairness you should say to them what will happen to them after that.'

'Ah, I see. You suggest I spell it out?'

'Yes, sir. After all, it is their future.'

'Quite. I take your point, Miss Parvic. But I'm not entirely sure this is the place or the time. What you suggest will be done, and better done, down in Mittelthal, at the depot there. If people ask, tell them all will be made abundantly clear, be fully explained, later on today down at the depot. OK? But do, do, underline what I've said about any fears they may have being groundless.'

'You refuse to tell them they are to be deported?'

'It's not a question of refusal; it's a question of timing.'

'No, I don't think so.'

'Well, you should. It's as plain as the nose on my face. That's all, Miss Parvic, thank you.' He turned sharply to his radio operator. 'Surely you've raised Brigade by now, Corporal?'

'I got 'em, only for them to go again, sir,' the soldier said.

I returned to my queue. Captain Surtees came across to me and suggested I need not travel in the lorries, I could ride in his Jeep. I said no, just that, *no* – not *no, thank you*. He shrugged and went away. Shortly before nine o'clock, when everybody was embussed at last, a young man suddenly leapt down and ran away between the deserted tents. Several soldiers gave chase and several shots rang out. At once people in the lorries began to cry and scream, while Captain Surtees went up and down the convoy yelling at the drivers to get started. At the same time the troop carriers came up to position themselves ahead and behind us. We never did find out what happened to the youth who ran away. I hope he lived.

As we approached Selsen, we passed another sort of convoy. But this one was what Jack would have called a very ragtag-and-bobtail affair. There were horse-drawn wagons, two unreliable motorcars, peasants with decrepit bicycles, many handcarts, even an old woman in black pushing a wheelbarrow. It was quite a procession. The whole village was going up to Grubenfeld for only one purpose: to steal what we had been forced to leave behind. They were going to loot everything. They would take our livestock, the tents which were heirlooms, our precious rugs, the white flour and the groundsheets the army had issued, even the hay from the haycock that the clearing of the cricket field had created.

Grinding in low gear through the empty village, I caught a glimpse of Jack. He did not see me, I think. Or if he did he gave no sign. I saw him step out and wave down Captain Surtees' Jeep. They conferred earnestly together as we in the lorries passed by. Then as I looked back I saw Jack jump into the seat I had refused. So he was coming with us? I didn't know whether to laugh or to cry. Whatever duties his colonel had given him, they could not, it seemed, be so very onerous after all. I wondered if Captain Surtees had told him about little Varya laid out in front of the church. With a shudder I realised she and her family had been left unburied. Unless the British had detailed a squad to do the job? They might have. After all, they were in charge of public health, weren't they? If not, then perhaps the thieves of Selsen might have enough conscience to do it.

But why had Jack elected to accompany us? Possibly it is indicative that, as I shook and trembled in that lorry, I did not imagine it was because of me. I assumed it was from shame or even a stern, Protestant sense that he must witness the worst, however much the cost; even if it meant never sleeping in peace again.

At the outskirts of Mittelthal we came to a crossroads with many signposts – or, rather, with many signs stuck on to it. Here the convoy stopped for a long time. Under the stencilled symbol of an axehead, painted arrows pointed to a cemetery, to something called PAC, to the army cinema and to a bath unit and clothing-exchange point. There were other signs in German and, of course, the original place names: one, Graz, I recognised as being in the not so distant Soviet zone.

Soon it became clear why we waited. Military police and traffic marshals were giving priority to another convoy coming from further west than we had. It was also longer. Many more people just like us were being transported to the transit camp before we were. When that convoy had passed we still waited and had plenty of time to become aware that in the background, among the trees of a public park, several armoured cars were standing with their heavy machine guns pointing at – or, as a soldier would say, covering – the crossroads. They were not exactly concealed, but on the other hand you could say also that they had been deployed in a discreet, even gentlemanly, sort of way.

The wait of the crossroads was bloody interminable. The crying of the kiddies in the three-tonners had particularly grated on people's nerves. Jack and Tom had become concerned for the 5th's morale. Especially when a colour sergeant came up, a reliable man if ever there was one, decorated at El Alamein, and advised them with the greatest respect that the blokes were getting a touch browned-off. They were starting to say this wasn't the sort of thing they ought to be asked to do and could either of them or the colonel please get the convoy moving again, sir?

Colonel Billy meanwhile had buzzed off ahead, so Jack went over and had another word with the MPs and was told the hold-up wasn't actually at the crossroads – which Jack could see for himself – but at the depot. 'It's documentation at the depot is the problem,' the MP corporal said. The bloody Russians kept insisting on a complete register and/or rollcall. The bastards wanted the identity of every single person being repatriated clearly stated. Apparently there'd been 'a balls-up with the hand-over of those Cossack officers yesterday. Not enough bumf to satisfy the Red Army,' they said. So with this lot – since there'd been this official complaint, 'if you see what I mean, sir? – the hand-over had to be 'bloody impeccable or our GOC'll get his poor old whatsit whipped off'. This time they had to make sure every man, woman and child was identified and classified and the only efficient way to do this was to check them immediately upon arrival at the depot. Only that way could they actually find out 'who we've bloody well got, right?' Jack saw the logic of this.

He went back and together with Tom and Colour Sergeant Guppy they went round and talked to the blokes, explaining what was happening. They comforted themselves with the thought that putting their men in the picture generally helped them to bear with a situation. Information was a real help. A recognised aid to understanding. At this stage Colonel Billy returned with the same story, reserving his surprise at seeing Jack until he'd finished and then saying mildly, 'It seems you've seen fit to bend my orders, Grandad?'

'Yes, sir. I knew you'd understand.' Jack grinned.

'Consider yourself reprimanded, Major Kempe.'

'Yes, Colonel.'

Both smiled. 'Right, well, that's that dealt with, Jack. I expect Tom's told you how things went earlier today? Up at Grubenfeld?'

'Not too bad, he says.'

'Could've been worse.'

They continued waiting. Jack realised he was virtually

chain-smoking so he forced himself to stop, only to automatically accept a fag from Billy ten minutes later.

To reach our destination we had to bump over a railway track. There we waited again to have our papers examined. Mine puzzled the officer in charge so I was ordered to stand to one side. I told him I wished to go to the Soviet Union with everybody else. He did not answer me directly. All he said was: 'Wait over there, please.' He kept my papers. This process with the papers was conducted in the open air as soon as we had climbed down from the lorries. It took a long time because the British seemed to be making painstaking lists of us. Everybody looked about with apprehension at the rows of windowless huts. We could see no sign of Brigadier Kolya and the other officers. It was as though they had never been there at all. Perhaps they hadn't? We had no means of knowing.

While we stood or sat in the sun we couldn't help noticing that the railway track we had crossed in order to enter the camp ran deep inside the wire, where it was overlooked by two watchtowers. The soldiers on duty in them were dark against the light. The line came to an end at some wooden buffers placed, you could say, more from a sense of administrative fitness than anything else. They would not have stopped a tramcar, never mind a train. They looked makeshift and charming.

Jack came to where I was. He said, 'There you are.' At first I was tempted not to answer. I knew he would hate my silence. He did. He said, 'Please, Tonya, please speak to me.'

So I said, 'I thought you were under orders to stay away

from us?' And, indeed, behind me I could hear a growing murmur from the rest of my people.

'I've just been having a word with that intelligence chap.' He jerked his thumb at the officer who had questioned me. 'And I've brought you back your bumf.' He seemed very nervous, almost stammering, which he never had before. I had already seen him talking at the trestle table where our identities were examined. I had seen him and the investigating officer glance across at me several times.

'Yes, he ordered me to wait here,' I said. 'So I have.'

'He was quite right, Tonya. With your identity card you're in the clear. There's no question of your being a Soviet citizen, because you aren't. You just aren't. Do you see? We cannot categorise you as such. If your father had been a Cossack, yes, but he wasn't, was he? He was a Serb. Correct?'

'My mother was a Cossack.'

'Granted. But according to Intelligence that doesn't count. Just as I said, didn't I? So there you are. You can't go. Allow me to return these to you.' And he held out my identity card and birth certificate.

I took them, but even so I said, 'I intend to go, Jack.'

'Nonsense. You can't. Ridiculous.' His voice was pitched higher by disbelief.

'I mean it. I shall go. I have chosen to go.'

'No, I'm sorry, my dear, but no. The minute the Russians see your papers they'll shove you smartly back to us. So you'll be wasting your time. And ours. Much the best to make the best of it. Right?'

I suppose there come certain times when you can take

your destiny into your own hands, even perhaps discover that you are holding it physically? Quite how many people experience this I cannot say, but I do know that at that moment I did.

I tore up my papers into little bits. Those grubby, precious, dog-eared things which made me who I was, stated my age and where I had been born, showed others what I looked like three years before with my hair tied back and my eyes full of doubt, and carried – most precious of all until then – the official Army Corps stamp mark on my ID card which confirmed I had been appointed as an interpreter to the British forces on 1 May 1945.

As I did it, Jack said, 'Don't, don't, don't.'

I said, 'There. No papers now. All gone. And no papers means I am a Soviet citizen, yes? That's the rule, isn't it? That's what the officer over there told me. Without papers it is goodbye.'

We stood among the scraps of card and paper as we had among the daffodils. I saw tears glisten in Jack's eyes but felt none in mine. According to him my gesture was pointless; there was no point in it at all, he repeated. I told him there was for me.

He took me firmly by the arm in order to lead me back to the Intelligence officer to see if they could issue a new card. I told him I would destroy anything they gave me.

He gripped my arm yet tighter and begged me to reconsider. He agreed the whole business was a rotten shame, an almighty shambles, but there was no need for me to be part of it. I wasn't a Soviet citizen.

That did it. I shouted, waving my free arm wildly, heads

turned, I screamed: 'Nor are these! None of us are! We're White Russians, Kazaks, Caucasians, anyone you like except Red Russians!'

His look and his voice hardened. He said, 'I won't let you do this, Tonya. I simply won't. You can't do this to yourself. And you don't have to try to shame me either. I feel bad enough as it is. As you know perfectly well, if you're honest, don't you?'

'I'm not doing this to make you feel ashamed.'

'You aren't? Then why? What for? Please, what for?'

I chose my words. 'I go because to stay would make me just like you, Major.'

At this he at once relinquished his grip on me. As if my very being had scorched him. But I think he might still have protested at me had we not been interrupted by the arrival of the train.

It came into the depot backwards, shunted by a rusting, wheezing engine with all its pipework on the outside. The wagons juddered past us, coming to a resonant stop well before those silly buffers. I counted twelve. They were the sort of slatted boxes used before the war to transport livestock: cattle, sheep or pigs – the latter often packed so tightly they had to stand on each other's backs – or else the more ordinary kind of workhorse, mule or pony.

On seeing the train, the people began to cry. The British soldiers displayed no emotion. The people were crying because so many of them had experience of what such rudimentary transportation foretold; enough of us had, at one time or another, ridden in such wagons for our reaction to unsettle those who hadn't yet. You, my dear reader (forgive my clumsy style, but I need to feel I communicate with a real person – I have learned enough never again to attempt to speak to an official or anyone in their 'official capacity'), you must know, please know, that many Cossacks among whom I had just deliberately included myself, many of us, for reasons about which we were not consulted, had worked in German labour camps to escape only when liberated by the victorious Red Army. That was why we feared to be sent to Russia so very much. Especially in such a train. We knew it would be no different, in fact worse, than the Third Reich. We knew that if we were not worthy of Stalin's vengeful firing squads we would be put to work in similar labour camps – but this time in Siberia – where output or long-term construction projects would take priority over human considerations.

I think Jack, too, was appalled by what he was seeing. He at least looked less composed than the other British. As he released my arm he said imploringly for the last time, 'I'm sure I could get you new papers, I'm sure I can swing it, Tonya. Let me try, please let me try, please.'

But I had made up my mind. I was, if you like, a fool. Jack certainly thought so. A proud fool, trapped by my unforgiving sense of what was right for me. I say this because I realise now that when I told him I was not condemning myself to misery in order to shame him I hadn't spoken the whole truth. No. I was utterly determined to shame him. I was young, I was arrogant, I was conceited in spirit. I was priding myself – I remember doing it so clearly – on being chock-full of condescension towards this dutiful English major with his imperial scale of moral weights and measures. I was inordinately proud of having seen more than he of what I called the real world.

It is possible I had, but is it really necessary to compare a tank battle holocaust in North Africa, for example, with slow forced labour in Saxony? Why weigh such sufferings against each other too jealously? Still, there you are, as Jack would say; that was me in those days, that was what I was, what I did. My excuse must be, can only be, that if then it was pride and folly I have paid for it since, many times over, I think.

For the very last time I repudiated his offer of new papers. This meant we just looked at each other quite dumbly. For one dreadful moment I thought he would try to kiss me – kiss me goodbye – but he didn't. No, instead he simply held out his hand for me to shake. He pushed it firmly forward, but still it trembled; an innocent, placatory gesture such as a child can be trained to do. I found I was unable to accept his hand so I didn't. I just shook my head, feeling so much it felt like nothing at all. He nodded as if he understood – perhaps he did? – then he turned from me and marched away, his shoulders hunched. I never saw him again.

The cattle trucks waited, empty, for an hour or more. Like us, they stood there in the sun. The general crying had stopped. The warmth of that early summer's noonday had dried our tears.

Eventually several new squads of Tommies arrived. They formed up around us while their NCOs opened the doors of the wagons. Another wait followed and then several officers appeared. Two of them carried loud-hailers. At their appearance the crying began again, but this time it gathered into a sort of keening noise: a wail in unison difficult to describe. I had never heard a sound like it before, nor have I since. It possessed so terrible a concerted quality you would have thought it had been orchestrated deliberately. In a sense it was – we were, were we not, being orchestrated by our own virtually hopeless future? I found that I was making the same sound. I had no difficulty at all in joining in. It was the only thing to do. And as our communal grief oscillated between the wagons and the huts, we found we were pressing closer and closer together. We were gathering in upon ourselves. It was most strange but quite spontaneous. Group compulsion really. Herd instinct. We simply held on to each other. Men, women, children and babies were beginning to cohere, to amalgamate into one mass of humanity. The word 'solidarity' was made flesh there in Mittelthal. We all pressed and clung one to another, became glued together by fear, in the face of those cattle trucks and those British soldiers – cattle themselves, responding to orders.

Next the officers came, the ones with the megaphones among them. The priests with us unwrapped the icons they carried and held them above their heads as rallying signs of comfort and protection. They began to sing, leading us from our primitive wailing to the life-giving fatalism of the psalms. I think our singing unnerved the soldiers a little. After all they were Christians too and, though Protestant, shared our beliefs.

As we began to sing the twenty-third psalm they began to address us through the megaphones. They spoke awkward, thickly accented Russian like the Intelligence captain who had inspected my papers. Their words, amplified by their speaking-trumpets, which were merely tin cones with handles, filled the air around us. They were difficult for us to understand but the overriding message was clear. Translated – old habits die hard now, as they did then – this, roughly, is what they said: 'We require you all to entrain immediately, please. Kindly assist us by boarding the train in an orderly manner. We are here to ensure that the correct procedures are observed according to international law. Please board the train now. Thank you for your co-operation.' That, broadly speaking, was the gist of those tin trumpets.

We took no heed of this genteel announcement. It was repeated three times, the officers with the megaphones patrolling uneasily around us. And still we clung together, still we did not move, still we sang *Dominus regit me* in a huddled, resonant mass.

The fourth time the message was bawled at us, the text was sharper. It introduced, predictably enough, a time element – if you can call it that. We were to board the train *at once*, without delay, immediately, or further measures would be called into play. But still they said please, 'please do as we request'. Oh, how those British minded their manners. We didn't. We had lost our manners now. Our singing became shrill, less tuneful, no longer concerted, and the babies and children began to add a raucous, eerie, skin-scraping descant. But despite our loss of social nicety we still cohered physically and we did not budge. Not one of us took so much as a step towards those cattle trucks. We were making our futile stand. Silence gradually descended over us.

A final appeal was made. But still no one moved. No one spoke. Then Father Sacha in the midst of us began to pray aloud – his voice rose out from us, rose above us – and all the other priests all about joined in and so did we. We were repeating the Jesus prayer, as we call it. It is very simple. It invokes the name and mercy of Jesus. That is all it does. It says, and we said, following Father Sacha and the other priests: 'Lord Jesus Christ, son of God, have mercy on me, a sinner.' Nothing else. Anyone can say it forever if they wish. It has a healing property, I've found.

An English officer – I'm glad to say I did not know him: he was not from Jack's battalion – yelled: 'B Company! Fix bayonets!' And the squad close to us slammed their rifles between their bent knees, jerked their hands behind their backs and produced bayonets from their belts, which they snapped into position on the end of their guns. All the other squads followed suit – you could hear the same order echoing round the camp. More orders were shouted and the soldiers performed another ugly ballet, adopting a lunging position with their bayoneted rifles poking straight at us. It looked like parade-ground soldiering but was no less terrorising for that.

What happened next is both clear and confused and that, I assure you, is not an idle paradox. For that was how it really was for us at Mittelthal. Each of us had a personal experience to share, to contribute to our communal hindsight later on in that goods train. History, if you can call what happened to us that, is forever two-faced. But why do I philosophise so feebly? Forgive me, it is because I am prevaricating. I recoil from reporting the next occurrence. Not because I'm sentimental about the English, nor because I am in general sympathetic towards them; I hope everything I have written so far demonstrates that I am not. No, I recoil because what happened next was horrible in a way that is universal.

No one was at fault except we all were. What took place was that while we as Cossacks were united in our refusal to move – we really did not wish to go into those wagons – the British military were obliged to make us enter them. To put us in regardless. 'A quart into a pint pot' was an English proverb I learned in my studies. And that was how it was. We had to go in because it had been decided we must – not by these Tommies, but by others we did not know, whom we had never met. Bureaucrats, English-style, who were neither friends nor enemies of ours but simply distant persons working in secure expectation of a pension and a tranquil retirement cultivating their gardens.

Some of the NCOs moved towards the rim of us to try and strongarm a first few of our men away. They were winkling out those deemed to be key resisters, I suppose. Our men linked arms, held back, kicked out, refused to be manhandled. Scuffles began. The people immediately behind this front line started to shout and scream. The soldiers' efforts became harder, tougher. One drill sergeant had a polished stick and he started to use it as a truncheon. At this, one of our men managed to kick him in the stomach. The sergeant doubled up, purple-faced with pain, and someone grabbed his pace-stick and hit out with it. Just to my left another man, locked in struggle with a corporal, bit his opponent's ear. The corporal screamed with rage, grabbed a rifle and used the butt of it to strike down the man who had bitten his ear. At once other soldiers moved in to drag the biter away. They hurled him bodily into a wagon and he was the first of us to board that fateful train.

The British were cursing us steadily now and soon more of our men followed the first, beaten and bloodied by systematic blows from the rifle butts. But still no bayonets had been used.

Now, however, the British tried a new method of persuasion, which was to stab at the ground in front of our feet. They used their bayonets as if they were hoeing the ground in spring. Perhaps they were all farmers' sons? Stab, stab, stab. This way they forced us back upon ourselves and, where before we had clung together in mutual support, now we found we were, in our refusal to move towards the train, climbing up and over *ourselves*. We would not retreat so we became instead a dreadful series of pyramids; human ant hills, if you like.

Such hysterical mounds of people – risen human dough – could not endure for long; soon we collapsed into a spilt, screaming sprawl and were easily swept up, dragged bodily away, to be pushed into the wagons. I saw a woman stabbed through her foot and the soldier who did it laughed. His eyes were bloodshot. We women covered our stomachs and breasts as best we could with our arms, for the soldiers, thoroughly roused now, were wielding their rifles like paddles. They were savage canoeists battling through turbulent waters – us. They would butt with the blunt end, cut and thrust with the sharp end. We were all of us bruised and bleeding.

As I was being dragged to the train I saw a small child, a little boy of three or so, being flung through the air above me. He landed on the wooden floor of the truck just before

I was pushed in beside him. Somewhere else shots rang out and people said later a man had broken free, only to be shot down.

All the while this was happening the megaphones continually brayed at us as if we were at a normal station and were entering those trucks of our own accord: 'All persons will entrain now. Please board the train now.' And just like the towers and walls of Jericho, we had come tumbling down. The result was that, after an hour or so of applied brutality such as I had associated before only with the Nazis, the British had herded us on to that train and slammed the doors shut. We could hear the soldiers snapping on padlocks outside. Inside, we were as crammed together as we had been before but now we did not sing, though many still prayed. One of the priests was crying: he had lost an icon of great sacredness, snatched from him in the struggle.

After that we waited again. The soldiers relaxed in the sun, smoking, chatting. We watched them through the slats. I thought they looked as if they would be glad to see us gone. Out of sight, out of mind. Except for one boy who came along pushing cigarettes one by one through to us.

Shut in like that we had no way of knowing just how long we would be kept there or how long the journey to the Russian zone would take. During World War II the simplest railway journey could last hours, or days and if anything the aftermath was even worse. But we knew that whatever the duration proved to be we had already been degraded forever. When ultimately we were released from those wagons we would emerge not merely physically soiled but stained in spirit too.

The blokes were playing pontoon for matchsticks as the train chuntered towards the Russian sector. Jack sat with Tom Surtees, both glancingly illuminated by swaying storm-lantern light. All ranks were packed in together, but this creaking wooden-seated passenger carriage was the height of luxury compared with the cattle trucks the poor old Cossacks had been herded into. Tonya among them.

At this persistent thought Jack hung his head. She had been cooped up in there since midday and now it was night. Her own fault, of course. Of course, of course, of course. The rhythm of the train, damn it.

Now and then snatches of their singing drifted in at him from the trucks in front. Terrible to hear because so beautiful. Of course. Oh no, they were singing that one. That tune. The ballad she had explained to him by the fire. The ataman's hearth. Oh, God in Heaven, what had he done? His duty, of course. Of course. Hoot. They were entering another tunnel. Sweet smell of smoke in the compartment. Their singing had stopped. Hoot. They were out again. Still no moon. A very short tunnel that time, considering the speed of the train. What was it? Ten miles an hour at most – if that. Hello, they had started again. Of course. Bloody brave of them considering. To sing. Tom had nodded off. Jack wished he could.

The train had stopped. Another wait. For what? An adverse signal, another train to pass or for nothing? Where the hell were they? Jack didn't know or care but he doubted their desultory journey had so far got them more than thirty miles. He shut his eyes, ordered himself to take a nap such as Churchill was famous for, tried to think of his wife and daughter, but all that came into his mind's eye was that little girl Varya. Up at Grubenfeld. Tom had seen her with her family laid out in front of the church. He hadn't known who she was, but from the description it sounded as if it had to be Varya. Unbidden, the words of the Lord's Prayer came into Jack's head. Who were they for? Himself, Varya, Tonya, or all of them together?

When dawn arrived at last it was gentle, luminous, promising a perfect day. The train moved forward again, only to halt once more on a steel bridge above a nondescript stretch of river. One of the men said it was a pity nobody had blown it up. Jack was inclined to agree. He and Tom got out for a breath of air and saw below a squad of Red Army soldiers with a couple of vehicles parked on the spread of pebbled shore beside them. At first they thought the soldiers were taking an early morning dip then they realised that several drenched corpses lay at the water's edge out in the early morning sun, and that the soldiers were dragging out yet another body from the river. Some were men; others were women, two were babies. They could only assume that these must have been Cossacks who had attempted escape or jumped in order to die from the train ahead of theirs. Such things were happening. Tom wondered without enthusiasm if they should order the escort platoon to line the track across the bridge until the train moved off again, but Jack said no, he reckoned their particular consignment was secure enough: the poor bastards were padlocked in. The train emitted a short, warning hoot and they climbed in again as their carriage trundled past. In the trucks ahead of them all was silence. They had reached the Russian zone.

The hand-over took place smoothly in a goods yard.

Tom, accompanied by several Red Army officers, supervised the opening-up of the trucks while Jack spoke to the reception top brass. Tom mentioned later that the stench on detraining had been pretty powerful and the people had seemed rather cowed. The receiving Russians had immediately hived off the men from the women and children. Yes, he had seen Tonya, but she had looked through him as if he did not exist. Tom thought it just as well Jack had had to do the social honours. He had been far better occupied knocking back the ritual vodkas. The Russians had checked all the male Cossacks meticulously against the lists the British had provided. They hadn't been quite so particular about the women and children, though they checked them before herding them into some waiting lorries and driving off. The men, on the other hand, were marched away under heavy guard.

Meanwhile, for Jack the operation had dissolved into a sort of godawful cocktail party full of big smiles, comradely guffaws and back-slapping among allies. One Russian captain spoke a modicum of English – he kept saying 'chin-chin, cheerio'. And laughed as if this constituted a heart-warming witticism. The vodka flowed and he wasn't saying no exactly. Nor was Tom, who had now joined him. So when the first, distant volley of shots was heard they both more or less accepted their hosts' explanation that not far away there was a rifle range used for training; the war might be over but the Red Army kept itself in battle readiness, chin-chin, ha-ha. Full of a mounting disquiet and yet more vodka, they didn't query any of the subsequent volleys either. Eventually they were taken across to another part of the yard to await the train that would return them to the British zone.

As they kicked their heels on a low platform of cracked and bubbled asphalt sprouting grass and dandelions, the chin-chin captain assigned to them as aide and supervisor suddenly clutched at his stomach, indicating, half in gesture, half in words, that he had been taken short. 'Excuse, pliss. Shit me soon,' he said and rushed away. Jack and Tom were glad to be shot of him.

They paced up and down the open platform in the sun. They were impatient to be gone. To put the whole business behind them. 'Sufficient unto the day,' Jack said at one stage and Tom nodded.

For no reason except to kill time during this hour of enforced idleness, Jack crossed the track to peer in through one of a row of broken windows in a dirty, run-down warehouse that stood opposite the platform. He was to regret doing so for the rest of his life. In his shock he turned and beckoned speechlessly to Tom to come and share what he had seen.

The space within was like a large, empty garage with a concrete floor darkened by years of sump oil and grease. There were brick pillars and pipework. Walls painted a dirty yellow. And blood. Blood was everywhere. It had mixed with the murky shine of the floor. It was spattered all across the walls. Great sprays and plumes of redness that had run down like tears. To one side was a small heap of discarded clothing: a crumpled jacket or two, some khaki gloves, several belts, a few worn-out boots. And one hat. A Cossack's hat. Jack recognised it the moment he registered it. The fur had got that familiar bald patch which had become a running joke between him and Brigadier Bakturov – the patch that looked like the Caspian Sea, that commemorated the old ataman's misspent youth.

He pointed it out to Tom. He said, 'Now we know.' Tom nodded.

After that they didn't speak at all, except in the course of duty, until they were back in their own sector.

I have often wondered what happened to Jack. And of course if he ever wondered what happened to me. Did he continue in the army after the war? Perhaps he rose to brigadier or even general? Or maybe he didn't? He was, when I knew him so briefly, already rather old for his rank. That, after all, was why his fellow officers, none of them more than thirty, nicknamed him 'Grandad'.

But my chief thought was always: had he managed to forget what he had done? To blot it from his mind? It is well attested that some people can genuinely forget their crimes. Consign them to a gulag of the mind. Or, if he had not been able to do this (I hoped he hadn't, naturally), then perhaps he had consoled himself with thinking that as a soldier he had simply obeyed orders? And thus was innocent. It is, ironically, a salient truth that in performing this evil the British had done nothing wrong.

I have asked myself these questions because for years, even after I was released from Vorkuta in 1955, I had a recurrent dream in which Jack appeared to have ordered his own court martial. Such wishful fantasies were, inevitably perhaps, typical of the labour camps, the atom factories, the mines where we female 'Soviet citizens' were put to work. All of us dreamt of revenge or redress, according to our temperaments. But of Jack's true state of mind or conscience I had no knowledge. Not then or since. Perhaps he often recalled what happened; perhaps he still does but does not give a damn?

But in my absurd dream he did. Always he begged the court to find him guilty. And always I would see his commanding officer, Colonel Bellgrave, flanked by Captain Surtees on his left and by that other officer who requisitioned our horses on his right. They would sit in judgement at a trestle table covered with a Union Jack, either in a flowery meadow – was this a dream pun upon the phrase 'a field court martial'? – or else in a tent; and, just once, they sat in our little church at Grubenfeld. But in all other respects my dream hardly varied. I, for instance, was always the prosecutor.

Jack would be standing to attention in front of the table, while I was free to be anywhere I chose. I was composed of lightness. Always the process began with Jack's colonel announcing solemnly that he was the president of this unprecedented court martial and that dear old Grandad could stand at ease. Always Jack refused. Always he remained as correctly alert as an exclamation mark.

Next Captain Surtees would rise and, leaning forward, place his fists on the table. His shoulders would hunch like a gorilla's and his knuckles would show white. From this threatening position he would tell us that it was not for Jack to accuse himself. That no British soldier could possibly plead guilty to doing his duty, could he? That would be a nonsense. Whereupon Jack would reply that he was not alone in inpugning himself, that he had me with him as both prosecutor and chief witness. I was about to argue the case against him and would establish beyond doubt his crime of obeying orders.

At this point Colonel Bellgrave always laughed like a gun, as did Captain Surtees and that other officer. Their mouths thundered out laughter, their bodies heaved like howitzers and the air around us reverberated as in an artillery barrage. When it was over the president of the court always said, 'Case dismissed.'

Now was my turn to speak. Now was the moment when I always stepped forward to say that for me, for my people, the Cossacks of Grubenfeld who had survived the Red Army shooting squads and Stalin's archipelago, this Major Kempe, our Major Owzat, would be a war criminal for all time. He had befriended us only to betray us. And he was right when he said he wasn't just accusing himself, although he should: no, we, the Cossack nation, were crying out from our past, our present, our graves even, to say that there exist some orders that men must never obey. Never. And Jack would nod, tears starting in his eyes.

But, as may be expected, his fellow officers always yawned in brotherly solidarity and Colonel Bellgrave, rising, always said: 'Thank you, Miss Parvic. Your case is unproven because if it weren't we too would stand accused. I therefore declare once again that this charge is dismissed and dear old Jack not guilty. He, like all of us in the 5th Bucks, did his bloody best in bloody awkward circumstances, carrying out his orders as required by King's Regulations. This court is adjourned. For ever.'

And they would salute and vanish, leaving me alone with Jack. We would regard each other. Jack's eyes at that moment always shone with truth at last acknowledged and as we moved to embrace, perfect accomplices in sorrow and shame, I, without fail, woke up.

I do not think it takes a psychologist to analyse this dream. Half of me likes to think it shows that, in moving the blame from him across to his comrades-in-arms, I have forgiven Jack. Also my particular affection has been translated into a comfortable generalised opprobrium. The other half of me likes to think (or, rather, is forced to admit) that I have had only myself to blame all these years. Jack tried to save me but I refused him and his help. In seeking to shame him, in my youthful desire to adopt an idealist's posture, I had wilfully created my own future.

I had intended to end here this brief memoir of how it was in May 1945, but suddenly, if not quite fortuitously, it requires a postscript. Or should I say a footnote to what is already a footnote to the larger history of war in Europe? I write this because I have just received a letter forwarded to me from the British Embassy here in Moscow. They know of me as an occasional translator and retired interpreter. The postmark on the envelope is from somewhere called Milton Keynes.

What I've withdrawn from it is a newspaper clipping from *The Times* of London. This reads:

> On Whit Sunday peacefully at home Major 'Jack' Kempe MC, late the Duke of Buckingham's Rifles, aged 85 years. Funeral private. Family flowers only. Donations if desired to: Refugees Worldwide. 1 All Hallows, Aylesbury, Bucks.

Attached to this clipping is a note from a Diana Hurst

née Kempe (Jack's daughter, clearly) saying she hopes it will reach me. In his later years, her father often spoke of me, she says, not knowing if I lived or not. She decided the most sensible thing to do was to send it to the embassy. 'Rather a long shot, but there it is.' She sounds very like her father.

If I had sufficient money I would be tempted to go to England. I still have never visited it. I should like to see Jack's grave. But the exchange rate puts this sentimental journey out of court. We may all be White Russians again nowadays but we are yet to be economically free. However, such restriction allows me to imagine Jack lying in an ideal English churchyard under ancient yew trees with rooks calling overhead and with me looking down at where he lies in peaceful earth. Now I can place my last offering on his grave: a bunch of wild daffodils. I feel I should like to speak but I know there is nothing further to say. Not now.

ACKNOWLEDGEMENTS

For information concerning Anne de Gaulle I have gleaned what I could from numerous biographies of her father but especially from *De Gaulle le Rebelle* by Jean Lacouture and *De Gaulle* by Bernard Ledwidge. The General's own *Mémoires de Guerre* and a chronology of his life issued by the Institut Charles de Gaulle have also been consulted. A pen portrait of Anne's mother Yvonne by her brother Jacques Vendroux proved helpful, as was an informative article by Susan Raven in the *Sunday Times* describing the family's wartime exile in England. A visit to Colombey-les-Deux-Eglises proved especially revealing.

No one can write about the events in Austria 1945 without acknowledging a debt to Nicholas Bethell's superbly documented *The Last Secret* and Nicholai Tolstoy's impassioned *Victims of Yalta*, while Alexander Solzhenitsyn's *The Gulag Archipelago 1918–1956* places this event in its terrible context.

Finally, I am grateful to my friend, David Alexander-Sinclair for his invaluable advice on all things military.